PRAISE FOR PAUL BLACK'S
THE TELS, SOULWARE AND **NEXUS POINT**

WINNER for genre fiction in the Writer's Digest's
International Book Awards.

WINNER and Second place for science fiction,
ForeWord Magazine's Book of the Year.

Finalist for the 2008 New York Book Festival.

"Dallas writer Paul Black makes his first foray into the world of science fiction with *The Tels*. It's a HIGHLY ORIGINAL novel set in the near future and IT MOVES AT LIGHTNING SPEED. Mr. Black has quite an imagination and puts it to good use. The MIND-BENDING PLOT centers on Jonathan Kortel, who is approached by a shadowy group called the Tels, who covet his telekinetic gifts. The ENSUING ACTION IS BIZARRE enough to read like something straight out of *The X-Files*."

~ *Steve Powers, Dallas Morning News*

"(*The Tels*) is WRITTEN SO SPLENDIDLY, at times I forgot I was reading science fiction – with the emphasis on fiction. The characters are realistic, and the hero is someone you relate to, worry about and wonder if he's going to be able to cope with the reality that is set before him. This is definitely ONE OF THE BEST SCIENCE FICTION NOVELS I've ever read...the BOOK IS REMARKABLE."

~ *Marilyn Meredith, Writer's Digest's 11th Annual Book Awards*

"...*Soulware* was a BRILLIANTLY EMBROIDERED STORY, mixing science and fiction in a plausible and entertaining way...I absolutely LOVED THIS BOOK!"

~ *Ismael Manzano, G-POP.net*

*"...it moves at lightning speed.
Mr. Black has quite an imagination
and puts it to good use."*

"I agreed to review the science fiction novel, *The Tels*, by Paul Black as a favor to my coworkers.... I had expected the handoff to come attached with a few snickers...I was truly amazed by how wrong I was. Not only did I enjoy the book, I almost feel guilty that I got to review it...The book is the kind of science fiction that I like to read, not weighed down with technical jargon that the average person cannot understand....The prose is light and catchy, but did not fail to bring the emotional hammer down when necessary. It's a character-driven piece that was WORTH EVERY SECOND I'D SPENT ON IT...get your hands on a copy of *The Tels*."

~ *Ismael Manzano, G-POP.net*

"The biggest complaint about science fiction is that there is always too much science and not enough fiction. In *The Tels* Paul Black brilliantly combines the two in a novel that is almost too plausible...Blending sex, government intrigue and a new reality aren't easy tasks but Black is up to it. Taking us for a ride through a world totally different from our own and yet with the emotions that aren't going to change between now and 2109...*The Tels* DOESN'T LET GO AND STAYS WITH YOU AFTER THE LAST PAGE."

~ *Leslie Rigoulot, Continental Features Syndicate*

"...I was totally hooked...*The Tels* is for anyone who loves a good story, with LOTS OF ACTION AND GREAT CHARACTERS."

~ *Jo Ann Holt, OC Tribune*

"A riveting science fiction novel...an imaginatively skilled storyteller."

"This story by Paul Black is as STRONG AND WELL WRITTEN as any of the stories of my heroes: Robert Heinlein, Isaac Asimov, Andre Norton, or Anne McCaffrey. He is one of those writers that we who worship this genre look for every time we pick up the novel of an author who is new to us...The CHARACTERS COME ALIVE for you. You feel right along with them. You can believe the decisions they make. And best of all, nothing is clear-cut and simple. The story brings us to a strong ending while leaving us with the desire for more...I recommend *The Tels* to every lover of sci-fi. Good work, Paul! Welcome to my bookshelves!"

~ John Strange, thecityweb.com

"Paul Black's ENGAGING PROSE promises big things for the future...."

~ Writer's Notes Magazine

"...a GREAT READ, full of suspense and action...."

~ Dallas Entertainment Guide

"A RIVETING science fiction novel by a gifted author...*The Tels* would prove a popular addition to any community library Science Fiction collection and documents Paul Black as an IMAGINATIVELY SKILLED STORYTELLER of the first order. Also very highly recommended is the newly published second volume in the *Tels* series, *Soulware*, which continues the adventures of Jonathan Kortel in the world of tomorrow."

~ Midwest Book Review

"*The Tels* is an addictive read...
manages to capture the reader in the first
ten pages...*The Tels* has it all."

"Black rises above the Trekkie laser tag spastics found in your typical sci-fi novels resting on the grocery store racks. His sensibilities broaden from machine gun testosterone to discreet fatherhood, from errant sexuality to wry humor. HE DELIVERS A CHARGE OF VENTURE RARELY FOUND IN FIRST-TIME WRITERS. And *THE TELS* HITS THE MARK as a solid adventure serial, leaving you hanging for the next publication."

~ *Brian Adams, Collegian*

"*The Tels* is an ADDICTIVE READ from first-time novelist Paul Black, a promising new storyteller on the sci-fi scene. He manages to capture the reader in the first ten pages. He introduces us to a set of intriguing characters in a totally believable possible future. There is a grittiness and sensuality to his writing that pours out of every word in the book. Whether it's his description of the preparation of a good meal, the seduction of a beautiful woman, or a fight to the death, *THE TELS* HAS IT ALL. Even people who don't read sci-fi will want to read this book. The action is great and would make one hell of a movie. Is Hollywood listening? Paul Black has a winner on his hands. I can hardly wait for the next installment."

~ *Cynthia A., About Towne, ITCN*

"*Soulware* doesn't miss a beat as it continues Jonathan's story, the story of his quest to find out exactly who he really is and why the Tels are so interested in him. The ending makes it clear that there's more to come, and readers who crave their science-fiction with a hint of weirdness can look forward to the next book in the series."

~ *Steve Powers, Dallas Morning News*

SOULWARE

PAUL BLACK

NOVEL INSTINCTS

NOVEL INSTINCTS PUBLISHING

501 S. 2nd Ave.   Suite A-100
Dallas, Texas 75226
www.novelinstincts.com

This book can be ordered on the web,
at www.barnesandnoble.com, www.amazon.com or at all major retailers.

ISBN: 0-9726007-2-8
Library of Congress Control Number: 2004097635
Printed in the United States of America.

Cover photo: PhotoDisc / GettyOne.
Author photo by Jeff Baker.

AUTHOR'S NOTE The Tels series is a trilogy. *Soulware* is the second book, and the reader should know that it is the continuation of Jonathan Kortel's struggle as he continues his quest to discover his power and destiny. Even though *Soulware* can stand alone as an independent novel, I would highly recommend that you read book one so as to fully enjoy the story from its beginning. If you're a fan of the first book, thanks for coming back and please enjoy the read. But if you are new to the Tels, get ready to enter a fascinating world that could be just around the corner.

FOR BRYAN

~

BOOK TWO
SOULWARE

JANUARY

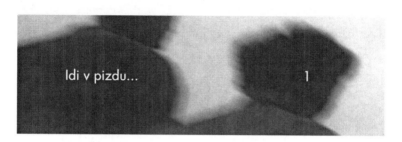

Idi v pizdu...   1

JONATHAN Kortel quietly sipped kapustnyak in his favorite booth, the three-quarter-circle one in the rear corner of the VIP section.

Nikita's was one of Moscow's oldest nightclubs – nothing fancy, but hell, what was fancy in Russia these days? Mainly, it was dark, quiet, and Jonathan felt a kind of kinship to its spavined black vinyl marked by a hundred years of patched tears and embedded effluvium. He had passed many a good time in this booth. He often thought that the owners should put up a small plaque in his honor. Lord knows he had spent enough digirubles to warrant it. Best of all, it was right under the VJ's cage. Just reach up and pass her some extra credits, and she would stream whatever you wanted. That's why he had always requested it. Asking was merely a formality, though. As soon as he called, they knew what he wanted.

And who he wanted.

But the best part about Nikita's? No one would bother him. Nikita's was deep in the heart of one of the world's darkest cities, and Jonathan could bury himself in the booth with the glow from the table candle as his only light. In a remote corner of the club.

Far from the world.

Far from the Agency.

He looked into his soup at the flecks of pork and fat and garlic. This was not biofood; this was real food from the old Russia, the Russia that had seen a hundred invaders since its birth in the ninth century. A flood of memories came swimming back in the bowl.

In a prior life he had been a successful programming chef, riding the crest of a revolution that had washed over all of humanity. The Biolution had changed life forever and had made the world a different place – a dangerous place, some felt. The fusion of organic peptides and nanobiotics had swept away all the old issues of bandwidth. Entire industries were changed virtually overnight. The Net was everywhere, which meant the world was in your pocket like it had never been before. But tonight, Jonathan Kortel was off line. Maybe permanently, if things could go his way.

He sensed the three Russian Tels the second they entered. He didn't know how he could sense others like himself; he just could. It was like a scent he could smell in his mind. These were big Russians. Powerful. Probably from their equivalent of the

New America Agency. They were simply known as the *u'ebitsche*. The Freaks.

They turned down the collars of their thick gray overcoats while they calmly walked past Zoya, the door girl. Fresh snow fell from their shoulders and melted into the warm, plush carpet that had covered the floor of the restaurant for five decades. They passed the main stage and its caviar bar, where the Moscow elite hungrily dug in and knocked down its precious vodka. They passed the VIP doorman, who stood oddly motionless, staring blankly into a world only he could see. The Siberian cowboys refused to meet the gaze of any patron, so focused were they on their target. They knew exactly whom they wanted and where he could be found. The club became coldly silent, as if Stalin himself had walked in and taken a table.

Jonathan meticulously separated the pork from the fat. The Russian Tels stopped at the narrow entrance of his booth. The tops of their coats were now soaked by the melted snow, and a wide trail of wet footprints followed them from the front door. Like trees from the frozen Siberian forests, they stood planted, watching Jonathan calmly slurp the sauerkraut off his spoon. These men were like the country itself: massive, cold, and as emotionally frozen as a Murmansk river.

Jonathan scooped another spoonful.

"*Govorite li vy po russki?*" the middle one asked. The creases in his cheeks deepened as a smile crept across his face.

Jonathan didn't grace him with his attention. He continued to eat his soup.

"I would think not," the Russian said, now in perfect English. "We have heard a lot about you, Comrade Kortel. I quite frankly thought you were nothing more than disinformation from your Agency, but I can see that you are real *and* quite human."

The one on the left grunted under his breath with what could have been taken as a laugh.

"Is it true, Jonathan..." he said as he leaned forward until Jonathan could smell his acrid breath. "I can call you Jonathan, can't I?..."

Jonathan took another spoonful.

"...that you're *faster* than light?"

A noodle slapped Jonathan's upper lip as he sucked it down.

The Russians looked at each other, then back to Jonathan. "*Idi na huy*!" [*Go to hell (penis)*: a mild insult] the one on the left exclaimed.

"He's nothing but a *pedik*!" (a male who is used as a female in prison) said the one on the right, and they started to laugh.

"*Idi v pizdu* [*Go to hell (vagina)*: a worse insult]," Jonathan said apathetically. He ripped off a hunk of bread to wipe his bowl clean.

The Russians stopped laughing. Their expressions turned deadly serious. The muffled pitch of black-market, handheld Light-Force bioweapons collectively whined under their dense wool coats.

"No," the one in the center replied, *"you* go to hell!" And with the grace of Bolshoi dancers, all three drew in sync.

The light from their weapons' discharges exploded like

an antique flash photograph and captured on the retinas of the patrons every terrible detail of the dank Moscow nightclub.

Jonathan calmly wiped his mouth with the linen napkin, leaned back against the cool vinyl and casually took in his would-be assassins. The beams of matter-shifting light protruded about four feet from each gun muzzle, suspended motionless. They emitted no sound and glowed white hot. He calmly leaned forward and lit a cigarette from the end of one of the beams.

"Now," Jonathan said, smiling around the cigarette. "Who did you say was going to hell?" He exhaled smoke into the face of the center assassin and settled back into the comfort of the booth.

The big Russian's eyes were wide with fear. "Forgive us—" He choked on the rest of his sentence.

Jonathan took another drag and sighed. He had grown weary of challenges. If someone had told him two years ago that the strange little "episodes" that had riddled his former life were just manifestations of his true telekinetic nature, he would have thrown them from his restaurant. But when someone finally did tell him, he didn't do a thing. Because ever since the Agency had approached him, he had been in denial of the truth. He was a Tel, and perhaps the most powerful one ever.

Jonathan slid gingerly out of the booth, knowing all too well the deadly nature of the Light-Force beams. One touch and he would be reduced to a biological puddle, hardly distinguishable from the puddles of water left by the Russian Tels' march through the club.

As he made his way through the tables of Muscovites, he

felt their stares burn deep into his soul. Being a Tel meant living in the world of rumor – that aberrant space between headlines and copy. He had become part of a secret family that had grown weary of a world consumed with petty conflicts and global egos. Still tolerant of human limitations, yet having no patience for their arrogant view of life, the Tels had come to look upon their human brethren with an admixture of pity and disdain, and Jonathan had become their point man, whether he wanted the role or not. But tonight, all he had wanted was a bowl of soup. With a side of solitude.

He neared Zoya, who stood next to the receptionist booth with his coat draped across her arm. She was the classic Slavic beauty: tall, solid, and with enough intelligence to cut someone off at the knees. They didn't exchange a word while he slid his arms into the sleeves and hiked the heavy garment onto his shoulders. When she stepped back, the coat's living fabric sequenced to the preset protocols of his body grid. It wrapped tightly at the neck, cuffs and legs, creating a personal cocoon against the harsh winter night. He took her netpad from her hand, entered his tip for the evening and watched as she read the amount. She slowly lifted her eyes and smiled a wide, red grin. He returned a slight smile and began to leave.

Knowing he had a serious "containment issue" at Nikita's, Jonathan stopped short of the front door and turned to the room of hardened Russians. They were all staring at him with the same dead expression inculcated by a culture that had seen it all. Every Tel knew that the key to their joint survival was complete and utter secrecy. Jonathan looked over to the three assassins still held in his grav field and knew he had serious breach. There was only one thing to do. He quietly slipped into phase.

As Jonathan came out of phase, his vision changed from white to a blur of color and, finally, into focus. He looked around at the 60 or so patrons and staff draped in various ways over chairs, or in crumpled heaps on the dense red carpet. All had been put into deep telekinetic sleep, and all would wake with a wicked headache and not remember the last five to nine hours of their lives. The three assassins' bioweapons had completed their discharge, the impact coming where he had sat just moments before. The center of the damaged booth was now a gooey, disfigured blob of congealing wood, horsehair and vinyl. It hissed as it slowly dripped and spread across the floor.

I'm going to miss that booth, he thought.

Zoya had fallen where she stood. He lifted her body and gently placed her in an overstuffed wingback. He brushed the hair off her forehead. His hands never left his pockets. He finished his cigarette.

Jonathan bent and softly kissed the top of her head, then passed the back of his hand down the side of her cheek. He let the tip of his finger stop gently at the edge of her mouth. *"Do svidaniya,"* he said reflectively.

When he approached the antiquated front door, he stopped and let his hand slide over its worn surface of knots and grain. It was real wood, from an actual tree, probably felled in the forests near Moscow more than 200 years ago.

Only in Russia, he thought.

The winter wind hit his face like a thousand tiny needles. The gale had whittled the snowflakes to ice, and even the high-tech thermo biofabric of his overcoat couldn't stop the brutal Arctic wind.

He had ordered a bowl of soup. What had come was a helping of grief for a life lived in shadow. He'd had his fill of it for two years, moving from one black assignment to another, shuttling between bleak apartments in a country that had never really crawled out of the collapse of Communism. His world now was a far cry from his prior life. It had its own rules, its own agendas and its own judgments. He had been warned that it would change him, but he had jumped into it anyway, arrogantly dismissing the possibility that *he* could be changed. He turned his face from the bitter wind and headed back to a cold and empty hotel bed. His netphone hummed deep inside his overcoat, and his nerves, even after all this time, still flinched from the knowledge of what that vibration meant. He let it hum through its answer sequence.

Jonathan Kortel was off-line.

"Fuck the Agency," he said to himself, and hailed the first cab that could move out of the busy Moscow traffic and get to his side of the street.

MARCH ~ 2 YEARS EARLIER

PAUL BLACK

The life left behind...   2

"**MR. KORTEL**?...Mr. Kortel?!"

Jonathan, his seat still trying to vibrate him gently awake, snapped back from a deep, thick sleep to see the flight attendant's face in his sleep station's vidscreen.

"I'm so sorry to disturb you," she chirped, "but you have a vidcall. Would you like to take it, or shall I have them call back after you freshen up a bit?"

"No, no. That's okay. I'll take it," he said, clearing his throat. His bed finished transforming to its seat configuration and settled into place.

The flight attendant smiled, and her image was replaced with the logo of Nations Air. Then James McCarris appeared, his slim face pressed to the edges of the small screen. "Ahh, did I wake you? Sorry, man. I can call back..."

"No, don't worry, James. I needed to get up. I think they're about to serve dinner anyway. What's up?"

"Well, for one thing, the unit director wants a debrief on Paris as soon as you get in tomorrow."

"Shit, James, can't it wait till Monday?..." Suddenly, the gigantic transcontinental Airbus jerked to one side and threw Jonathan against the bulkhead. "What the hell?..."

James's face instantly was replaced with the flight attendant's, her smile calm and bright. "Please take your seats, ladies and gentlemen. We're experiencing a little turbulence. We should be out of it shortly. And for you folks exercising on the second level, please stop what you're doing and take an available seat until we enter clear air. Thank you."

With the Biolution, the giant modern commercial airliner had become more of an airborne mall at 48,000 feet. Flight control, thrust and stabilization were now a fine art. Planes didn't fly, they slipped through the air, and to experience a bump, much less a jolt that knocked you against your seat, had been almost unheard of for 30 years.

James's face returned. "Everything okay there?"

Jonathan cautiously surveyed the cabin. "Yeah...yeah, I think we're okay." He slowly turned in his seat and faced the vidscreen. Both Tels were silent, remembering a similar jolt that had ended in tragedy.

Jonathan settled back into his seat, its living fabric nestling him in First Class luxury as it recalled the memory of his frame. "Now, what were you saying?"

"Oh right, there was one other thing..." James hesitated.

"Yeah?" Jonathan pressed.

"...we found Tarris."

Jonathan stared into the inky blackness of the airspace high above the Atlantic. They were slicing through the boundary zone between the atmosphere and the edge of outer space, high above the weather that wrapped the earth in a blanket of sporadic turmoil. Even though the need for a crew to fly the huge aircraft had vanished over 20 years ago, it was comforting to Jonathan that a human was still required in the cockpit. His thoughts drifted...

Tarris had been more than just a boyhood friend: He had been a brother figure and, many times, a father figure.

When the first wave of the Biolution hit, it took with it certain industries that had been the foundation of the world's economy. When the ability to create synthetic oil and its thousands of byproducts became a reality, the need to pump the planet dry of what was once its most important resource dried up. So, too, did the power of the Arab world. Checkmated in a global chess match, the Middle East never saw it coming. The resulting demotion in world ranking had pushed radical elements of the Arab world to show the infidels one last demonstration of anger. But this was not going to be your average terrorist act. Sadder than the World Trade towers, deadlier than the Jerusalem incident, more heinous than the Olympics of 2044, the detonation of an untested biothermonuclear weapon not only obliterated the Hawaiian Islands, it robbed Jonathan of a childhood and the parents who would have shared it.

Tarris had not been the best surrogate brother or father, but he always had been there when Jonathan needed him. Growing up parentless in the Midwest had left a scar on Jonathan's soul, and Tarris had filled the void when questions about life, or love, had overwhelmed him. Years later, when the inevitable realization of his telekinetic nature had overthrown his orderly life, Jonathan had sought out his old boyhood friend.

Tarris had introduced Jonathan to the urban myth of the Tels and their secret culture. He also had unknowingly set into motion a sequence of events that drew Jonathan into a battle between two rival Tel leaders. Like telekinetic Mafia dons, Jacob Whitehorse and Armando Zvara fought their own personal battle, with Jonathan as the prize. Each knew that Jonathan might be the next step for their kind, but each had his own agenda and his own view of where Jonathan fit into the Tel world order.

Whitehorse had been the founder of the Rogues, a radical group that had left the Agency to pursue a platform of helping their human cousins throughout the world. They secretly intervened when necessary – helping the downtrodden on the world stage. Whitehorse had used Tarris to get to Jonathan, and in doing so, he had leveraged the love of Tarris's life.

Always the good Rogue, Georgia dutifully took the assignment, but didn't foresee that she would fall in love with Tarris, the man she had been sent to set up. When the plan to bring

Jonathan into the Rogues via Tarris turned into Jacob Whitehorse's personal vendetta against Armando Zvara, things turned deadly. Whitehorse was blinded by his hatred for the Agency and vowed that if he couldn't have Jonathan, no one would. Arrogantly, he had underestimated Jonathan's telekinetic potential, and in a desperate attempt to force his decision, Whitehorse had threatened the only thing that mattered in Jonathan's life: the woman he loved.

Pushed by a series of deadly events and driven by fear for his girlfriend, Jonathan had unleashed a telekinetic ability the Tel world had never seen before. With the death of Whitehorse at Jonathan's hand, the stage had been set for him to "cross over" to the cold hard reality of what he was.

When Jonathan chose to join the Agency, Georgia felt it was time to come clean with Tarris, her lover. It didn't go exactly as she had planned. Tarris felt betrayed by the only woman he had ever truly loved – a woman who had overlooked the fact that he was paraplegic and loved him for who he was. Crushed by the deception, Tarris left Georgia. He disappeared, leaving behind his life as one of the top independent developers of biogames. He left his beloved compound in the New Mexican desert and never looked back.

To his lover.

Or his boyhood friend.

"Jonathan? Hey Jonathan, are you with me?" James asked from the vidscreen.

"Yeah." He stared out the window. "Is he...all right?"

"Not really, unless you think being strung out on Jack is all right."

Devil's Jack was the biodrug of choice for heavy riders. Tarris had battled with addiction all his life. He had stayed clean for many years, until the truth about his lover tipped the scales.

"Is he bad off, James?" He already knew the answer.

"Yeah, well...I guess he's surviving. I mean, he's living off his royalties. Man, he's buried himself really deep. You know it's taken us a year to find him. This guy is so good he's firewalled himself into oblivion. He made it so hard to trace his money flow, we gave up for a while. Shit, he should come work for us!"

Jonathan kept staring.

"Well, I'll let you go. Enjoy your dinner, and we'll see ya when you get back." James made a click sound with his mouth and the vidscreen cut out.

"Later, James," Jonathan said to the blank screen. He never heard the answer to his question.

. . .

The flight attendants began to prepare the First Class cabin for dinner. Jonathan had ordered the salmon and was interested to see how the biofood would be prepared. As a former programmer, chef and proprietor, he was always curious how other chefs worked. When the attendant served his dinner, the presentation and the smell seemed strangely familiar. The texture and flavor combinations had been programmed to his specific genetic requests, but as he ate, there was a palatable *deja vu*. He motioned to one of the flight attendants.

"Yes, sir. Is there a problem?" The attendant squatted down in the aisle to meet his eyes.

"This dinner is excellent. Do you know who the chefs are, or what programs they may be using? I'm very curious. The flavors are so unique."

"I don't know, sir, but I can certainly ask the head steward. He probably knows." The attendant hurried toward the forward galley.

Jonathan continued to enjoy his dinner, savoring the salmon and the delicate hint of saffron in the rice.

"This flight's dinners have been prepared in our Chicago facilities, sir," the attendant said on his return. "I was told that we are featuring dishes from different Chicago restaurants. I believe yours is from..." (he pulled a napkin from his pocket) "...oh, yes...Kortel's. I've never been there, but I've heard the food is fabulous. Is that the information you were wanting?"

Jonathan went numb. He quietly pushed the dinner forward, picked up his merlot, and turned his attention out the window. It was Saffron Salmon from kitchen Kortel. It was his old partner's recipe.

. . .

The lights dimmed throughout the cabin as the flight

attendants collected the empty dinner trays. Jonathan sipped his wine while the plane slipped through the night. His thoughts drifted back to his old restaurant and friend.

And to the life he had left behind.

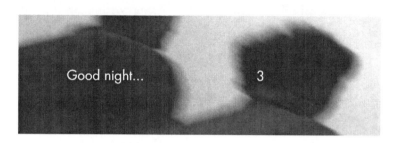

Good night...   3

JONATHAN clicked off the vidscreen, folded it tight and returned it to its compartment in the seat in front of him. Throughout the cabin, most of the individual lights were turned off as the First-Class passengers slept off their sherry-glazed ducks and crème brûlées. He couldn't sleep. Only two lights – along with a woman's across the aisle from him – were on. Younger than most trans First-Classers, she had taken her seat back in Orly. He had noticed her immediately, and couldn't help occasionally glancing over. With her curly blonde hair and tall frame, she reminded him of someone he had once been very close to – someone who had changed his life. He watched intently as she engaged in something most people had given up years ago, a ritual that had disappeared with the postal service and land-based telephone. She appeared to be writing a letter.

Abruptly, she put down her pen and turned in his direction. Like a schoolboy caught in class, Jonathan quickly shifted his attention to the window. After a few moments, he slyly glanced back and found she had returned to the business of writing. She turned to fish something out of her purse, and her elbow knocked her antique pen off the tray table. Jonathan considered mentally catching it, but instead, he decided to pick it up with his hand and introduce himself.

"Excuse me," he said, sliding over, "you dropped your pen." He had snatched it before it could roll under the foot of the snoring passenger behind her.

She met his advance with quiet, cool blue eyes that disappeared into slits when she smiled. Her curly hair fell over her forehead. "Thank you," she said with an unfamiliar accent. She took the pen while tucking her hair behind the edge of her ear. "I've lost a million things on these huge planes."

"I can relate. I've lost a ton of things, too. It looked like a beautiful antique, and I thought you might miss it. Besides..." He glanced at her writings, then back to her. She met his look with the beginnings of a wary smile. "...it would be a shame for you not to finish your...letter?"

She completed her smile and clicked the pen's cartridge into place. Her fingers grazed the paper. "Poetry, actually."

"Really? Poetry?"

"What? You find it odd that I?—"

"No, no. Nothing like that. I think I'm more...I mean, I thought it might be, you know, something personal."

She began to laugh.

"What? What did I say?"

She looked over, her eyes slivers of blue framed by the most perfect complexion. She covered her mouth as if she were ashamed of laughter. *"Hvordan yndig, deres flirting med meg,"* she said more to herself than to him.

"Hvorfor ikke? Det er ikke daglig de møter en vakker, intelligent kvinne," he replied.

Her laughter waned, and he was again looking into her crystalline blue eyes.

"Thank you," she said cautiously, her English returning. "Where did you learn Norwegian?"

"My work demands that I know a number of languages." He held her gaze just long enough, remembering a similar face and a similar look. His smile fell away, and he began to slide back to his seat.

"Excuse me," she said, "are you all right?"

"Hmm?" he questioned. "Yeah, it's nothing. It's just that you remind me of...ah, I'm sorry to have disturbed you." He resumed his sliding.

"Who...*is* she?" she softly questioned.

He stopped. "Excuse me?" he asked, slowly looking back.

"You know, who is she?... Who did I remind you of?" She sported an intuitive half smile.

Jonathan sheepishly grinned, embarrassed at having been

so obvious. He leaned on the armrest of his seat. He stroked the hair he had let grow under his chin. "Was I that obvious?"

"Well...no. I mean, I could just tell..." She smiled nervously, like she was trapped in a conversation she might not want to have.

"I'm sorry if I embarrassed you."

"No, not at all...please, tell me about her."

"Nah, it's boring–"

"No, please," she pressed.

Jonathan's attention was caught by a cute little girl playing with a toy horse in an aisle seat two rows ahead of him. His mind flashed back to the last moments he had with Tamara – the girl who had taught him how to let go of his pain – and her daughter, Nicole, playing at their feet in the restaurant where she and Jonathan had talked, and laughed, and decided to let their walls down. Possibly, even, to love one another. The thought of her crashed against his heart.

"Although," he said reflectively, still staring at the little girl, "I sure did love her." He glanced back.

They sat staring at one another, as when two strangers acknowledge the same feeling toward something with a laugh or nod of the head. Jonathan sensed, momentarily, a shared feeling. A shared pain. That she had also lost someone. Someone important. Someone she had loved.

"Tell me about her," the stranger urged again.

"Well..." Jonathan hesitated. "No. No I can't. It's a very complex story, and one that I can't really go into."

"You can with me."

Jonathan's look questioned her.

Her smile returned. "It's all right. People talk to me every day...it's part of my job...to listen to people."

"Are you a psychologist or something?"

"I've studied psychology, but I'm not a psychologist. I'm in the priesthood, actually."

Jonathan felt himself staring.

"What," she asked, "are you that surprised?"

"No, no, it's just...that..."

"That a priest can't be pretty?" Her grin returned.

"No...I mean, maybe...wait..."

She began to laugh, and Jonathan joined her.

"I'm sorry," Jonathan said, "I didn't mean to be offensive."

"Don't worry, I get this more than I care to admit."

"So what, ah...faith are you?"

"Catholic," she replied with an edge of pride.

"That's right...that was passed last year."

"It's been a long time coming, and our new Holy Father has a more progressive point of view than his predecessors."

"But you're Norwegian...I thought Norway was mainly Protestant."

"There're a few of us in Norway, probably more than you think."

"Say, um, how did you get?..." He pointed to her seat.

"They had overbooked, and this was the only seat left."

"Really? Well then, I guess congratulations are in order for your ordination."

"Oh, I'm not a priest yet. I've just been ordained into the Transitional Diaconate. I have another six months of studies to complete before I'm ordained into the Permanent Diaconate. But thank you. Now, weren't you going to tell me about this woman I remind you of?"

Jonathan was already feeling the fatigue from his Paris assignment. He hadn't talked with anyone about Tamara since the last time he had seen her – at their breakfast spot two years prior, where he saw firsthand how brutal the Agency could be.

"All right then," he said, letting his guard down. "But will you have a drink with me, or is that not allowed?"

She smiled and nodded. "Obviously you haven't been around many Catholics."

. . .

The huge plane was quiet as most of its 800 passengers slept or read. He told her about the life he had led in Chicago, his partner at the restaurant, and the girl who had entered his life and shown him what it was to love. He told this complete stranger about Tamara's life as a single mom and about little Nicole, an exact miniature of her mother. He remarked to the stranger that she had eyes similar to Tamara's, which went to slits when she smiled. He had loved that trait. She blushed at the comparison.

He continued to tell how they had met, and how most people hadn't understood why he was so drawn to her. Why neither of them could explain their deep, passionate need for each other.

Beyond just sex. Even beyond love. Their feelings had been almost instinctual. He also explained what Tamara did. She was a dancer, and not your Broadway kind, either. Tamara was the kind that preyed on the insecurities of men and women and parted them with their credit faster than their netbanks could transfer the funds. Even with her high marks in art history, she couldn't escape the lure of easy money. Combined with the need to care for her child, it kept pushing her back into a life she despised. He didn't even get into the Nevada thing – that she had turned tricks at an age when most girls were worrying if their major was going to get them a decent job. Even though they had both known that it would probably never work out, they had gone for it nonetheless. They both had let go of their bags and jumped aboard a relationship that was sure to become a train wreck.

"Why did it end?" she asked.

"Because..." But Jonathan caught himself. He had never told anyone before about his true nature. He hesitated and took a large drink of Scotch.

"Because why?" she pressed.

"Because I discovered something about myself, and it changed my life." He couldn't meet her eyes.

"Oh, it can't be that bad," she offered. "You seem pretty normal to me."

Hardly, Jonathan thought. He glanced up and met her questioning look. "I shouldn't really say any more. I'm sorry to have taken up so much of your time." He turned away, but felt her hand at his shoulder. He slowly faced her and was met again by her eyes. This time they were filled with a profound care.

"Is there something you'd like to...confess?" Her voice was quieter and had a taken on a more serious tone.

Jonathan smiled slightly. "No, it's nothing like that. Don't get me wrong, I've done some questionable things....It's kind of required in my world now. But why my relationship with Tamara ended is, well...you wouldn't believe me even if I told you."

"It's not about whether I believe you, it's about whether God will forgive you." Her look seemed to cut to his soul. She leaned over and said, "And He *will*."

"Thank you, I'm sure He will. But what I discovered about myself has nothing to do with sin....It's a little, ah, out there."

She politely folded her hands. "Please, go on."

There was something about her sincerity that caught him off guard. *What the hell*, he thought, *she'll never believe me*. "Okay." Jonathan took a large gulp from his drink and faced her. "I'm telekinetic," he said, and the sensation of relief rippled though his being.

The stranger just stared at Jonathan for a second, then her expression changed, like the temperature in her body had suddenly fallen 20 degrees. "I see," she said, nodding her head in a professional manner.

Jonathan pensively pulled at the patch of hair under his chin. "I told you it was out there."

"I have to admit, I've heard some strange things before, but this does qualify as one of the stranger. Who else have you told?"

Jonathan laughed slightly to himself. "You don't

understand...there's a lot of us out there. Possibly a couple of thousand–" Jonathan stopped himself, knowing he was seriously breaching Tel protocol.

"What's the matter?" she questioned.

"It's weird," he said. "I've never explained it before, I mean...we're not supposed to."

She gave him that look again. "Remember, this is between me, you and God. What we discuss here is in complete confidence."

Jonathan didn't know whether it was the fatigue or the third Scotch, but the idea of divulging the Tel world to this woman seemed the perfect panacea for a life lived in secret. "I'm not sure where to begin," he said.

"Well," she replied, settling back against her seat, "why not start at the beginning."

He thought for a moment. "We call ourselves Tels....It's short for telekinetics, and we were discovered at the end of the old war – you know, World War II. Back then, they thought we had developed from the extreme conditions of that conflict, which is partly true. Humans have been evolving for thousands of years. But with us, the race took a left turn, so to speak. For some reason, nature decided to click on this ability, probably driven through stress, like the soldiers experienced in battle. It's adrenaline, you see, that triggers the effect, as we call it."

"So...what is this *effect?*" There was a new edge of skepticism in her voice.

"We can manipulate gravity. We're like lighting rods – conduits, if you will, for gravity to flow through. But it's our minds that can alter its properties. Imagine if you could isolate and displace the gravity around, say, a car. Then that car would begin to levitate off the ground. And say you could also control, with pinpoint accuracy, the force within the field of displacement. Then you could move that car around like a toy. Now, not all Tels can do the same thing. There are 10 different levels for the various degrees of strength. Most Tels are between 4 and 6. Some never make it beyond 3 – they can't move much more than a suitcase. But at Level 8, our highest level, they can do some amazing things."

"So, what happened to the Tels after the war?"

"The major governments created departments for us. Sort of safe harbors for the early ones. It also gave the scientists an opportunity to study the effect. As our population grew, so did the size and complexity of the different departments around the world. They kept us a secret...I mean a deep secret. Nobody knew. In America, the early ones were kept at a remote Air Force base in the Southwest. As the level strength grew, we became more of a threat than a experiment, but this is where it gets a little gray for me. I think one thing led to another, and a decision was made between the world departments to go underground. I won't bore you with how they did that, but today, we number around just under a thousand worldwide."

"What level are you?" she inquired.

Jonathan paused. "Me? Uhmm, I'm a little different."

She raise an eyebrow.

"Yeah, it appears that I don't fit the mold. You see, when

the Recruiters—"

"Recruiters?"

"It's how we're discovered. They're a special team. Recruiters will go and study a Potential, what we call a person with the gift..."

She scrunched her face, confused.

"Sorry, the ability. Anyway, they'll study Potentials for a month, a year, however long it takes to confirm they have the gift. Then they'll extract them from society. The age of the Potential dictates the method of extraction. Young ones just...disappear. With older people, they fake something – kidnapping, dying in an accident, whatever—"

"You mean to tell me that you just take a baby from its mother?!" she said on the verge of outrage.

"No! No! Nothing like that. It's thoroughly discussed with the parents before extraction. I mean, you've got to admit, there's no way someone with an ability like ours can function in regular society. Some have tried, but it never works. They always come back—"

"But what about the secrecy thing?" she questioned. "Don't these parents now know about the Tels?"

Jonathan apprehensively looked away.

"What?..." she pressed.

"A high level Tel can also...*impair* a person."

Her look questioned him again.

"Erase their memory, either in fragments or all of it. How do you think we just collectively disappeared one day?"

The stranger sunk back into her seat, staring ahead. Jonathan took a slow sip of his Scotch.

"You never answered—"

"Nine. I'm a Level 9, or so they think," he replied, not looking her in the eye.

"So," she said, "how were *you* extracted?"

Jonathan grinned. "Oh, I found religion."

She started to laugh.

"What? What's so funny?"

"Nothing...religion, that's all. It's just funny."

Jonathan started laughing also. "Yeah, I'm *supposedly* in Nepal right now, at a temple."

"At a...temple?!" She burst out laughing.

He laughed with her. "Well," he said, sharing the moment, "there's more if you're interested—"

"Interested? Why yes," she encouraged. "Please, go on."

"When I was discovered, I guess I was something of an anomaly. The Agency, the New American organization – the one I belong to now – their Recruiters really wanted me. But so did the Rogues. They're sort of a splinter group. A bunch of high-levels from the Agency who got fed up with all the protocol and agenda this, agenda that, and took off to form their own group. Anyway, things got a little ugly. I won't go into all of it right now, but trust me, it got to a dangerous point, involving my best friend, my old business partner and..." His voice trailed off as a memory surfaced like a body that had spent days underwater.

"Are you okay?" she asked tentatively.

"Hmm? Yeah. Just remembering..."

She gasped. "Tamara!" she said, realizing the inevitable conclusion.

"Yeah," he said, nodding, "Tamara."

"Did they?... "

"They did. She, along with everyone else, had to be erased."

The stranger's look softened, as if she actually were buying his tale.

"It's okay...really. It was for the best." He sipped his drink. "So," he proclaimed, cutting the edge off the somber moment, "what do think of my bizarre little story?!"

The stranger, her resolve returning, took a gulp from her wine and went with his lead. "Honestly, I think you're in need of some professional help. This is a little out of my league. I really should get back to my writing." She started to pull the antique pen nervously from her purse.

"Whoa there. Easy. Just a minute, come on now." He motioned for her to stop.

The stranger tentatively returned the pen to her purse. "Please," she whispered from across the aisle, "I'm still in seminary...I'm very new to all this, and I'm feeling very uncomfortable. I know that what you've told me seems very real to you, but with the proper help, I'm sure you'd be able to work out whatever it is you need...to work out....Look, maybe it would be best that I move my seat." She began to collect her things.

"Well, if you're going to move," he warned, "you'd better

be careful. We might enter some unexpected turbulence." Suddenly, the plane seemed to jerk.

She stopped what she was doing and looked at him gravely. "You didn't just do that...did you?"

Jonathan kept facing forward, calmly sipping his Scotch.

"Oh, that was good. That was funny! You really had me going there..." She laughed nervously.

The plane bounced.

She grabbed her wine before it tipped and trained him with a look of utter disbelief. The color had drained from her face.

Jonathan glanced over and raised an eyebrow.

She slammed the rest of her wine.

"Go ahead and blink," he whispered as he leaned across the aisle. "When you do, I'll move the plane, just a little. It'll appear to the pilot like a little rough air."

She pulled back with a "Yeah, right" look on her face.

"Come on, it's okay. I'm not joking. Really, try it."

Determination came over her face. Challenging him, she leaned into the aisle and met his gaze for 20 seconds, then blinked.

The plane again bounced. Her smile disappeared. She sat back into her seat and glared.

"Sir?" Jonathan said to a flight attendant with a chuckle, "I think she'll have another!"

The stranger wasn't laughing.

"Ah, come on. That was funny! You've got to admit. The look on your face was priceless."

"Did you...did you just really do that?" she asked.

Jonathan nodded with a sudden seriousness.

Her expression shifted like this news had hit somewhere near the foundation of her faith.

The flight attendant placed another merlot in front of her. After he left, it rose off the tray. "Oh, good Lord!" she yelled and grabbed the drink.

"Shhh. Easy. It's okay." He glanced at the attendant, who had shot them a look. "Let's not make this an event, all right." He glanced about the cabin to see if anyone else had noticed.

The stranger looked away.

"Hey, don't be scared," he reassured. "We're not here to hurt or do anything bad."

"You talk like you're not human...like you're something else. You are human, aren't you?"

Jonathan hesitated for a moment. "Technically yes, we're human. But in some ways, we're very different. For one, some of our genetic code is different. The resequencing that..." He stopped. He had never explained the science behind their gift. He wasn't sure if he really understood it himself. He could tell he was about to lose her. He smiled. "Look, this isn't coming out right. Let's just say that yes, we're human, but we're developing into something else. Something more *advanced*." He leaned forward, as if he were about to tell her the most important secret ever, and whispered, "We believe that it could be the next step for humanity. Who knows the possibilities?"

The stranger pulled back in her seat, and Jonathan could see fear in her eyes. He had seen it before with Hector, his friend and partner in his restaurant in Chicago. When Jonathan had told him of who he was, what he had become, he could tell that a chasm opened up – himself on one side, and Hector on the other.

It happened to all Tels.

The stranger lowered her head and stared at her wine. "I think I really should move now," she barely managed.

"I don't even know your name," Jonathan said, just realizing it.

The stranger regarded him painfully. Jonathan could sense she was grappling with this new revelation, and it appeared to be testing her faith. "Oh, my name?" she questioned. "Heavens, I can't believe we never introduced ourselves to each other. I'm sorry, my name is Freja–" She froze.

Jonathan leaned back against the seat and studied her eyes. He had never looked so closely into the eyes of someone he was about to erase. He took a slow sip from his drink. The stranger sat motionless, like a holoimage stuck on pause – her mouth caught in the middle of her first name, Frejasomething. It didn't matter. When she woke up, she would find herself in her seat with a glass of wine, figuring she probably had drank too much. She would attribute the headache to the tannins.

Jonathan leaned forward and began his "surgery." He narrowed a grav field to the width of a needle and began applying pressure to the part of her brain that directs short-term memory, and he watched her eyes for any signs of his invasion. They didn't vacillate or dilate. They remained motionless. Quiet. Clear. Blue.

When he finished, he slowly released her, and as she came

out of his mental grip, her eye muscles shut in response to the telekinetic sleep he had induced. He caught her head before it hit the tray table and turned her face gently to one side. He neatly arranged her hair. His hands were still swirling the ice in his glass.

"Is she okay?" the young flight attendant inquired.

"Oh yeah. Just a little too much – you know." He made a motion like he was slamming down an imaginary drink.

The attendant smiled, turned off her light and continued down the aisle.

Jonathan turned his attention to the window and the blackness of the sky. A twinge of guilt cut through him. He thought about her reaction, when she pushed back from him in fear. He glanced down at his netwatch.

11:14:58 pm GMT. Habit. He was supposed to have called in an hour ago.

"Fuck the Agency..." he said under his breath...and yawned. His seat sensed the change in 127 of the 200 different anatomical aspects it was programmed to monitor and began shifting into sleep mode. He leaned back while it reconfigured into a bed. He looked over to the stranger, who was quietly sleeping with her head on the tray table.

"Good night, Mother Freja," he whispered. "Sweet dreams."

P A U L   B L A C K

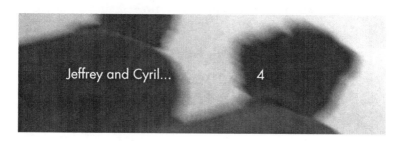

Jeffrey and Cyril...   4

"HERE you go, Mr. Kortel," the driver said, piloting the MicrosoftFord out of traffic and up to the curb.

"Thanks, Mazza. This is good right here." Jonathan patted the young Tel on the shoulder. "More training today?" The car opened his door, and he stepped to the curb.

"Yes, sir. Hopefully moving a level by the end of this year."

Jonathan leaned in through the passenger window. "I wish you the best, man. I know you'll do well in the displacement field tests."

"Thank you, sir!" Mazza said, smiling, and he raised his right hand as if to high-five. But when Jonathan raised his left, their hands never touched. The Tels met each other halfway with their grav field, a mental high five. Jonathan liked the kid. He was 18 years old and, like himself, an orphan. They had that special connection. Nothing weird – just a connection. Like their high five.

"Hey, Mr. Kortel?" Mazza asked, catching Jonathan before he pulled out of the window.

"Mazza, I've told you a billion times, call me Jonathan. What's up?"

"How was...Paris?" His expression went serious.

Jonathan knew why he had asked. Paris had been a "dirty" assignment, one that meant having to displace a person.

"No, Mazza," he said coolly. "I didn't dis anyone."

Mazza nodded his head knowingly. "Yeah, I knew you were a little apprehensive."

Jonathan leaned into the window. "I didn't know you were telepathic–"

"Well...sir...I...I didn't mean to imply that...that you were...ah–"

Jonathan mentally grabbed the boy by the neck and pulled him gently toward him. Mazza instantly shut up. Jonathan glared into Mazza's eyes and smiled, then released him with a jerk and pulled out of the window. "Oh, by the way," he said with a glance back, "you were right. I was apprehensive." He smiled and saw the young Tel was visibly shaken. "You little fucker, you're going to be good. You've got a keen sense about you. Work that seventh sense, man. It'll come in handy someday."

Mazza smiled with relief.

"Hey," Jonathan assured, "I'm just messing with you.

Remember, you need to be ready...for anything. It's a tough world out here, and we seem to be the only ones who can get anything done these days. Know what I'm talking about?"

"You're right about that," Mazza said with the confidence that he had scored big with (if the rumors were true) the most powerful Tel ever.

Jonathan glanced up at the tall metal letters throwing their backlit argon blue at the top of the building. His pant legs whipped about in the wind. *Citenikelet Investments.* He snickered. Some thought they were a Finnish or Dutch firm, while others thought the name was just one of those trendy non-meaning marketing words, arrived at through thousands of dollars by "branding doctors" from the turn of the last century. It was more like a private joke of the New American Tel founders, who knew that they could move through the world's information net undisturbed as an investment firm. They had learned a long time ago that the basis for the world's rhythms was its global financial dealings. Its wars, famines, government overthrows – all driven by the ebb and flow of money and, ultimately, the power that accompanied it. Like some globalwide peristalsis, money moved power through cultures. In New America, *Citenikelet* closely monitored the wave.

In the early 1960s, when the imminent confrontation between the world Tel agencies and their respective governments loomed, the Tel leadership decided that the best course of action was not conflict, but complete disappearance. By erasing any evidence of their existence, both physical and mental, the Tels and their culture vanished as if they had never existed. Now they would live without the fear of reprisal and develop their culture in secret, away from their human cousins, who, by the mid-1960s, were dangerously close to wiping themselves off the face of the earth. The Tel leadership watched from the shadows a world locked in global struggle, until it became increasingly clear that a paradigm shift had taken place in human evolution. Once considered only random mutations, the Tels soon realized their true purpose: to save humans from themselves.

During the late 1960s, they organized into various legitimate corporations. In Europe, they were a food conglomerate. In Russia, they were into manufacturing. And in America, they were an investment firm. From these platforms, the Tels needled out and infiltrated all aspects of society. By strategically placing their people in key positions, they could exercise their own unique influence, hidden puppeteers reshaping a world that was hell-bent on destroying itself.

The first assertion of Tel influence impacted the world in 1963, with the changing of Khrushchev's mind about the nuclear missiles in Cuba. Deftly executed by the Russian Tel agency, it averted what could have been the third and final World War. Like their space agency counterparts, the Russian Tels had beaten the Americans to the world stage. But by the early 1980s, the American Agency discovered that the real money wasn't in political power changing. It was in the corporate sector.

At the beginning of the 21st century, many of America's

high-tech corporations had ridden out the wave of the Internet revolution and were desperately searching for the next big "discovery" that would catapult their industries out of a floundering world economy. Many companies had built their fortunes on the backs of cheap brainlabor from India, who at the time still held the virtue of an education in high esteem. The American Agency had also ridden the wave of the Internet, investing wisely and creating a war chest that could, if necessary, sustain them through the lean, post-boom years. The American Tels, acting through their investment front company, began researching thousands of small start-ups, that, like decades before, had been the catalyst for the digital revolution. They discovered a small Indian bio-tech firm that was researching a bizarre concept about a new branch of science that could bridge the world of chemistry and technology – where living cells would be programmed to inject insulin into a diabetic's bloodstream or be incorporated into a bandage that would analyze an injury and heal the wound. Injected into a soldier, they even could detect when a toxin or agent was released. Taking a chance, the American Tels invested heavily in the firm and, after a period, became its sole funding source. Years of clinical trials and failures went by until e a researcher named Majit Singh developed the first fully functioning, living biochip. Its early processing power was close to a billion times faster than conventional chips. Thus was born (what the TVid pundits termed) the Biolution, with a *Citenikelet* front company owning all the patents.

For nearly 150 years, the Tel world had orchestrated its influence over a planet that was preoccupied with breast size and music videos. The Tel world was stable and hidden, which led them to believe they transcended any "outer world" laws or politics. Level 8's had set the standard and brought a sense of hierarchy and order. That is, until Jonathan Kortel came onto the scene with his faster-than-light field imaging, powerful enough to move 500-ton commercial airliners like model toys. With the arrival of a Level 9, the ground rules shifted, and the Agency might have had something it never possessed before – something that would allow it to manipulate the world order even further.

A weapon.

"Good morning, Jonathan," the receptionist beamed from behind the desk.

"Morning, Tessa. Is he in?"

"Oh yes, and he has Jeffrey with him."

"And how is Jeffrey?"

"He's in one of *those* moods. If I were you, Jonathan," she grinned knowingly, "I'd keep your field up."

"Greaaat. All I need are those two on my ass," he said to himself as he walked past a sea of biocubes, their human occupants busily jacked into the world's financial markets.

"Hey, Jules, how's the Global 200?" Jonathan yelled.

"Like a bull," the young associate answered, pulling the netgear from his face.

"And the Pac 50?"

"Like crap."

"Really?"

"You should know," Jules replied with a smile. "You tanked it last month." He wiped his brow and replaced his netgear; its fiber optic implants clicked in sync as they reestablished their connections.

"No shit," Jonathan said to himself. *Just a little influence on the right person,* he thought, *can always move market attitudes in your favor.* He turned the corner to the elevator bank and offered his eye to the retina reader. "Twentieth floor."

"Yes, Jonathan," it responded in its feminine metallic voice. "And how are you this morning?"

He didn't answer. He had grown tired of responding to public AI's, with their widely reported "collective netconscience," as if they really cared how you were.

. . .

The 20th floor was one grotesquely giant office: Takeda and Trumble's private sanctuary, appointed beyond anything that could remotely pass for civilized taste.

"Good morning, gentlemen," Jonathan said.

"Good morning," Trumble replied, not looking up from his netpad.

Takeda, silhouetted against the morning sun, didn't respond. There was an awkward silence while he stood at the huge bank of windows that ran the length of the floor. Without changing the direction of his gaze, he reached back, and Trumble's netpad flew into his gloved grip.

"Really, Cyril," Trumble scoffed.

Takeda reviewed the data, his back still to the room. Jonathan stood at the landing, his hands calmly in his pants pockets. Trumble sat at a long, steel-legged couch, his arms folded in disgust. More awkward silence.

The HVAC system engaged, and a rushing softly emitted from the wall vents. Trumble cleared his throat. "Today. And take off those silly gloves. You look like some Hong Kong drag fag."

Takeda released the netpad. It floated to Jonathan, who caught it about two feet in front of him. He spun it in the air so that he could view the screen. He played with a chip card in his pocket.

"Excellent work in Paris," Takeda finally said. He turned and walked to the center of the room. "And I wear these gloves because I hate the discharge effect, Jeffrey. You *know* that."

Trumble waived him off.

"Thank you, Cyril," Jonathan replied.

"Are you *comfortable* with the...results?" Trumble asked Jonathan.

Jonathan mentally moved the netpad back to Trumble, who was still waiting for a reply. He caught the tiny device with a casually outstretched hand.

Jonathan knew what the question really meant. "No," he cautiously replied. "I'm not."

"I don't blame you," Takeda said, "but I'm sure it was a last resort. Or so you said."

"The labor talks went as planned, but one of the French

minister's bodyguards...let's just say he confronted me. I'm sorry that I overreacted."

"Yes, well...that was unfortunate," Takeda lamented, sitting down at his massive desk. "Control is one of our most important strengths. Maybe we've pushed you too much. After all, you're young, and you're still getting your mental legs as it were, yes?"

"Yes, quite," the older Tel agreed. "I remember when I was on assignment—"

"Jeffrey, *please*," Takeda snapped. "Don't start with that, *thank you*."

Trumble waived him off again.

"Sovann?" Takeda asked into the air.

A holoimage of an Asian woman appeared on Takeda's desk. "Yes, sir?"

"Make a note, please, to pay off the mortgage on the home of a...Jeffrey, what *was* that guard's name?"

"Mmm...oh, yes," Jeffrey began. "Le Flure. Lieutenant Henri Le Flure. It's all in file PS24563—"

"Yes, yes, I know that! Sovann, it's all in case number PS2456326. Tell them to make it appear to be a loan payoff to his family...from insurance, you know, like we did for that other case, the Jordanian fellow. I doubt his family will argue against it. Thank you, dear." The image vanished.

"Always the generous one," Trumble said, standing to leave.

"We may be serious about our business," Takeda declared, "but we're not without morals. Let's not forget that."

Jonathan just smiled.

Both Takeda and Trumble were Level 8's, and very adept at precise field movements. They had run the American Agency, along with the board of Overseers, for a decade. Trumble had been the first Level 8 to display tendencies toward Level 9. But the exercises had always fatigued the Brit, and his potential was never realized. When the two met almost 30 years ago, it was like a telekinetic firestorm. Had it not been for the partnership of Armando Zvara and Jacob Whitehorse, they could have been the longest governing Tels the Agency had ever known.

Twenty years ago, Zvara and Whitehorse were young Turks whose brand of telekinetics swept the Agency elite off their grav fields. They displayed an uncanny ability to second-guess situations and deliver remarkable solutions. Zvara advanced faster, and became the youngest Tel ever to be named head of the Agency. Over the years, though, the acquisition of power proved to be the undoing of Zvara. As well, he had developed an interest in something equally undoing – a love for Whitehorse's wife.

"Jonathan, please take some time for yourself, will you?" Trumble straightened his tie and eyed him like a father. "We have great plans for you."

"Thank you, sir," Jonathan acknowledged with a slight smile. He entered the open elevator and spun back to the room. "Gentlemen," he said with a tilt of his head, and the doors closed.

The HVAC system ended its cycle, conspicuously draining

the room of sound. Takeda didn't respond. He sat quietly behind his desk and pulled at the tight, black micropore around his fingers. He intently stared at the closed elevator doors.

"If he discovers his true strength," Trumble sighed, "he will be beyond us."

Takeda cracked his knuckles.

PAUL BLACK

Now I've got you...   5

"FINALLY..." Kaya said softly to herself.

She leaned back in her chair and pulled her wavy black hair into a makeshift ponytail. The steady glow of her netport was her only light. She was tired. Worn by the search. For more than a year she had hunted, but not like her ancestors. She hadn't crawled through the prairie grasses of the American Southwest like her great-great-great-grandfather. Her hunt had been through the gigaquads of data that coursed through the world's information net like water through the rivers of her ancestral lands. She hadn't had much to go on: a rumor, a comment. It had all started with a netcall in the middle of the night, a message that pierced her heart like an arrow hitting its mark.

"Your father is dead."

Like her parents before her, Kaya's genetics had separated her from the general population. She had inherited the gift, but had disappointed her father by treading a different path. She had chosen a life outside of the culture and away from him. She had wanted just to be normal.

Kaya stared at the vidscreen with tempered relish. Here was the data she had spent hundreds of hours tracking down. She had hacked her way through multiple firewalls and deeply encrypted telenet security portals of the world's most secretive culture, and now that she had finally broken through, it was as though she had parted the thicket to view an open field – her prey before her, defenseless and unaware. She leaned forward, narrowing her eyes and clenching her jaw as the image of her father's killer quivered on her vidscreen in pixelated glory.

"Now I've got you," she said in the quiet darkness of the room. Then, like her ancestors before her who drew their bows and released death, Kaya Whitehorse clicked the download button.

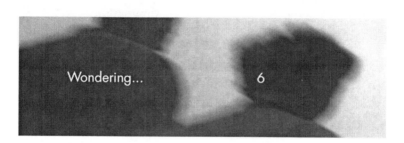

Wondering...   6

JONATHAN mused where he should go. He had never been to New Rio, with its Carnaval and its contest between *escolas de samba*. He had read that the *Cristo Redentor's* new location was even more breathtaking. Higher up. Closer to God.

"Stop on four."

The elevator slowed to a crawl, then halted. "Fourth floor, Jonathan."

As he walked through the open environment, people didn't look up; they just followed him with their eyes. Feigning preoccupation, they tracked him, sizing him up – judging him against what they had heard and what they now perceived. Jonathan rarely stepped onto the fourth floor. Conversations there stopped as he walked past, but it didn't really bother him. He had become used to it. Here on the fourth, people could at least pretend not to notice him.

He passed the ring of outer offices that encircled the pit of netcubes like a Roman amphitheater. In the pit were the new Tels, who hustled in the world markets during the mornings and trained for their levels in the afternoons. Like a giant financial commune, everyone started in the pit. Jonathan had been the only exception.

Approaching the row of Recruiter offices, he slowed as he passed Armando Zvara's. It was sequestered in the corner, silent and sepulchral, and still as Zvara had left it when he and James McCarris had departed for assignment more than two years ago.

Jonathan stepped into the doorway of James's office. "Jimbo," as he preferred, was at his netport slashing someone to his knees. Jonathan leaned against the door frame and folded his arms. A young woman patiently waited in one of the side chairs while Jimbo ranted. Her back was to the door. He smiled at Jimbo, motioned toward the girl and mouthed, "Should I come back?"

Jimbo, still in the the thick of his argument, shook his head. "...that situation is going to be a big bucket of assholes....I don't care, just get it done!" He clicked off the netport. "Jonathan, come on in." He gestured toward the girl. "Look who's coming back to the fold."

The young woman turned in the chair, and her dark, shoulder-length hair fell over her face. She brushed it back and smiled a smile that Jonathan hadn't seen in a long time. He missed that smile.

"Georgia..." he said, and a warmth moved across his heart. "What are you doing here?"

She stood, and her smile grew to the point that her bottom lip curled down in a way that revealed what she might have looked like as a little girl. Her dark, nearly black eyes locked onto his as she wrapped her arms around him and pulled him close. They held for a moment, the air about her redolent with a fusion of rosemary and clary sage. It filled his mind with short little memory trips. He breathed her in; she gently kissed him on the cheek.

"Jonathan," she said, leaning back from their hug. "It's so good to see you." Her hand went to his face.

"God, Georgia, you look great. What...what are you doing here?"

"Coming back to the fold," Jimbo said.

"Oh?" Jonathan questioned tightly. "And what brought this on?"

"She's seen the error of her ways," Jimbo said, cutting her off before she could answer.

"I came back because I was asked." She shot Jimbo a look and curtly smiled.

"Hey, don't blame me. You can stay with the Rogues if you want," Jimbo said, folding his arms. "But, come on, if you—"

"*Really want to make a difference, you can't do it from some compound in New Mexico.* Yes, James, you told me. But if you must know," her voice went soft and serious, "I do want to make a difference in the world. And after Whitehorse, the Rogues have been fractured, at best. No, it's time I got off my butt and started doing something. You know...give a little back. We've been given a great gift, after all."

The men exchanged glances.

"So, Jonathan," Jimbo said, "what can I do you for?"

"I'm thinking about taking some time off, and I wanted to ask you about that place you went to on vacation. You know...the island, in the Caribbean, with that beach house..." He snapped his fingers. "Come on, what's the name again?"

"Tortola?"

"Yeah, that's it. You said it was heaven on earth."

"It's the best. You have got to go! Georgia, you ever been?"

"No, no I haven't. Look guys, I have to run, but Jonathan, call me...please. I want to catch up. My number's in the system now."

Jimbo, ever the Southern gentleman, stood. Georgia hugged Jonathan again. "Please call me," she whispered in his ear. She squeezed his arm and stepped back. Jonathan let his right hand glide down her arm till their hands met. They held for a second, then she hurried away.

"You tell her about Tarris?" Jonathan asked, watching her hurry through the pit.

"Hell, no. I don't think she wants to know, to tell you the truth."

"She still looks great," he said without taking his eyes from her. "And by the way, thanks for finding Tarris. I know that was a pain in the ass for you."

"It wasn't, really," Jimbo assured. "Just more of a challenge figuring out his net patterns. He is one cagey *hombre*."

54

"That's for damn sure," Jonathan said. "You're still not going to erase him, right?"

"No, don't worry. He's way too fucked up to be any threat," Jimbo said, stretching. "Besides, if we closed in, he'd probably just lose us."

"No shit," Jonathan replied and intently watched Georgia step into an elevator.

"Hey, man, what are you thinking?" Jimbo asked.

"Oh, nothing..."

"Bullshit. I know you, Kortel. You're thinking about how great she looks, and how you'd like to get some of that."

"To be honest," he said, still staring at the spot in front of the elevator, "I was thinking about the last time I saw her...at the airport in Albuquerque."

"And?"

"And how she and I had this connection thing going." He glanced at Jimbo, who was looking at him with half a smile working. "What are you looking at?"

"A *connection* thing?"

Jonathan waved him off. "Give it a rest. I was with Tam at the time. We never did anything–"

"But?"

Jonathan reflected back to the time he had met Georgia. There *had* been something special between them. He had felt it from the moment he first met her. But he cared too much for Tarris, and would have never done anything to hurt him...or Tamara. "But what?"

"*But,*" Jimbo said now in full smile, "now that it's been close to two years since she and Tarris were together, and with Tam—"

Jonathan shot him a harsh look that said, "don't go there."

Jimbo nodded and his smile quickly disappeared. "I think you get my drift."

"I get your drift. It's just..."

"Jonathan, come on. I saw how she looked at you. What's done is done. She and Tarris have been split longer than most marriages. Let it go and ask her out. You need to get laid. Besides, when did you get all full of morals?"

Jonathan sighed. "Maybe I will. Hey, you wanna grab a drink after the meeting this afternoon?"

Jimbo nodded and said yes, as well as one could in the course of a yawn, then intently returned to reading his file.

"What's got you so interested there, another strong Potential?"

Jimbo leaned back and pointed to his screen. "This one's a 10-year-old boy in Lawton, Oklahoma, who had been so frightened by the artillery practice at Fort Sill that he lifted one of the old projectile-firing howitzers from five miles away and threw it like a fucking football. Or, at least, that's the rumor running around."

Jonathan whistled. "They're getting stronger younger, aren't they?" He began to leave, but paused and turned back. "Say, James. Where are they going to assign Georgia?"

"Hmm?" he questioned. "Oh, she's going to be a Recruiter."

"Really? And who's she going to be under?"

Jimbo, his attention apparently still in Oklahoma, only grinned.

. . .

"Bar of Chocolate" was one of Washington's most fashionable restaurants. Housed in an old candy factory, the turn-of-the-century building had been retrofitted for the huge bandwidth requirements of bio-tech interface cooking. Its new owners had removed much of the original processing equipment and created multilevel "personal food environments" where patrons could dine from practically anywhere in the restaurant and always have a spectacular view of the Potomac.

Jimbo and Jonathan secured a small table in the corner of the outside patio and cooled their eyes in the urban flow. The air was relatively warm for spring, and the late afternoon sun cut long shafts of light through the area. Being Friday, the sidewalks were filled with freshly released office types. These biped symbols of corporate sovereignty wore their blackest of blacks and descended into the "Chewy Nougat Center": the huge bar inside the restaurant. Here, they could drink and smoke and hunt for the lifemate – or, at least, nightmate – of their dreams. A girl in a tight biotex jumpsuit strolled past Jonathan's table. The living pattern of leopard spots undulated as if the suit were the skin of a real cat. The accuracy of detail wasn't as important as the perception, because most people didn't know the difference. The leopard, along with about a thousand other endangered species, had gone the way of the dodo. Given the kind of light upon her, the effect was eerily real, like a sick genetic experiment gone horribly wrong. Still, the whole package was oddly erotic.

"Now there's some split-tail," Jimbo noted. He took another swig from his beer.

Jonathan shot him a look.

"Hey," Jimbo said, "I can't help how I was brought up."

"I know, you're just a good ol' country boy." Jonathan sipped his drink. "I wonder what kind of work *she's* doing tonight?"

Both men keenly watched as she preened for the crowd, but just before she reached the front doors of the restaurant, she stumbled backward like she had slammed into an invisible wall. Her purse spilled onto the sidewalk, and she almost fell off her heels. She quickly pulled herself together and gathered the essentials of her life – netpad, lip enhancer, various credit and debit chips – back into the purse, and her spots, which had retreated from the trauma into one giant black island in a sea of orange, cautiously began to shift back into pattern.

Jimbo laughed into his beer.

"Did you do that?" Jonathan asked.

"I couldn't resist. I was hopin' to set one of those bad boys free."

"You're such an asshole."

"That I am, Jonathan. And proud of it." He laughed with an air of pride that seemed rooted in some deep history of Southern justification.

"So tell me about this place you rented," Jonathan inquired. "It's on the west side of the island?"

"Yeah, it's a killer house, man. All tricked out. Owned by some Texan — you know the type. The artwork alone was worth the trip. They rent it for damn near nothing, considering you're on the ocean and you get a maid, a cook and a driver. You've got to go, Jonathan. And if you can, take a girl. Man, it's the best place on earth for a little fun in the sun, if you know what I mean."

"I hear that. So, it's right on the beach?" he asked, reflectively sipping his Scotch.

Jimbo nodded.

"Sounds like the place. I'm due some major R&R. That Paris assignment was fucked. Real fucked."

Suddenly, a high-pitched snap echoed about the small shopping canyon. Jonathan looked across the plaza and saw installers hoisting a giant KFBC sign up the front of an old brick building. The snap echoed again.

Jonathan followed the cabling up to the top of the hoist and saw its multistrand interlacing unthreading at the coupling near the roof. The safety wires, which should have been taut, had way too much slack. Another snap echoed. One of the installers on the street desperately began waving people off, but at this last snap, the sign broke free. The giant annijection face of Colonel Sanders started to fall, still smiling and selling the accolades of simfried, cloned chicken as it scraped down the front of the building in a spray of electric gold sparks. The leading edge caught a windowsill and crumpled, which splintered the sign into large, jagged fragments.

Plastic and metal showered the crowded sidewalk. The force of the impact caused the trailing edge of the sign to fall away from the building, and the street-level installer frantically began shoving people out of the way. The safety cables snapped with two loud cracks. The installers gave up and ran. A woman screamed.

In the single moment that it had taken for the situation to spiral out of control, Jonathan had begun to go into phase, but a waiter, spinning at the scream, fell into his lap and broke his concentration. Pushing him, Jonathan jerked his attention back to the street and was startled by what he saw. Like a bizarre post-modern sculpture, the sign and its splintered fragments had slowed to a crawl above the plaza. Jonathan whipped around in his chair.

"Nice catch, slick," Jimbo said with a grin.

"I thought you caught it," Jonathan said, surprised.

Jimbo's grin instantly disappeared. He jumped to his feet and pointed to the plaza. "Look!"

Jonathan spun around. "What the fuck?!" he said, and watched in horror as the sign resumed its freefall. The plaza instantly fell into chaos. People scattered in panic, screaming and stumbling. In a situation like this, the protocols of containment demanded that a Tel deal with the people first; finesse dropped out of the equation. Jimbo instantly phased and telekinetically hurled people out of the impact zone, their legs continuing to kick as if they were on solid ground. Some landed in merciless heaps, while others just kept running. The sign slammed into the pavement, transforming a thousand pounds of annijection plastics and metal into hundreds of pieces of jagged, high-velocity shrapnel. Jonathan tried desperately to envelop the spray pattern and prevent its radius from expanding, but the trajectory angles were vastly too complex to calculate in the milliseconds it took for the sign to disintegrate. Several of the deadly pieces evaded his field and sprayed omnidirectionally across the crowded sidewalks, each shard carrying with it a little element of the Colonel's promotional enthusiasm. Jimbo caught a 10-inch, delta-shaped slice of the Colonel's left cheek inches from the back of a woman's head. It dropped harmlessly to the ground. Jonathan deflected three shards comprising most of the beard and tie as they flew in formation toward an Asian family who struggled with a baby carrier. Diligently, Jimbo and Jonathan stopped as many of the pieces as they could, despite the randomness of their sorties of mutilation about the shopping canyon. One sliced through the shoulder of a boy, sending him to his knees in screams of agony. Another carved a perfect triangle from the calf of a man eating at a biomeal cart. He retched as he collapsed from pain.

While the dust settled, Jimbo and Jonathan stood motionless in a sea of hysteria. Jonathan snapped back from phase and turned to congratulate his friend. A high-pitched whipping sound dopplered into the threshold of his hearing.

He shoved Jimbo out of the way.

The multi-pointed fragment careened through the air and halted between them, right where Jimbo's head had been. For a second it hung motionless, a hideous example of their premature celebration, then it dropped to the ground and splintered the

Colonel's right eye into a triptych that winked sickeningly back at them.

Both Tels took their eyes from the Colonel's and slowly looked at each other.

"Thanks..." Jimbo said, still in shock from what might have been.

"I-I didn't stop it," Jonathan acknowledged.

Jimbo frantically pulled out his netpad and began to sweep the area for who – or what – had stopped the fragment from plowing through his head.

"What are you reading?" Jonathan anxiously asked.

Jimbo didn't say anything and continued scanning.

"James?!"

"Got it...no, wait, yeah, no...wait. Damn!" He slapped the netpad against his fist. "I had 'em, but then the sigs just dropped to zero. I mean instanfuckingtaneously. They never drop like that. There's always some background res floatin' around."

Jonathan searched the area for anyone who might appear out of place. The panic in the canyon began to subside.

"You don't dis gravity at the levs I saw and not leave at least a little res," Jimbo said. He tapped the netpad against his fist. They both slowly sank into their chairs. *This*, Jonathan conjectured, *had been at least a Level 7 effort*. The heavy sign, falling at a high rate of speed, along with its vertical force – not to mention the erratic spray pattern of fragments – made for a challenging telekinetic field displacement.

"No," Jimbo said, still tapping his pad, "something's not

right here...not right at all."

Jonathan watched the crowd build around the debris. The installers busily scurried about and gathered pieces to haul away in their truck. Some people had rushed to the aid of the few who had been struck down. The faint screams of sirens began to fill the air. Soon, the whole area would be swarming with EMS, police and local netnews TVid trucks, their junior reporters all jockeying for the unique paranormal angle to their 10:00 filler segment.

Jonathan picked up his drink, now more water than Scotch, and gulped it down. There had been no bulletins issued about any foreign Tels in Washington, and he seriously doubted any Level 7 Rogues would just wander into the nation's co-capital without being detected. Besides, he should have sensed the Tel's displacement a mile away. He watched the cleanup and wondered. Jimbo kept tapping his netpad.

PAUL BLACK

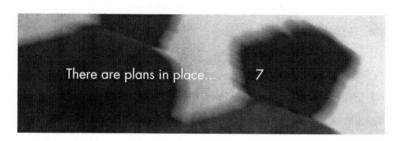

There are plans in place...   7

"**STOP.** Play back my last sentence."

"So, in conclusion, the transfer of 32 million shares will balance the portfolio in favor of the acquisition. I am not concerned..."

"Stop. Change that to: will balance the portfolio *toward* the possibility of acquisition. Resume."

"...that this transfer will signal a change in direction. Rather, it will strengthen our position and allow us to guide the future of the company more easily. If acquisition occurs, then, to the victor go the spoils. Please call me when you have had time to discuss this with your board. Take care and give my best to Leigh. Yours truly, Cyril."

"Good. Send that at 3:30 this morning with the usual protocols."

"Yes, sir. Will there be anything else?"

"Yes, resume the concerto...no, wait. Play something Mozart...mmm, ah, no. Play Pachelbel, the Kanon-Albinoni. Yes, yes, that will be excellent." Cyril Takeda leaned back. The oily water and bubbles swallowed him up to the neck. He mentally reached for his wine. The adagio began.

It was almost nine o'clock in the evening, and Takeda was beginning to relax. He glanced at the TVid, with its split screen of PREM and Kuwaiti Exchanges, and clicked it off. He was sick of the markets. He needed to languish, if even for an hour, in the sanctuary of his own thoughts. No netcalls. No decisions. No interruptions. He slowly closed his eyes.

. . .

"Cyril?..."

The adagio was playing.

"Cyril?!"

"In here."

Trumble threw his overcoat onto the bed, reconsidered and outstretched his hand. The coat flew back, and he hung it in a cavernous room the two of them called a closet.

"I had the most dreadful evening. Three long, boring hours with Ortiez and Toliver. Those Senate subcommittee boys can be the worst," he lamented. He entered the 1,000-square-foot master bath. The 500-gallon tub was the focal point of the room. It rose from the floor entombed in a marble platform, and was practically a Mayan altar with its eight-foot palm trees and natural rock waterfall. "I believe we made an impression on them, though."

Takeda didn't look up, apparently lost in the bouquet of his wine. "Did you convince them of our urgency?"

"Yes."

"And will they now vote their...conscience?"

"Oh, I'm *sure* they will."

Takeda laughed.

"As I was saying, those Senate subcommittee boys...God, is this what we pay for? They're a joke. All they're concerned about is their damn reelection." Trumble yanked at his tie, and it slapped out of the collar. "We need to move out of this town. Somewhere quiet—"

"Like Nice?"

"Possibly. I was thinking more tropical. There's that island we were looking to buy. I believe it's still available—"

"*Please*, Jeffrey. Don't start with that again. You know how I hate the bugs." Takeda disappeared under the bubbles.

Exhausted, Trumble eschewed his upbringing and threw his clothes into a pile at the base of the TVid. He began studying his face in the large vanity mirror that hung in the middle of the dressing area. On the other side of the room, a long white robe left its hook. As it floated, its arms and body filled with the rush of air, creating the eerie appearance that a ghost had donned the robe and was sneaking up on Trumble. He reached back his arms, and the robe gently slipped onto his body. He tied its thick sash around his waist and resumed his study of the mole that had competed for attention on his face for the last 30 years.

Takeda's head broke the surface of the water. "Why don't you just get that thing removed? They've had the technology for, oh, I don't know...200 *years*."

Trumble didn't answer. Takeda rolled his eyes and slipped back under.

"Cyril, I'm worried."

"What?!" Takeda asked, bobbing amid the islands of bubbles and wiping the foam from his face. "What are you worried about now?"

Trumble hesitated. "Jonathan."

Takeda nodded knowingly.

"He's a smart, ambitious boy," Trumble continued. "He's going to discover his true nature soon. We can't hide it from him forever. He is, after all, our future, and it would be in our best interest to nurture that potential. Am I right?"

"Does he still believe his plane incident was...*unique*?"

"As far as I know he still thinks that it was an Extreme Condition Situation, and he hasn't reproduced that kind of grav intensity again, either in the lab or in the field. At least...not yet."

Takeda eyed Trumble. "How's his training going? Are they still holding him at level?"

"Yes, yes, they are," Trumble said. He tore himself away from the mirror. "But all it's going to take is an assignment where another ECS comes up and he'll begin to develop again. And this time, we're not going to be able to contain him. Look at what he did to that French security man. My God, all he did was look at the poor fellow, and his head practically imploded."

"Oh, Jeffrey," Takeda said, "so he overgrav'd. It's a natural reaction—"

"Piss off, Cyril. There's nothing natural about it. The boy's becoming downright unstable. You know that! Remember the bus in San Francisco? It was one of the worse containment issues we've ever had to deal with. My God, I think we still are! I swear, sometimes you defend him like he's your own damn son." Trumble returned to his mole.

"Jeffrey, you know we must protect Jonathan from himself. But don't worry ..." He took a sip from his wine. "...if Jonathan does begin to develop again, there are plans in place. You know that...Jeffrey?..."

Trumble didn't respond.

"Is that...*jealousy* I'm sensing?"

Trumble continued to analyze his mole.

"Jeffrey Trumble, are you—"

"You're not telepathic, Cyril."

"*Jeffrey?*"

"No, I'm bloody well not!" Trumble reluctantly faced his partner.

Cyril Takeda rose out of the water like a leviathan standing up into the clouds. Large clumps of bubbles began to rise and hover around his body. He smiled a slow, devilish grin.

"My God, Cyril," Trumble mused. "What's on your mind, hmm?"

Takeda stretched out his arms. "Come here, *lover*."

Jeffrey Trumble smiled as the robe slipped off his body and glided back to its hook.

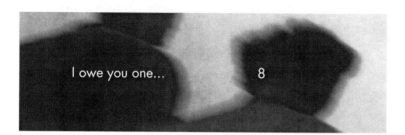

I owe you one...   8

JONATHAN approached his Georgetown walk-up.

"Are you going to need a ride when you leave on your vacation?" Mazza yelled from the driver's side window.

"What? Oh, yeah. Sure...I'll call you."

"You okay there, Mr. Kortel?"

"Yeah, Mazza, I'm okay."

"Still thinking about the sign?"

"Yeah. There's something about it that bothers me..." He turned back to the car.

Mazza, his arms folded, was leaning out the window. "It's 'cause you didn't pick up on the other Tel before the grav field was created, isn't it?"

Jonathan thought for a moment. "You're right, I should have picked up on it. And what really disturbs me is that this was a Level 7 display. We haven't had any Level 7's in D.C. for months. I mean, it was a powerful grav flux, and James didn't even capture it with his netpad. I don't get it."

"Could be a Rogue, or maybe the *u'ebitsche*."

"Nah. They wouldn't enter the D.C. Zone. That's way too ballsy. No, this was something else." He looked quizzically at Mazza.

"An Indie?" Mazza asked, raising his thick, Baltic eyebrows.

"That's what I'm thinking."

Mazza whistled.

Indies were advanced Potentials who not only recognized their ability, but thought they could master it on their own. They came around only once in a lifetime, and of the 11 known Indies in the history of the Tel world, just one had even survived. The Tel ability was an efficacious addiction, and without proper training and guidance, the sheer intoxication of it could quickly spiral someone into deep trouble. Some were injured or killed in reckless, self-induced level tests. For others, the tremendous stress of overuse debilitated their bodies to the point of death, or, worse yet, left them sucking their meals through a tube the rest of their lives. The only person to have lived a "normal" life never really developed to her full potential. By the time she was discovered, she was in her late 50s, and had so many psychological scars from dealing with her ability – which kept her on the fringe of society all of her life – that it had been impossible to integrate her into the Tel culture.

If this had been a true Indie display, as Jonathan feared, it was imperative for the Agency to find this person before he or she caused irreparable damage. Even worse than someone being hurt, the Tel culture could be widely exposed, and the containment issue would grow exponentially with each passing day.

Jonathan shrugged off his thoughts. "Well, it's not my problem. It's James's now. I'm on vacation. Good night, Mazza. I'll call you when I know when I'm leaving."

He watched Mazza drive off and began walking up the steps. As he approached the landing, a searing pain shot through his head like a needle piercing his skull. The intensity drove him to one knee. He clutched his forehead and almost vomited over the side of the stairs. Then, as fast as it had appeared, the pain vanished, leaving a thick, gritty sensation, as if a chemical had been released and was spreading into every recess of his brain. He slowly stood up, shaking from the voracity and suddenness. He wiped a little sweat from his brow and tried to swallow, but found his throat dry and raw. He reached for the doorknob, but his vision was blurred. A strange sensation of seasickness was creeping through his body. He gingerly sat on the top step and cradled his head in his hands. He had been warned that as he developed he might experience sudden and severe headaches.

After a minute, the sensations passed, and his vision returned. Collecting himself, he entered his home and slowly walked down the hallway toward the kitchen, only to stop twice as the sensations returned and briefly held him in a state of *mal de mer*.

"Lights, Max," he ordered. He stumbled to the refrigerator.

"Jonathan, is there something wrong? Are you ill?"

"No, Max, I've just been thinking too hard."

"Sir?"

"I'm just having another reaction...probably from those grav exercises I did before Paris." He collapsed onto a stool and leaned heavily on the counter. "Water, Max. Cold, with ice." A glass slid into view in the front of the refrigerator, and the plexi door moved aside. He put the cold drink to his forehead and quietly sat as the condensation numbed the residual pain.

"Do you need your medication?"

"No, Max, it's passed." He swept the glass from side to side. "Do I have any messages, here or at the loft in Chicago?"

"Yes, sir. Here you have one net message from James McCarris, one from SATVid Plus, one from Georgia—"

"Stop. One from Georgia?"

"Yes."

Jonathan sipped the water and closed his eyes. "She leave a message?"

"No."

"An ID?"

"Yes."

"Recall it."

He placed an ice cube to his temple. Georgia's holoimage appeared on the countertop.

"Hello, Jonathan...hey, what's wrong?"

"Oh, nothing. Just a bad headache. I saw that you called, but you didn't leave a message."

"I didn't want to bother you."

"You're never bothering me, Georgia, you know that. What's up?"

"I was wondering if you..." she hesitated, "...wanted to have dinner...tonight?"

The pain all but disappeared. He opened his eyes. "Yes...yes, that would be great. What are you hungry for?"

"I'm new here. I have no idea where to go in D.C."

"Are you up for high energy, or quiet conversation?"

"Maybe a little of both."

"I know just the place." He popped the ice cube in his mouth.

. . .

The bar in the Chewy Nougat Center was circular and seemed to have no visible means for the bartenders to enter or exit. Yet, they appeared and disappeared as if choreographed with the driving beat of the club's music. People shimmered around the bar like a mass of neon tetras, edging in and out of the hot shafts of light that cut from floor to ceiling. Standing out conspicuously were the Net Keepers, an androgenous government army of tech masters who kept the world's T-12 lines in order. Their silver, Czech-made Micro-Night Shades, which kept them continuously jacked to the net, reflected the shafts of light and sent prismatic ovals fluttering about the dark room. Peppered into the throng were the Potomac People, the new symbol of power in Washington. Sporting jaunty yellow bow ties, they looked tragically lost against the midtier business types scaling the walls of corporate dominance, where bioaugmentation wasn't a luxury, it was a rite of passage. This legion of narcissism perched their manufactured beauty strategically at the bar, where they flaunted their surgeons' visions of the perfect human much as one might have sported a fur or a diamond a century earlier. Their casual perfection reflected an amalgam of interpretations, all desperate followers of a constantly shifting "ideal" paraded in the faces and bodies that populated the popular media.

Jonathan observed it all from the comfort of a booth he had secured with a little Tel influence. He rarely called upon his ability to obtain something as inconsequential as a good table, but tonight was special. She was special.

He spied Georgia swimming through the teeming sea of black, her tall, thin frame effortlessly parting the full-length trenchcoats and drably patterned knee shirts popularized by the German netbands. Her mock turtleneck pullover was the color of an old school bus. Its ribbed stitchwork gave the appearance of an old silicon circuit board. Her thigh-high boots were made from the finest genetically grown eel, and they made her appear taller. He watched her as she searched the bar. She wasn't looking for him, she was sensing for him. He had thrown up a field wall around himself, just to make it interesting. He let her circle twice, then dropped the field. She instantly turned in his direction and caught his stare through the crowd. She smiled and wagged her finger.

Strutting up to his booth, she stopped and put her hands on her hips. "Very funny, Mr. Kortel."

"Just testing," he replied. He leaned over and kissed her cheek.

"This is a great place," she said, settling into the booth. "Do you come here a lot?"

"Yes. As a matter of fact, James and I were here yesterday and a really strange thing happened—"

"Drinks, food, candy or oxygen?" the holowaiter asked, suddenly appearing.

"Ah, Oban. No water, just lots of ice, thanks," Jonathan answered.

"I'll have a vodka tonic. House is fine, thank you very much." Georgia studied the pixelated holoimage that glowed its simgirl likeness in the darkness of the bar. Its manga eyes bright and spread wide, each cast its own curved rectangle of phony light reflection. Its spiked pink hair reverberated as the raster lines twitched every 3,000 cycles. Vintage.

A human waitress passed through the image, disrupting the connection. "Thanks, Kasis!" it snipped in a shrill electric voice that reminded Jonathan of old Japanese anime. "Okay, one house vodka-t and one Oban, no H20. Solid." Suddenly it was gone, and the booth darkened.

Georgia shook her head.

"Hey," Jonathan said, "you wanted a little high energy and a—"

"Oh, if you want food or whatever, just press the big red button there," the holowaiter said, suddenly reappearing and pointing across the booth. It disappeared without a sound.

"Well," Jonathan exclaimed, still staring at the space formerly occupied by the holowaiter. "Hungry?"

"Yes, I am. Let's see what the Chewy Nougat has in the way of some dinner." Georgia pressed the red button, and two holomenus appeared in the center of their table. She tentatively touched hers, and it flipped through its pages. "So, mister big-time biochef, what do you recommend?"

"*Former* big-time biochef," Jonathan said. He smiled at her through the holomenus. "I like the burgers. They're big, dumb and..." he leaned forward, "...taste like they're damn real."

"Really? How do they manage that?"

"It's in the programming. But how they get their ground beef texture is beyond me. It's very impressive work."

Kasis slid up to their booth. She smiled tersely as she reached through the holomenus and placed their drinks in front of them. "Enjoy," she quipped, turning back toward the bar while spinning her tray with her index finger. She stepped off the platform and was swallowed by the fray.

"Friendly here, aren't they?" Georgia said sarcastically, and she took a sip from her drink.

"Yeah, but you can't beat the show."

Jonathan and Georgia settled back, each studying the other. "It's good..." they both said simultaneously. They laughed.

"Go ahead," he said.

"It's really good to see you, Jonathan. It's been too long."
She focused on him with a presence that he didn't recall ever
seeing from her.

"You, too. You look so, so..."

"Healthy?"

"Yeah, healthy. What have you been doing?"

"It's what I haven't been doing." She pensively swizzled her
drink's ice with a finger. "I haven't been with Tarris, for one."

"I wondered about that. What happened, you know...after
he left?"

"I just laid low. After he disappeared, I stayed on at the
compound, but only for a few weeks. I got a place closer to Taos.
It was a lot easier to get to and from the casino."

"Why'd you leave?"

Georgia reflected. "Too many memories."

"Yeah, well. I know what that's about," he said,
remembering.

"I heard about Tam—"

"All right," interrupted the holowaiter, "do we know
what we'll be having tonight, or do you need a little more time?"

"Yes," Jonathan said. "We'll both have the burger. Hers
will be dry, prepared well-done, and mine will have everything,
medium-well."

"Good choices!" the holowaiter exclaimed, and its pixels
blurred to nothing.

"You remembered," Georgia affectionately said, leaning
onto the table.

Jonathan moved closer. He remembered the feeling they had shared when he said goodbye to her at Tarris's compound. They took long, slow sips.

"I heard about Tamara," she said tentatively. "I'm sorry that had to happen."

Jonathan's attention shifted to a young couple at another booth. They were kissing. "Me, too," he said softly.

"It's a shame they had to erase her—"

Jonathan motioned for her to stop and shook his head. "Let's not go there, if that's all right?"

Georgia smiled. "Sure. I'm sorry to have brought it up."

"No, no...it's all right. I'm over it now. It's just..." He searched his drink as if it contained his answer. Georgia took his hand. "Never mind," he said. He gently squeezed her fingers. "So!" he declared, pulling away from her. "You're going to be working with James?"

"Yes, this ought to be interesting." She brushed some hair off her face. "How's he doing these days?"

"Still basically the same ol' Jimbo, but he's changed some." He ruminated on the crowd around the bar. "We all have."

"Kasis will be right out with your food. Do we need a refill, hmm?" the holowaiter asked.

Startled, they both nodded without looking up.

"Oh, sorry. Bad timing." The booth darkened again.

. . .

Kasis brought their food and another round. While they
ate, Jonathan told Georgia about his time at the Agency. He
talked in depth about the training she could expect – and about
the politics that drove the world's most secretive culture.

"God, Jonathan. It sounds like they've been keeping you
busy. Have you had any time off?"

"As a matter of fact, no. But I'm going to take some time
here in the next couple of days. I'm thinking of going to Tortola.
Know anything about it?–" Suddenly, the same sharp pain that he
had experienced on his steps sliced through his head. "Oh, shit,"
he groaned, grabbing at his temples.

"Jonathan?" Georgia asked, alarmed.

The pain intensified. It drilled down into the core of his
brain and embedded itself deep within his mind. "My...my
medication," he said, trying to retrieve it from his inside coat
pocket. He began to slip into unconsciousness. He slumped forward
onto the table, but was violently thrown back against the booth.

"Oh, Jesus, Jonathan!" Georgia jumped to her feet but
was instantly slammed back against the booth and held firmly in
place. She watched in horror as Jonathan's eyes rolled back and blood
ran from his nose over his mouth and chin. He went limp and began
to slide onto his side.

Georgia instantly went into phase and created a field flux
wall around the booth. Struggling to his side, she could feel the
attacking grav field punching against her telekinetic strength.
She propped Jonathan up, wiping at the blood with a napkin and
stuffing his nostrils in a desperate attempt to stop the flow.

"So," the holowaiter declared, "how's the food?" Its glow was wavering from the gravitational distortion and filled the booth with a nightmarish cerulean hue. "Oh!" it said, glaring down at them, "gotta go!"

Jonathan was now leaning heavily against Georgia's shoulder. She wrapped her arm around him and began slapping at his cheek. "Jonathan, don't leave me," she pleaded firmly. "Come on, come on. Don't go under!"

He slowly surfaced. The pain had ebbed, but he was disoriented and struggling to breathe. "Oh, shit," he coughed, straightening. "What happened?"

Georgia felt the grav pressure evanesce off of her field. "I don't know, but let's get the hell out of here," she said into his ear and helped him out of the booth. Keeping her guard up, she scanned the bar with her netpad for anyone or anything that might appear out of the norm.

"Be careful," Jonathan said above the pounding beat of the music. "They might triangulate on us."

She shot him a look, and quickly reshaped her field to plow through the crowd around the bar. "How are you doing?" she asked as they crept along. Her grav field shoved people aside like the bow of a boat carving through an ice flow.

"Better," he answered hoarsely.

"You have any strength yet?"

"Some."

"Good," she said, slipping into professional mode, "we might need it."

They emerged from the crowd and headed toward the front doors. "Everything all right here?" the holowaiter asked, suddenly blocking their path.

"Will you please get the hell out of here!" Georgia said. She expanded her field and disrupted the image's connection.

"Bitch!" the holowaiter shrieked. Its pixels dispersed into a cloud of electronic vapor.

Leading Jonathan out of the bar and toward the parking area she asked, "Did you drive?"

"No...no I didn't." He straightened and tried to collect himself.

"Let me take you home." She handed the valet her chip card.

Jonathan swept back his hair and wiped at the blood that had spread over his shirt. He noticed Georgia's sweater was stained as well. "Sorry about your clothes."

"Hey, don't worry. Let's get you home and cleaned up." She kept scanning the parking area for anything unusual. "I don't feel safe exposed out here in the open."

"That was pretty fast phasing you did in there," he said. "I owe you one."

The valet pulled Georgia's car around, and they climbed in. She pulled into the Interway traffic, while Jonathan dug the medication out of his coat pocket. He placed the small pneumatic infuser to his neck and clicked the injector. It made a short hiss sound. He settled back against the seat, finally able to relax.

"Jonathan, what happened back there?" Georgia asked.

"Just give me a moment, please, while the medication

takes effect." He folded his arms across his chest and closed his eyes. The cabin fell silent as the car sped through the narrow Georgetown streets.

"I didn't know you were that strong," Jonathan said, breaking the silence. "I mean, that sure felt like a Level 7 grav field you put out. I thought you were only a Level 6." He kept his eyes shut. "It takes something seriously major to jump a level like you did."

Georgia, her attention focused on the road, didn't respond. "Two levels...actually," she finally said, just above a whisper.

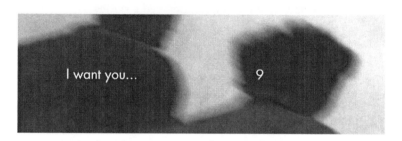

I want you...   9

THE task lights in the kitchen intensified and brought the richness of the marble countertops into full detail. Jonathan sat on a stool, his head having a viscid feeling, as if someone had poured a bag of Polycrete into his skull to slowly harden.

Georgia went to the refrigerator.

"*Deja vu...*" he said to himself.

"What?" she questioned from inside the freezer.

"Oh, nothing." He rubbed his temples.

"What did you mean back in the bar when you said 'they might triangulate on us'?"

"I've had migraines all my life, but lately, I've been getting these monster ones. The guys in the lab say it's normal, especially with all the exercises they've been putting me through. That infuser has some drug that's supposed to neutralize the effects, but it doesn't feel like it's doing shit tonight."

Georgia placed a cold gelpack against his forehead. "There, how's that feel?"

Jonathan closed his eyes and forced a smile.

"I'll take that as a 'Thank you, Georgia, that feels sooo good!'" She stepped back and folded her arms. "You haven't answered my question."

"Tonight didn't feel like one of those migraines. It felt different...like we were–"

"Being attacked?" Georgia said with an edge of sarcasm. She wiped at his chin and neck with a warm towel.

"That's just the Rogue in you talking." Jonathan tilted his head back and pulled the gelpack over his eyes. "No. It felt more like being...tested."

"That didn't feel like any test to me. Here, let me get you some water." Georgia turned back toward the refrigerator.

Jonathan gently grabbed her arm. "Hey," he said, his eyes still covered. She stepped between his knees. He let the gelpack fall from his eyes into his lap. He placed it on the counter. She was conspicuously averting his look. "*Two* levels?" he questioned. He reached for her other shoulder.

Georgia sheepishly smiled that smile. "A girl's gotta do what a girl's gotta do."

He softly brushed some hair behind her ear and let his finger follow the line of her jaw. He held his touch at the bottom of her chin. Her smile fell away, and they instinctively leaned toward each other.

"Jonathan," Max interrupted, "you have a netcall."

"Who is it?" Jonathan snapped, reluctant to release the spell of nature.

"James McCarris."

His eyes met hers. Her grin returned.

"Okay...but no visual." He leaned back and put his finger to his lips.

"Jonathan?"

"Hey, James, what's up?" He folded his arms. Georgia walked around the counter.

"I've got that info on Tortola you wanted. It should be in your netmail."

"Great, thanks. I'll let you know what I decide."

"Hey, Jonathan?"

"Yeah?"

There was a pause. "You don't mind...you know, having Georgia working with me...do you?"

Jonathan glanced over to Georgia, who was leaning on the counter. She smiled and shrugged. "What do you mean?" he replied.

"I always sensed that there might have been something... you know...between you two—"

"James," Jonathan interrupted, "don't worry. I don't have any issues with Georgia working with you. I think she's a great lady. And no, there's nothing between us, okay?"

"All right, thanks...I just wanted to make sure. I'll catch up with you tomorrow. Good night."

"See ya, James." Jonathan shook his head, hopped off the stool and headed around the counter. "That guy, I'll tell you, he can be the biggest—"

Georgia, her back to him, was removing her blood-stained top. "No offense," she said, pulling the bright yellow sweater over her head, "but I want to get to this blood before it sets." Her long black hair fell across her shoulders. "Now..." she slowly turned to face him, "...where were we?"

Jonathan gathered her to himself. He unhooked her bra and let it slide gently off her breasts. He kissed her neck and savored her perfume. "That stain," he exhaled, "will just have to wait."

• • •

A candle's flicker sent hypnotic streaks of mikado and maize to dance upon the dark walls. Jonathan lay on his side watching a small bead of sweat slide down Georgia's back. He leaned over and let it roll onto his tongue. He had tasted her and wanted more.

Georgia shuddered. "God," she whispered, rolling to face him, "don't get me started again." She reached for the edge of his jaw and let her fingers glide down its line. Then she dragged her finger down his chest and over his stomach, until she found what she wanted, and squeezed slowly, letting her nails dig to the border of pleasure.

Jonathan moaned and softly kissed her. "You know," he said, "I've thought about you."

"Me, too," Georgia whispered. "I often wondered, you know, where you were, what you might be doing." Her fingers went to his chest and playfully entwined themselves in the hair he had at the top of his sternum. "You're getting gray."

"The hell I am," he said, looking down. "I'm only 31."

"Made you look." She laughed.

He reached over and pinched her nipple.

"Ouch," she giggled, "not fair."

"Ha! Made you...say...ah...ouch, or something..."

Georgia rolled her eyes.

"That didn't work, did it?"

"No," she said, falling back against the pillows, "but nice try, Mr. World's Most Powerful Tel." She rubbed at her breast.

Jonathan lost his grin and sat up.

She ran her hand down his back. "Hey...what's the matter?"

He didn't answer.

"What? Tell me."

"Remember me telling you this afternoon about James and I seeing something weird?"

"Yes, why?...What happened?"

"It's bugging me. I mean, we're outside the Bar of Chocolate having a drink, just watching the world, when this huge sign they're putting up across the street snaps free from its guides and falls. This is a huge sign. It's got to weigh at least half a ton." He rubbed his face at the memory. "And just as I phase to catch it, it stops, just for a second, like it's in a grav field...I mean, it had to be in one." He turned and faced her. "I thought James had caught it, but he thought I had. Then it crashes, and all hell breaks loose. I mean, we jumped into a Situation 6 mode so fast....There's pieces flying all over the place. It's a really screwed up ECS. And just when we think we've caught them all, this fragment flies right for James. I shove him out of the way, and the damn thing freezes right in front of our faces! James gets his pad out and scans practically the entire eastern seaboard, but it doesn't show a damn thing."

"My God. Do you think it was the Rogues?"

Jonathan shrugged.

"Russians?"

"Nah...it was *weird*."

Georgia sat up. "An Indie?" she asked quietly.

Jonathan didn't answer.

"Shit..." she softly exclaimed.

"Yeah. That's what I thought, too," he said. "Until tonight."

They both watched the candle slowly die, bringing the frantic dance of the shadows to a quiet and serene halt. The flame hissed into oblivion when it drowned in its own wax. A thin line of smoke rose from the charred wick.

Jonathan thought back to the bar. "What happened tonight?" he asked the fresh blackness.

"I think someone was after you."

"Maybe," he said. He picked at the dried blood inside his nose. "Welcome to my world."

"What? You mean this has happened before?"

"Yeah, sure. I've been challenged...oh, I don't know, a dozen times now? I had one last week...in Paris."

"God, Jonathan." She sat up behind him and wrapped her arms around his chest. "Have you been hurt?"

"Nah, I'm always too fast for them. It's kind of unfair." He swept his fingers through his hair. "Until tonight, that is."

Georgia hesitated. "You know, tonight sure felt like a Rogue move."

"Really?"

"Yes." She nestled her chin on his shoulder. "At least two. One for me, and one to get you."

"And a third for good measure?"

"Possibly..."

"And you know what's really weird about all this? I should've sensed them coming."

"Don't be too hard on yourself. I felt a lot of displacement in that bar. There were a lot people and energies moving around. They just caught us off guard. Are you going to report it?"

"I usually don't report the ones that happen on my time."

Georgia pulled his head around to face hers and frowned.

"Look," he said. He wrapped his arm around her waist. "There are a lot of reports to fill out, not to mention the debrief. Besides, I'm on vacation."

"At least go and get checked out. Please...*for me?*"

"Okay. If it makes you feel any better, I'll go in and have Franks run some tests...just to make sure." Jonathan pulled back and looked at her through the darkness. He could barely make her out. The slight bump at the bridge of her nose. The silhouette of her thick black hair. The little cleft at the base of her chin. Georgia leaned close to his face. He could feel her breath against his lips.

"Come here," she whispered with all the seriousness of a woman who was used to getting what she wanted. She leaned closer, her lips grazing his. "I want you," she barely uttered and gently pulled him back down onto the bed.

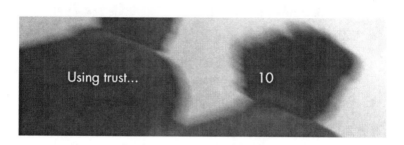

Using trust...   10

JAMES McCarris wasn't a big man. It wasn't his size that intimidated people; it was his demeanor. James was the kind of man who could get things done without the added influence of height or muscle. He wore his 5-foot-11, 195 pounds like guys who were 6-10, 280, and he usually did it smiling. Like an alien in a sci-fi vid who grinned at an expendable extra while its tail was sneaking up from behind, James McCarris could smooth talk anyone into thinking he was becoming their new best friend. He was a true Southerner. From the real South. The "Old South." And if you said you were from the South in New America, you could mean the Yucatan. And James McCarris wasn't from Old Mexico, he was from Savannah – where men still rose to their feet when a lady entered a room. That's why he asked most people to call him Jimbo.

Glancing about Takeda's office, his eyes darted from the desk to the painting to the sofa and back to the desk. He shifted his weight back to his left foot. He passed his fingers through his wavy red hair, thinking that this time it would be perfect.

"James!" Takeda said as he entered the room. "Please, have a seat." His black-gloved hand gestured like a claw at one of the oversized chairs in front of the desk where he ran the Agency.

Jimbo knew not to lean back. Anyone who did ended up looking like a child in the huge chair – their legs off the floor and body sunk into the soft, overstuffed cushion. Just the way Takeda planned it.

"How are the Recruiters these days?" Takeda asked.

Jimbo's back straightened at the simple question. He knew Takeda never asked simple questions. "Doing well, thank you, sir," he replied with no hint of the suspicion that was welling inside him.

"James, relax. This is not an inquiry. The Recruiter Unit is one of the most important divisions we have. And, I must say, since you've taken charge, people are *very* pleased."

"Thank you, sir."

Takeda leaned back into his chair and intently studied the Southerner. "I've finally read your report....We are sorry for the deception about Zvara, but it was at his request. Too much history, you know," he said with a smirk. He leaned forward and moved a file pad to its correct position on the desk. "We paid for the surgery."

Jimbo grinned just a little.

"You have to admit," Takeda continued while he pulled at his gloves and glanced out the windows, "learning under him did have its rewards, did it not?"

"Yes, sir. It did."

"There, I knew it. Well, he's gone. Such a pity. He was a bit..." he trained his attention on Jimbo, "...unbalanced."

"A bit."

The room fell silent as Takeda scrutinized Jimbo's bright blue eyes. Jimbo didn't flinch.

"James," Takeda said, abruptly standing. He walked to the windows and stared out over the Potomac. The morning sun defined the river with glittering ripples that lacerated the reflection of the trees on the Virginia side. "I need to discuss something that's a bit...*sensitive.*" He placed his hands behind his back. "Jonathan Kortel is very important to us, and I'm sure you would agree that his well-being is essential to this organization. We all like Jonathan very much, and we don't want any unwanted influences distracting him from his studies, do we?"

"No, sir."

Takeda paused for a moment as he took in the view. "Would you say you're *friends* with him?"

"Uh, yes," Jimbo replied, on edge from the odd line of questioning. "I got to know him during my assignment, especially when he crossed. I think we've become fairly close."

"And would you say he *trusts* you?"

Jimbo hesitated. "Yes...yes, I think he does."

"Good," Takeda said, never looking away from the window, "because we might need to use some of that trust."

Jimbo's back straightened even more.

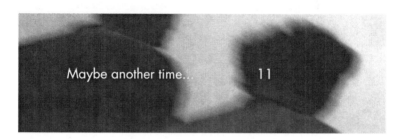

Maybe another time...   11

"...**NINETY**-three, ninety-four, ninety-five, ninety-six, ninety-seven, ninety-eight, ninety-nine...one hundred."

Jonathan relaxed onto his back, his knees up and his ankles tucked tight against his butt. He looked at the foundation cracks that ran like gray rivers from the subcontinent of the ceiling to the shores where the walls met the molding. NNN was clicked in, its morning news anchors droning on about regen'd pork and the recent FDA findings that it could cause colon cancer in cloned lab mice. They segued to the next news segment: "...those poor mice. Isn't it a shame, CeCe? In other news, scientists have discovered a shift in the biodegeneration curve that has been occurring in the former Hawaiian Islands–"

"Off!"

The vidscreen instantly cut to black.

Jonathan put his fingers to his wrist. *Pulse rate was good,* he thought, and sat up.

"Sir," Max said, "your car is here."

. . .

Jonathan threw his gear bag hard into the backseat and followed it, landing on his side. The car shut its door.

"Mazza, this is one fucking beautiful day!"

"Ah...yes, sir. It is," an unexpected voice said from the front seat.

A jolt like liquid electricity shot through Jonathan's nerves. He sat up. "You're not Mazza! What's going on? They didn't tell me about a driver change!"

The carbon-smoked, ballistic-proof window behind the driver slipped down into the divider wall, which forced the rate of time inside the car to accommodate its slow, even speed. A girl with long, curly dark hair turned and acknowledged Jonathan. "Good morning, Mr. Kortel. My name is Sasha Kuntar. Mazza has been reassigned. I believe he's moving up."

Jonathan cautiously studied her. She was foreign, but with a look he couldn't process. Her sharp cheekbones set off a pair of dark green eyes – the kind Jimbo called "bedroom eyes." Her hair was curly – not in an ethnic, tangled sort of way, just curly. Maybe Italian, or possibly Arabic. "Let me see your pad...Sasha," he asked warily.

She passed him her netpad. It floated through the opening and stopped, suspended in front of his face.

He carefully studied her file. "Okay...okay, thanks." He leaned back against his bag. "And I like to keep the window down....You know, that elitist crap. I hate that."

The car glided through the morning traffic, and Jonathan caught a reflection of Sasha in the nav screen. She was staring at him intently.

"Sorry about back there," he said.

"Sir?"

Her face appeared on his vidscreen. She looked pretty, to him, in spite of the distortion. "My swearing...I apologize if that offended you."

Sasha nodded, and a slow smile spread across her face. She shifted her attention back to the road, and the screen cut out.

When they went over Key Bridge, he caught her staring again. He leaned forward into the window and folded his arms. He could smell her bath rinse, or whatever she used. It was citrusy, but not heavy, with a sexy edge to it. "So," he asked, watching the road out the front window, "what have they said?"

"Sir?"

"Call me Jonathan, please." He patted her shoulder and felt her muscle under the light mesh of her coat. She was hard and athletic. "I'm just asking because I've caught you looking more at me than the road."

"Well," she hesitated, "come on. I mean, you're Jonathan Kortel. Everyone knows about you." She turned to look at him and smiled. A sensor buzzed.

"Ah...the road?" he said, gesturing.

"Sorry." She jerked the toggle and the car vaulted back into position. "You are just a little intimidating."

"But...?"

"But you're not what I thought."

"Oh? What'd you expect?"

"I don't know exactly. You're more...more," she looked back again, this time keeping the car fixed in position. "Sweet."

Surprised, Jonathan pulled back. "Sweet?..."

"Okay. Bad word choice. How 'bout...gentle?"

Jonathan's expression questioned her again.

"This is not how I wanted this to go." She slapped the top of the toggle.

"It's all right, Sasha...I think I know what you're driving at." He laughed. "I bet you thought I'd be this big hairy asshole kind of guy, all tough and full of himself – right?"

"Well..."

"Hey, look," he rested his chin on his arm, "I'm pretty new to this stuff, too. I'm still trying to get my level strength under control. In fact, that's my training on Mondays, Wednesdays and–"

"Fridays," she finished. She glanced at him out of the corner of her eye. "I know your complete schedule. But I thought you were on vacation."

"Yeah, I haven't figured out where to go yet. So in the meantime, I thought I'd get in a session with Franks. That's why I called the service."

She nodded, keeping her attention on the road. An awkward quiet filled the cabin.

"So," he asked, breaking the silence, "where are you from?"

"Around..."

"Around where?"

"I'm a military brat. We moved around a lot. My father did real special ops stuff. I didn't really know him well."

"What was he? Army NetForce?"

"You could say that. He was all over. Always off doing something he couldn't talk about. You know how dads get..." She suddenly caught herself. "Oh, sir. I'm...I'm so sorry. I—"

"Don't worry, it's all right. I'm used to it, really. I appreciate the thought, though." The cabin fell silent again, as Jonathan leaned back against the seat and watched the Virginia landscape rush by.

. . .

They left the Interway, and Sasha resumed control and piloted the car down some rural roads to the satellite campus of *Citenikelet Investments*. Tracked since they entered Virginia, when they approached the campus, their displacement signatures identified them to the Agency's system, and the gates opened automatically. Their signatures were like fingerprints, displacing gravity and registering a pattern as unique as a voiceprint or a DNA sequence. Sasha drove to the main testing lab and pulled the car around the back.

"You've been studying up on me," Jonathan said. He

collected his gear bag and stepped from the car.

"I don't blame you," she replied. "I'm sure you get tired of all the attention."

"It gets a bit much, the staring and all."

"I'll see you in three hours. Have a good session." The car shut its door, and Sasha drove off.

Jonathan approached the lab, or "gym," as everyone called it. Its name seemed appropriate, given that the mental exercises that took place in it were as strenuous as anything performed in a physical workout. The equipment was definitely not your typical health club, though. Reading his dis sig, the doors slid open.

Ashton Franks had been an Agency man for most of his life. He was one of the only Level 8's teaching Advanced Field-Flux Technique, and since Jonathan's arrival at the Agency, they had gotten along almost like father and son. Franks looked up from behind a biomed scanner, his handlebar moustache seeming whiter than usual. "G'day to ya, Jonathan!" the Aussie bellowed.

"Ashton," Jonathan replied. "Did you get my message...about running some tests this morning?"

"Oh, my dear boy. We're...ah, off-line for a bit," he said awkwardly.

"You weren't when I scheduled in."

"Right, yes...well. We've had a bit of a snafu in the systems...ah, the field harmonics and such," he answered nervously. "We can't test our star pupil without the harmonics in calibration, now can we?"

Jonathan looked around, and upraised faces quickly

disappeared into work stations. "Yeah...right, Ashton. No, we can't." He scrutinized the senior Tel. "Maybe I'll go try the Grav Center."

"Right, then," Franks said. "Come back when we're up and running. G'day to ya." He wiped the bottom of his moustache with the back of his hand and went back to calibrating the scanner.

. . .

When Jonathan entered the Grav Center, he found that it was booked for the day, which seemed odd, because the system had shown that it was available from 10:00 to 12:00. Again, he received a conspicuously nervous reception from the center's director. Resigned that the morning was a bust, he called Sasha. Her image came up on the netpad's vidscreen. She was working out at the Training Center.

"How's your testing going?" she asked, breathless. She appeared to be biking through a lush countryside in one of the Center's virt booths.

"It's not."

She frowned while she peddled furiously. "What happened, Franks spill his coffee in one of the TCV panels?"

"Just some systems glitch. How's...ah, where are you?"

"I've programmed a beautiful day here in France. You should join me."

"Nah, I think I'll just head back home. How much longer do you have...I mean, I wouldn't want to interrupt the *Tour de France*."

"About another 30 minutes," she said, crouching down to enter a steep curve. "But I can bring the car around immediately if you'd—"

"No, please...finish up. I'll meet you up there."

Sasha looked over, smiled, then raised her butt and bore down on the pedals.

. . .

Jonathan slowly approached Sasha's virt booth and began watching her on the monitor. It displayed the occupant in the context of the program, and he intently followed her through a series of sharp curves. Her body leaned and shifted in perfect sync with the bike.

"She's an excellent rider," said a voice from the equipment. Probably the guy monitoring the virt booth.

"Yes, she is," Jonathan answered, not taking his attention from the monitor.

"You want me to shut the program down, Mr. Kortel?"

"No...no, that's okay. Let her finish."

"You know, you could step in."

"While it's running? That would be way out of line."

"Not for Sasha....She's tough. She can take it."

Jonathan hesitated. "Well...I really shouldn't."

"Come on, let's have some fun." The seal to the inner service door broke with a hiss, and Jonathan hesitantly stooped through the service hatch.

Entering a running virtbooth was like stepping into another reality. Jonathan emerged beside a rural country road near the outskirts of a small French village. "Where are we?" he asked casually, knowing that without a holosuit, he would be a disorienting visual for Sasha. The holoimage of the village began passing through him.

To Sasha, it appeared that he suddenly materialized in the tall grass that skirted the road and sped right along with her. In reality, though, he was standing on a 50-foot by 50-foot virt-holo grid. "What?!..." she yelled, startled by his sudden appearance.

He gave a sheepish little wave.

Sasha slammed on the brakes. "Shit!" she exclaimed. The bike jerked to the right and slid into the gravel shoulder. Her front wheel dug into a large hole, which catapulted her over the handlebars. Her legs flew over her head as the bike cartwheeled down an embankment. Jonathan telekinetically caught her in midflip and held her motionless above the pavement. He had grav'd all of her except her head.

"This is not funny!" she screamed, suspended upside down.

Jonathan was laughing.

"Off program!" she ordered. The holosystem shut down with a mechanical groan, exposing the room's true appearance.

"Oh, that was good," Jonathan said, still laughing.

Sasha just glared at him from her telekinetic purgatory.

"Lighten up, for God's sake," he said. He stepped over to her. "You're the one who applied the front brakes."

"Let me down!" she ordered sternly.

"Oh, I don't know. You look kind of cute all sprawled out, with your legs going every which way." He turned his head to mimic hers. Sasha's hair was a spray of curls, and her back was arched to the point that it looked almost disjointed. "Damn, you're flexible!"

"Jonathan," she said, calming. "Please...this hurts."

"Oh, sorry." He gently lowered her and released the grav field just as she touched the grid's surface.

Sasha collected herself while the biofabric of her holosuit reshaped to the preset contour specs of her body. Jonathan watched the fabric move across her frame like a snake's skin.

"There," she said, adjusting her breasts, "that feels a lot better." She looked up and caught him watching.

"What?" He knew full well what her look meant.

Sasha put her hands on her hips. "Enjoying the view?"

"Well, now that you mention it–" Suddenly, Jonathan felt what seemed like an invisible fist punch him, just hard enough, in the stomach. He instantly flexed, but the suddenness had caught him off guard, and he stumbled back.

A slow smile crossed Sasha's face.

"Cute," he said, coughing. "I'll admit, I deserved that."

She slowly walked over and folded her arms. "Yes, you did."

"Nice focus," Jonathan said, straightening. "Your field flux was as tight as I've ever felt. What level are you again?"

"Oh, I'm just a...ah, Level...4," she said, helping him to his feet.

"That's funny," he said. He tucked his shirt back into the front of his pants. "I barely sensed your displacement before you phased. How did you manage that little trick?"

"It's, ah, something I kinda worked out on my own," she replied, clearly disturbed by the question. "I'll bring the car around." She hurried from the booth.

. . .

The cabin was quiet as the car skimmed along the road's surface: The only sounds were the systems interface clicks that broke the silence every five miles as the car dialogued with the vast Interway network of the D.C. Zone grid.

"Hey," Jonathan said, "I'm sorry for startling you in the virt booth." He watched Sasha's reflection in the front nav screen.

His vidscreen flashed to life; her face filled most of it. "I shouldn't have punched you," she replied.

"No." He turned his attention out the window. "I deserved it." Clicks followed by sharp processing sounds emitted from the dash panel. Jonathan gingerly rubbed his stomach.

Sasha moved out of traffic and pulled onto his street, piloting the car to the curb in front of his home. The car opened the back door.

Jonathan threw his gear bag onto the sidewalk and crawled out of the backseat. He motioned for her to lower the window. It slid down to slowly reveal her face: her hair, still in a wild state from the bike accident, her eyes, bright with life, her mouth, deep dimples on each side. She smiled with a look that asked, "Yes?"

"You were right, you know," he said, hefting his gear bag.

"What do you mean?"

"I should have joined you for the ride."

Her smile returned. "Another time."

He nodded in agreement and began up the stairs, but turned back to catch the argon window raising. It stopped, and all Jonathan could see were Sasha's eyes and hair. "Say—" he began.

"I'm 24-7," she interrupted. "Call the service if you need a ride anywhere." Her eyes squinted slightly, a suggestion of a smile. For a second, they took in each other.

"Take care, Sasha."

The squint again. "I will, thank you."

The window resumed its journey. A wide-angle reflection of his brownstone and the darkening sky above replaced her face. There was a sucking sound as the window slipped tightly into the frame that rimmed the driver's door. A light rain began to fall.

A message from the past... 12

JONATHAN fell into his favorite chair and eased back; its memory cradled his body as a thousand times before. Rain drew tiny streaks down the antique panes of glass, and as he looked through the 200-year-old windows, he wondered about the people and families that might have been in the room.

"Sir," Max said, "you received two messages while you were gone."

"Play back," Jonathan replied through a stretch.

Georgia's image appeared on the coffee table. She was holocaptured from the waist up and was in a thick robe with a tall collar that seemed to swallow her head. "Morning," she said while she vigorously tugged her hair. "You've got me using towels now

— it's a nice change to the microdryers. I'm meeting with James at three o'clock, but I wanted to see if you were interested in connecting tonight, maybe for dinner?" She stopped rubbing and stepped closer, her image swelling in the fixed frame setting of the holo projection's parameters. She lowered her chin and smiled that smile. "Call me." Her image disappeared.

"God, you're sexy," Jonathan said under his breath. "Next message."

"Yes, sir. It is audio only."

That's odd, he thought.

A gray static, like a distant antique cell phone connection, filled the room. *"Jonathan...this is a warning."* The unidentified male voice was low and measured. *"You can not trust anyone. The Agency is not out for your best interests. They will suppress your growth. They fear you. Your potential is vast, beyond anything ever imagined. You owe it to the world to reach your true level."* There was a pause as the static ramped up and flooded the room again. *"Be careful, and remember...trust no one."* The message cut out, leaving a steady hiss.

Jonathan shot upright in the chair. "Max, what's the ID origin on this transmission?!"

"Unknown, sir."

"Is it traceable?"

"No. It was encrypted and had a multi-fragmented band dispersion rate. Its origin code degraded point three milliseconds after connection."

"Play it again."

Jonathan listened to the message a dozen more times. With

each playback, the voice seemed familiar, but he couldn't place where he might have met the man or heard the voice. A crack of thunder rippled through the neighborhood, and the rain began to pelt the windowpanes in waves. Jonathan leaned back into the chair and carefully listened to the stranger's voice, trying to distill its inflection, cadence and rhythm. He thought back through all the people he had met over the last two years and desperately tried to remember their faces and voices. He moved to the edge of the chair, searching his memories for any indicator or trait that would expose the messenger.

"Max, play the first two sentences again."

Max dutifully complied.

"Isolate the second sentence."

Jonathan closed his eyes. *"You can not trust anyone..."*

"Isolate the words 'can not.'"

As Max replayed the words, Jonathan strained at every syllable, even listening to the space in between the words for any clue to their origin. The voice was serious, and devoid of emotion.

Or contractions.

Jonathan opened his eyes as realization hit his soul. "Zvara..." he said quietly to himself, and a rumble of thunder rattled the panes of glass in their 200-year-old frames.

PAUL   BLACK

It appears that way from the data...   13

"YOU haven't touched your soup."

"Hmm?" he responded, still staring into his bowl of lobster bisque.

"Your soup," Georgia repeated. She pointed with her knife. "You haven't touched it." She put another forkful of Caesar salad to the test.

Jonathan shrugged.

"What is it? What's troubling you so?" Her face was lit softly by the candlelight, which set her cleft in a deeper shadow and gave her a slightly mannish appearance.

He met her question, hesitantly began to speak, but went back to stirring.

"Jonathan, please. Talk to me. I haven't seen or heard from you in days–"

"I don't know who to trust," he blurted. The stirring continued.

"What?..."

Jonathan sorrowfully looked up.

Georgia shrugged questioningly. "What are you talking about? You can trust me. Jonathan, come on, of all the people–"

"I received a message a few days ago."

Georgia's demeanor shifted. A seriousness came over her and she leaned back into her seat.

Jonathan rubbed his face and likewise sat back. He breathed a heavy sigh. "I could barely make out the message, it was so encrypted and distorted. But it was clear enough. It said that the Agency is suppressing my growth....That, that they're afraid of me. That my potential is vast, and I owe it to the *world* to reach my potential."

Georgia listened intently and took a sip of wine.

"Why would it say the world and not the *Tel* world?"

"I don't know....Maybe you're reading too much into it."

"And it said to trust no one."

"Hey," she said, "you can trust me."

"Guess who sent it," he said gravely.

She shrugged again.

"Zvara."

Georgia's eyes flared. She flinched as if a cold chill had run down her spine. "Jonathan," she gasped, "are you sure? I...I thought he was dead."

"Apparently not. I'd do a voiceprint comparison, but I don't have a vid of him to compare it to. Only the Agency does, and that's restricted, even to me. Hell, I've spent the last two days searching the archives trying to find one."

"Couldn't you request a sample?"

"Under what pretense? No, that would draw a lot of attention. I think they track my movements....It's something I've always suspected since I arrived."

"They wouldn't me. I could—"

"No!" he said, biting off her words. "No, no way. I'm not going to get you involved."

"Jonathan," Georgia reached over and took his hand, "I've been involved ever since Taos."

Jonathan smiled at this and gathered her hand into his. "It means a lot to me that you say that," he said softly, "but really, I don't want you to get hurt."

She read his anguish. "There's more, isn't there?"

"Yeah. Over the last few months, I've noticed this weird energy when I step into a room, more so than the usual looks. This seems..." he struggled for words, "...calculated."

"How so?"

"Like just the other day, the system said that Franks was available, but when I show up for those tests – the ones you wanted me to get – suddenly he's shut down. Says there's a system glitch, and he acts all nervous. Real odd. So I go over to the Grav Center, and it's closed, and I get the same funny reaction from the Center's director as I got from Franks...and I considered Franks a close friend." He pensively swirled the wine in his glass. "It's been like this for the last two or three months. Then I get this message saying not to trust anyone, and I'm being suppressed." He let go of Georgia's hand and retreated into the corner of his chair. "And these headaches are getting worse." He reached for his wine.

"Come on now, don't go all paranoid on me. Let's do some digging and see if this message is the real thing. Let me snoop around. They're not going to watch me. James has me doing grunt work, just to get familiar with the systems and procedures. It's real desk stuff. I can do some hacking, and they'll never know what happened."

Jonathan frowned from the top of his wine glass.

"The Rogues weren't just do-gooders. I was a pretty damn good hacker when I needed to be."

"All right," Jonathan conceded, leaning onto the table, "but *be careful*."

"Oh, don't worry about me," Georgia said slyly. She leaned close to his face. "I'm a big girl. I can watch out for myself."

"Oh, you are, are you?" He slid his finger down the front of her lips. She bit his finger and licked the tip of it.

He smiled. "Oh, yeah...I bet you are."

. . .

Georgia deftly navigated the Agency's massive information grid, hopping from node to node with the care and agility of a cat burglar sliding from one windowsill to another. Hacking the Agency's network meant patiently unlocking the heavily walled security structures of the system's bioprocessing molecular supercomputers. Georgia knew she'd never get further than the outer layers, but that was as far as she needed. Information such as a vid of Zvara resided in the shallows, which were heavily protected but not invulnerable. Anything deeper would require the expertise that came only with age and a history of time served in a correctional institution. To traverse the virtual domain of the Terra-Cray platform, Georgia was required to carefully encrypt her digital footprints. Such encryption made her travel through the domain slow and arduous. She masked her sojourn as data retrieval for the Recruiter Unit, which allowed her to enter and exit sensitive files virtually without question. She found Zvara's file buried deep inside a case area that would have been caked with dust in the physical world. Untying the string of code like a safecracker in an aged celluloid gangster film, she broke through the firewall and entered the file.

Before her was the life of one of the most celebrated Tels in history. It was all there: the impoverished childhood; the rural family background; and the original Recruiter notes, complete with data analysis and real-time grav readings – even a detailed account of his faked death, arranged by the Agency when he had turned 16. The extensive file confirmed Armando Zvara had been a prodigy and, until Jonathan, the most powerful Tel ever, as well as the most feared.

Lost in the fog of forgotten information, Georgia suddenly

felt the breath of someone directly behind her on her neck. She ripped off the virt headset, almost taking a clump of hair with it. It hissed and whined as the fiber optic connections tore loose from their jacks. She spun around as the face housing separated into its standby components.

"Jesus, James," she exclaimed, and pulled her hair off her face. "You scared me half to death!"

Jimbo straightened and folded his arms. "Why's your vidscreen off?"

"I assumed the data you requested was sensitive."

"Not really." His eyes searched her face.

"I'm sorry. Have I breached protocol?" She smiled that smile.

Jimbo relaxed. "No, it's just odd." Suddenly, he reached across her and clicked the screen to life.

Georgia whipped around and watched the vidscreen pixel up; she prayed she had been quick enough to the download. Her nerves shivered like they had life of their own. The first page of a bio on a Potential that Jimbo had requested appeared.

"See," he said, placing his hands on her shoulders, "this is a kid out of Mexico City. We think he might have the gift, but the preliminary data says he's probably just a Displacer. Definitely nothing special..." he leaned down behind her ear, "...or sensitive." He squeezed her shoulders, and his fingers dug deep into her collarbones. "Don't worry; the data you're retrieving is your basic background crap. I'm going to run to a meeting." The headset levitated off the table and floated into her lap.

"Is this a hint?" she asked.

He smiled. "I'll see you later."

Georgia quickly reviewed the data transmission after he left. Zvara's file was now nestled deep inside Max's core, and the transmission stream had been successfully encrypted. Finally able to breathe a sigh of relief, she leaned back in her chair and wondered if Zvara had really sent the message. She bit at her thumbnail as she stared at the blank vidscreen. *If Zvara was alive*, she wondered, *what was he up to, and why now?* She gingerly rubbed at her collarbones.

. . .

"Were you able to retrieve his file?" Jonathan anxiously asked the holoimage.

"Oh, you bet," Georgia confidently replied. "Once I'd sequenced the code structure for the preliminary levels, it was like a house of cards."

"Now I know why you're so good in the casinos."

"That's right," she said smugly.

"Did anybody notice you in the system?"

"Jonathan, *please*. I've been breaking code since before you knew what a grav field was. You'll find it in a folder named Zman, inside Max's base function area. It's pretty interesting. I think I got most of it before James interrupted me."

"What?! He doesn't suspect anything, does he?"

"No. I sweet-talked through it. He thinks I'm the good little Agency girl."

"Don't underestimate him. He's dumb like a fox."

"Don't worry. Ten years with the Rogues taught me a lot." She stepped closer, and her image grew in the holoframe. "Hey," she said coyly, "what are you doing later?"

Jonathan smiled, knowing what that look meant. "Oh, I don't know. What did you have in mind?"

"I was thinking a little drink, a little dinner." She smiled that smile.

"Okay, okay, I'm getting the picture." He chuckled. "Sure...I'd like that very much. I'll see you, when? Seven?"

"I was thinking..." she grinned again, "...now?"

"Jeez, Georgia, don't you have work to finish?"

"I'm almost done, and James isn't coming back."

"All right, I'll see you in two hours."

Georgia giggled devilishly, and her image vanished.

"That girl is going to wear me out," Jonathan mused. He reclined and folded his hands behind his head. "Max, you'll find a new file near your base functions."

"The Zman file? Yes, sir. I have it."

"Good. Display it and make sure your security grid is as tight as it can be. I don't want you scanned by any third parties."

"Yes, sir."

Max displayed the extensive holochive, and for the next hour, Jonathan intently scanned Zvara's file. The psychotic so often portrayed in cocktail party discourse emerged from the data stripped of his myth. As he studied further, Jonathan began to distill a clearer picture of the infamous Tel, learning more about the man and his tortured life.

"Max, this is fascinating...I never realized his early childhood was so violent. I have a whole new concept of this guy. He's not really the devil that his mythos makes him out. He's more of...a..."

"Victim?" Max offered, with all the emotion an artificial bioconstruct could deliver.

Jonathan knew that Max was an intuitive AI, designed to evolve beyond the sum total of its programming, but the answer was still brutally accurate. "Yes, Max. A victim is exactly what I was thinking."

"It appears that way from the data," Max continued without prompt.

Jonathan read on. Much of the holochive he already knew. Zvara was a legend, and most of his life had been covered in his Intro classes. It was no secret that the Agency leaders had pushed Zvara from an early age. Believing that he could ascend to a Level 9, they had driven Zvara relentlessly. There were even rumors that Zvara had been augmented. Yet as Jonathan skimmed the vast holochive, he sensed that there were elements missing. Certain areas seemed fragmented, with subtle gaps that appeared to have been altered or smoothed over. He studied the files, and diligently searched for a pattern to the incongruities.

After an exhaustive hour, he gave up and retrieved one of the many interviews with Zvara. "Max, compare the voiceprint from the audio net message I received to the voice track in this vid from the Zvara file." Jonathan relaxed against the chair and began watching the interview. It looked like it must have been conducted sometime during Zvara's last year as head of the Agency. Gone were Zvara's youthful grin and boundless energy. The man in this vid looked old and tired, more like the Zvara Jonathan had met two years prior, even with all the surgery. He studied the great Tel and wondered...

"I have finished comparing the two voiceprints," Max announced.

Jonathan froze the vid, catching Zvara just as he turned to the camera. "Are the two from the same person?"

"Inconclusive," Max replied. "There is too much degradation in the net message to accurately evaluate. There is a 26.7 percent match rate on 234 evaluation points."

Jonathan toyed with the small patch of hair under his lower lip and figured that if Zvara were alive, he would know more about what the Agency might be doing to him than anyone else. The image of Zvara looked out from the vid. His mouth was caught in a stern half-frown, but it was his eyes that made Jonathan flinch. They had an intensity that was penetrating, and as Jonathan looked into them, he began to feel a strange kind of kinship with the man many had called the Master.

"Sir?" Max questioned, which brought Jonathan back to the moment. "Do you suspect the Agency might be doing to you what it did to Zvara?"

Jonathan grinned with the profound clarity of the simple question. "If you mean are they pushing me to be some kind of supertel, then, yes, Max...I believe they are." He rubbed at his temples. "Max, how did you arrive at that conclusion?"

"Because..." there was a slight pause as the bioconstruct expanded again beyond its sum total, "...the trend represented by the data bears out this conclusion."

PAUL   BLACK

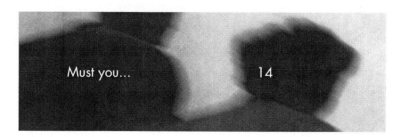

Must you...   14

"ARE you sure?"

"Her encryption codes were difficult to break, but by tracing her inception points, we're fairly certain of the download path."

Takeda reflectively stroked his thin beard; its white tip barely touched the top of his vest. "What do you think, Jeffrey?"

"He's probably just curious. Jonathan is an intelligent young man. I'm sure he's just trying to understand his future. After all, Zvara *is* the closest thing to a contemporary that he has."

"Had," Takeda corrected.

"Yes, quite." Trumble cleared his throat. "I wouldn't be too concerned. There's nothing in the file that pertains to the augmentations, is there?" He glared at Jimbo suspiciously, his eyes grossly distorted through the lenses of his antique glasses.

"No," Jimbo answered cautiously. "Not that I'm aware of."

"And what about this girl?" Trumble asked.

"She's harmless," Jimbo replied.

"She won't be too much of a *distraction?*"

"Doubtful. If anything, she'll probably do him some good."

"Well then," Takeda declared, "if you two aren't worried, then I'm not. Thank you, James."

Jimbo headed to the waiting elevator.

"James?"

He spun on his heels at Takeda's beckon. "Sir?"

Takeda leaned on his desk, sinuously weaving his obsidian-esque fingers together. Like an assassin focusing on his mark, he rested his index fingers on the front of his upper lip and trained his gaze intently at Jimbo. "You are *sure* about the file...aren't you?"

Jimbo instantly felt the incision of Takeda's telekinetic force. It burrowed deep into his mind, which created an odd sensation that wasn't quite pain, but definitely not pleasure. He secretly fought the reflex to blink because the acknowledgement of Takeda's presence would destroy any status he had in the eyes of the Agency leader. "Yes, sir," he assured, falsely calm; "I'm certain."

Like removing a hat two sizes too small, Jimbo felt Takeda release his mind. The suddenness caught him off guard, and he jerked back onto his heels. He tightened every muscle he had and strained to stop his movement.

Takeda's eyes flared slightly.

"Thank you, James," Trumble said. "Keep up the good work."

When the elevator doors shut, Trumble removed his glasses in disgust. "Really, Cyril! Must you be *so* theatrical?"

"We have to keep them honest, Jeffrey." A thin smile spread across his face.

Trumble rolled his eyes.

PAUL BLACK

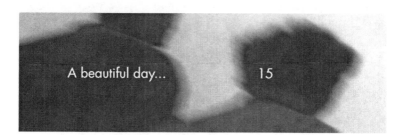

A beautiful day... 15

JONATHAN and Sasha approached Virt Booth 12. It was early, and the training center was vacant of the usual student crowd engaged in everything from the practical application of telekinetic quantum dynamics to recreational fly-fishing in the foothills of Aconcagua.

"Hey, Kreet," Sasha said into the panel to the left of the booth's door, "do you have my program loaded?"

"You are locked *and* loaded, Miss Sasha."

"Killer. Thanks, Kreet." She threw a glance at Jonathan. "Are you ready to get after it, Mr. Kortel?"

Jonathan's grin said "bring it on," and he yanked the handle to open the door. A click followed by a series of little pops accompanied his pull and the door glided effortlessly, its true weight disguised by a movement that resembled viscous fluid.

Entering a holobooth was like stepping into a coral reef, minus the water or distortion that came with navigating a thick haze of pollution. The booth's holo-optics were composed of 300 million biocones that covered every square inch of surface. With each step that Jonathan and Sasha took, the living optics quivered in slow-motion ripples that mimicked the surface of a shallow gray puddle.

Sasha cautiously put her bike down while Jonathan stepped to her side and gingerly positioned his bike between them.

"I realize once the program is running, we jump all over this stuff," he said, strapping on his helmet, "but it still unnerves me to walk on it when it's in this state."

"I know," Sasha agreed. She adjusted her gloves. "It's like we're intruding on their space. Even though I know they're not sentient, it still creeps me."

They paused as their virt headgear analyzed the contours of their heads and began conforming.

"Augh!" Sasha exclaimed. "I wish my helmet was back from service. These off-the-shelf models never get my shape right." She started blindly, fiddling with the headgear's control panel.

"Here, let me help you," Jonathan said.

"Back off!" She pushed his hand away. "I can handle it."

"You're in a mood this morning. If you weren't so rough on your equipment, your helmet wouldn't be in service."

"Really, Jonathan?" she replied sarcastically. "I didn't know that."

"Oh, come on," he said; "lighten up." He situated himself on his bike and threw a challenging look to her. "So, Miss Kuntar, are you ready for a little ass-kicking?"

Sasha positioned herself for holostart. "The real question is, are *you?*" She snapped her optic visor into place.

Even though Jonathan had been in virt booths a hundred times, holostart still unsettled him a bit.

"Hit it, Kreet!" Sasha yelled.

The booth droned for a second, as if some unseen force was exhorting it to do what it didn't desire. Then the grid exploded with the input surge that fed the holosignal to the biocones at a trillion gigaflops per second. They were enveloped in an intarsia of virtual dimension.

New York City.

"What the hell is this!" Jonathan yelled over the noise and confusion of Central Park North. His bike teetered at the edge of a littered malodorous gutter. A bright yellow cab laid on its horn behind him.

"Bite me!" Sasha yelled at the driver.

"Bite...me?"

"It's slang from the period."

"And what period is this?!"

"New York City, late 20th century!"

"Why?!"

"No shit!"

"What?!" Jonathan exclaimed over a police car that rounded the corner with siren screaming.

Sasha hopped to the ground. She shuffled toward Jonathan and grabbed his shoulder, supporting him as he balanced on his bike. "No Biolution!" she said into the side of his headgear. "No Interway or network hubs. These people knew how to move. They fought the traffic. It was like a game to them!"

"What people?!"

"Messengers!" A screech of tires from a FedEx truck sliced the air. "Bike messengers!"

Jonathan now noticed how the booth's matrix had interfaced with their virtsuits. Sasha was wearing period clothing for a spring day in New York, probably the late 1980s. Her short pants were made from some organic material – denim, Jonathan thought it was called – and her sleeveless shirt sported the letter "I," a cartoonish heart, and the letters "NYC" running across her chest. Sasha also wore a backpack, like the kind Jonathan had seen in old paper magazines. It was filled with an assortment of cardboard tubes.

Sasha answered the question in his eyes. "This was their uniform, I think."

Jonathan dismounted his bike to look himself over. He was wearing long, faded blue pants that were frayed at the bottom and made of the same material as Sasha's cutoff shorts. His right knee protruded from a tattered square hole. The patch for it hung by a few threads and flapped erratically in the brisk, chilly wind. His left pant leg was rolled up past his ankle, and the program also had created a hooded garment of soft, thick fabric. It had long sleeves and thin drawstrings that dangled from two holes on either side of the neck. On its front was a graphic lightning bolt that bisected the letters AC on the left and DC on the right.

"AC, DC?...What am I, an electrical engineer?" he asked.

"I don't know," Sasha replied. "Maybe."

"I look like a 'streeter,'" Jonathan declared. He noticed another large hole in the seat of the pants. No detail overlooked, he now sported bright red underwear.

"Homeloss, actually," Sasha said.

"Homeloss?"

"Yeah. They were called homeloss people. They lost their homes in the weird 20th-century economy. That's why they became bike messengers."

Jonathan shrugged. "Works for me."

The cabby blared his horn again, this time holding it down. Sasha spun and angrily gestured with three fingers under her right eye.

"Sasha," Jonathan said, laughing; "he's not going to be programmed to know what that means. You need to get in the spirit of the times!" He turned and flipped the driver off.

Sasha laughed and joined him, gesturing at the driver. "Bite me!" she yelled.

Jonathan straddled his bike. "It's actually 'fuck you,' but nice try." He felt at the pack on his back. "Let me guess, we've got to deliver these somewhere, right?"

"Right," Sasha said. "And the first one there wins."

"Where's there?"

"You know Manhattan?"

"Yeah," Jonathan said, looking around at the canyon of buildings.

"You know where the Daimler Building is?"

"You mean the old Chrysler? Yeah, sure."

"That's *there*." Sasha swung her leg over her crossbar and began teetering in place. Jonathan followed.

"Ready?!" she yelled.

Jonathan nodded.

The cabby laid on his horn again, and Sasha took off toward the entrance of the park.

"Fuck you!" Jonathan yelled at the cab. He snapped his optic visor into place and sped off after her.

Without the controls and safeties of post-Biolution transportation, 20th-century New York traffic, with its unpredictability, made for a formidable challenge. As they jammed through the streets, Sasha maintained her lead, darting and swerving to avoid the onslaught of pedestrians, delivery trucks and the errant car door (which would open to release yet another obstacle into their agonistic game). Sasha jumped a curb and dove through a curtain of cucumber-colored slickers. She rounded a corner wearing one of them for headgear. Jonathan followed, almost slamming into one of New York City's finest. "Hey, you!" the holojection cop said. "Watch it, you damn kids!" It was now obvious that Sasha had programmed an array of elaborate obstacles so perfectly integrated into the program that distinguishing them from the base scene was virtually impossible. And all of them, Jonathan figured, accomplished without a stochastic subroutine.

Sasha cut a hard left and nearly clipped a Yellow Cab (its driver yelled something only known in the Sudan) and sped into Central Park. With Jonathan drafting tightly behind her, they flew like one against the traffic of East Park Drive. Jonathan barely maintained his position as Sasha weaved in and out of the in-line skaters and joggers. The holoprogram was so accurate that the people actually reacted to them. At the Lawn, Jonathan shot around her and hugged her left side. She looked over, smiled, and slammed into his bike. He wagged his finger at her and sprinted ahead. She closed in on him and deftly rubbed her front tire against his back tire. Jonathan tapped his brakes and ejected her from his bike. They jockeyed like this for a hundred yards, one testing the other. Suddenly Sasha surged ahead, but Jonathan quickly gained and rode up beside her. He stuck his tongue out at her. She answered. A small orange disk abruptly entered Jonathan's peripheral vision. It appeared to sail right along with him before it ricocheted off his helmet and caused him to almost lose control.

"Shit!" he exclaimed.

"That was a freebie!" Sasha yelled. She angled toward the Boat House.

"I think you mean Frisbee." He laughed at her destruction of the period vernacular.

"What?!"

"Frisbee...that was a Frisbee!"

"How do *you* know?!" Sasha asked.

Jonathan's humor began to wane. "Because," he said, slowing his bike, "I had one as a kid." He left the street and rode into the grass.

Sasha, still at full clip, looked over her shoulder and saw Jonathan hop from his bike. She braked to a crawl, turned, and rode back to Jonathan. She jumped from her bike and let it continue riderless until it crashed with a little semicircle twist flip. She peeled off her headgear, and its couplings hissed in protest. "What are you doing? We're only halfway through!"

Jonathan, his bike on the ground next to him, back tire still spinning, was staring into a small grove of dogwoods.

"Ah, Jonathan?" Sasha badgered, hands on her hips.

Jonathan kept staring. "It's so weird..." he said under his breath.

"Not really. I was beating your ass!"

Solemn and distant, he kept his attention on the trees. "Why?" he said more to them than to her.

"Why what?" she asked sternly.

Without word, Jonathan pointed. Sasha followed his finger and recoiled at the sight. There, at the base of the thickest trunk, was a three-dimensional image that floated a foot off the grass. It gently quivered like a bedsheet hanging in a light breeze. The eerie image portrayed a boy and a man playing catch with a Frisbee. The setting was tropical, with a glimpse of a beach between the palms in the background. The boy laughed as he caught the Frisbee, and the man ran over and tackled him. They fell, laughing and rolling. It stopped and replayed.

Sasha intently watched it three times. "What the hell is that?" she asked. "Do we have a glitch in the system?"

"No," Jonathan said somberly, "we don't."

"And just how would you know?"

"Because," Jonathan said, pointing to the boy in the image, "that's me."

"What?!..." Sasha exclaimed.

Jonathan finally turned to Sasha with a quizzical, sorrowful voice: "Why do these happen?" he asked.

Sasha, hearing his anguish, was at a loss for words. "I, I...didn't know, I–"

Jonathan gestured for her to stop. "It's all right," he said. "My mind creates these images. They're like a manifestation of my subconscience....I don't know how, though. And no one knows about them – except James, that is, and now you."

"Jesus, Jonathan. I had no idea. This is incred–"

A flock of birds overhead startled them, their squawks muffled by the distance. Jonathan and Sasha watched them circle for a moment, then smiled to each other. There was no need to say how wonderful it was to see a flock of birds – again.

Sasha gasped. "Jonathan, it's gone!"

"I know."

Sasha's hair whipped in the wind. Jonathan parted it from her face. She took his hand. Jonathan circled his other hand around her waist and pulled her closer. Sasha slowly reached to touch his face.

"Coming through!" An out-of-control in-line skater screamed and careened toward them. Sasha and Jonathan jumped apart just in time for the girl to tumble between them.

"Sorry! Sorry!" the blader said, picking herself up. She

tiptoed out of the grass and rejoined a pack that was blading *en masse* down East Park Drive.

"Well," Jonathan said, looking about and trying not to acknowledge what might have happened, "it's certainly a beautiful day here in New York..."

Sasha reached for his arm. Jonathan resisted, but finally acquiesced to her overt show of caring.

"Jonathan," Sasha said quietly, "is there something you need to talk about?"

He looked away, but she pulled his face around. He painfully nodded, took her hand from his face and gently kissed the top of it. "Thank you," he said, not taking his eyes from hers.

She returned the gesture with a soft smile.

"Come on," Jonathan urged. He tugged her toward her bike. "Last one to the Chrysler has to buy lunch."

Sasha held her ground, pulling him back in midtug. "Tell me..." she began, but hesitated.

Jonathan questioned her.

"Please tell me," she continued, "about...Hawaii."

Jonathan smiled at her request. "Yeah, sure, that would be nice. Besides," he said, walking back to her, "I was going to beat you anyway."

Sasha playfully punched him in the stomach. The squawks from the flock were louder now, and the two of them lifted their faces in awe as the birds descended into a clearing 20 feet from them. For a brief moment, it felt as if they were actually in New York.

Before the Biolution. Before the Terror Years.

· · ·

The door to the virt booth shut with an odd little "clunk," not the expected sound from a door that held a quarter ton of bioholo processing packs and nearly three miles of fiber optics.

"Thanks, Kreet," Sasha said.

"*No problemo*, Miss Sasha. You guys have a good time?"

Jonathan grinned at Sasha.

"Yeah, Kreet," she answered. A smile crossed her face. "We had a nice time in New York."

"Most people do. We'll catch ya on the return."

Jonathan and Sasha rolled their bikes into one of the large storage lockers that took up most of one side of the staging area. They were quiet as they hung their headgear, and he could sense an awkward energy between them. Sasha stepped behind the translucent wall of the women's dressing area, but just as Jonathan rounded the wall to the men's area, a sharp pain carved between his two main frontal lobes. The sensation was excruciating, like a lobotomy performed with no anesthesia. He crumpled to the floor.

Lying on his side, Jonathan looked through the gap between the floor and the bottom of the wall. He could see Sasha's figure through the translucent divider wriggling out of her holosuit. He tried to speak, but the sheer intensity of the pain gripped him in a state of paralysis. He could only manage garbled, choked sounds as he clawed at the wall. He caved. A small puddle of drool formed on the floor and spread toward his cheek. His toes began to curl.

"Jonathan," Sasha said flippantly, "since I was kicking your butt in there, I think we can conclude that you'll be buying lunch today. Agreed?"

Jonathan could barely move his eyes to watch Sasha's backlit image against the scrim wall. With every ounce of strength he could rally, Jonathan forced his throat open and made a noise that sounded vaguely like gargling.

Her figure stopped undressing and turned. "Jonathan?"

He couldn't muster the strength to answer.

Sasha's figure moved to the edge of the wall, and she poked her head around the corner. "Jonathan, are you listening?..."

Jonathan's arm had dropped into the space between the two dressing rooms. His hand lay palm up; his fingers twitched in spasm as nerves misfired throughout his body.

"Jonathan!" She ran around the wall and knelt beside him. "Oh, my God, what's happening?!" she said in quiet panic, and pulled him off the floor and into her arms.

Curled tightly from convulsion, Jonathan's arms had bent so that his elbows almost touched, and his hands had contorted in on themselves. His brow and hair were soaked. He couldn't turn his head, but his eyes were still able to move in their sockets. He looked up at her like an infant in its mother's arms.

She swept his hair from his forehead, but when she touched him, the grip of the seizure abated.

"Oh, shit," Jonathan moaned. He coughed and spat. He turned away from her, but Sasha kept touching him as he crawled out of her arms. He curled up on the floor, shaking and clutching his head. He began to cough uncontrollably.

"Please," Sasha urged, "let me call a med team."

"No!" Jonathan exclaimed between coughs. "I-I'll be fine. Just...just give me a moment." His breathing returned to normal and he began to regain his composure. He quietly lay on the floor while Sasha stroked his head.

"Hey," she said softly, "look at me, please."

"I...I really shouldn't."

"Why?" she tenderly questioned.

"Because," he said with an odd little sound that came across more like a cough than a laugh, "you don't have on a top."

Sasha quickly examined herself. In her instinctive reaction, she had rushed to his aid topless; the holosuit peeled halfway down to her hips. She quickly covered her breasts with folded arms. "Excuse me, I, ah, need to finish getting dressed." She rose to her feet. "Are you going to be okay for a second?"

He nodded, still averting his eyes.

Sasha returned to her dressing area.

Jonathan said, "Don't be embarrassed. You're beautiful. Very beautiful."

Sasha paused just behind the wall and grinned to herself.

Jonathan closed his eyes and curled his body tighter. With his brain throbbing and his mind filling with suspicion and fear, he gingerly laid his head on the floor. All he could think about was the Zvara holochive with its haunting glimpse of a proleptic future. Overwhelmed, he silently began to rock.

PAUL BLACK

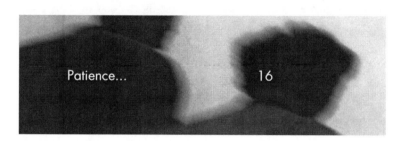

Patience... 16

JACOB Whitehorse had taught his only child that patience was the virtue of a great hunter. In the late summer of her 12th year, he brought young Kaya to his ancestral homelands of the Southwest, where, for eight weeks, he educated her on her Indian heritage.

Kaya learned to survive in the harsh New Mexican environment, living off the rugged land that, for the most part, hadn't changed since her ancestors roamed it more than 300 years ago. She grew to admire her father as he instructed her in the "old ways" of their people. During the days, they hunted for mule deer and black-tailed jackrabbit, and she discovered that the depth of a paw print, the angle of a broken branch or the direction of a blood trail could help track prey. At the end of each day, they built their camp wherever their hunt had taken them. When night fell, her father passed on their people's language and lore, and often, before Kaya slipped into sleep under the expanse of the New Mexican sky, she wondered about the Indian children and how they survived such a hard life. She learned to understand her father's passion for preserving their people's teachings, and by the end of their trip, she was fiercely proud of her heritage. She also could fell a deer at 50 paces.

The instrument panel of Kaya's vehicle suddenly chattered as the system conducted its routine dialogue with the D.C. Zone Interway. "All connections are secure and operational," it said, snapping her back from the memory. The car idled with barely a hint of vibration on the quiet street. Kaya settled against the pilot's seat and watched her prey ascend the stairs of his Georgetown walk-up.

She was always struck by Jonathan Kortel's physical appearance. He wasn't particularly tall or strong in stature (although his gait revealed that he worked out). He had a youthful look, but not in a "baby face" way. Many considered him handsome, though much of this was born, Kaya suspected, from his dry wit and natural charm – in truth, there wasn't anything really special about Jonathan Kortel at all. And this, more than anything else, is what enraged Kaya. She often wondered how a man like this could have killed a legend like Jacob Whitehorse.

She intently watched Jonathan unlock his front door. Every part of her being wanted to lash out, and it took all of her strength not to jump from the car and level her weapon. She rehearsed the words of her father: *Patience, Kaya. Practice the art of deception. Track your prey until it thinks you're no longer following it...then strike.*

Jonathan Kortel began to enter his residence, but turned as if he had heard her thoughts. He keenly surveyed the street; the dim porch light slid across his face so that Kaya could make out his eyes. He looked pained somehow, his posture sullen. "This is the Infinite Tel?" she mused in the quiet of the cabin.

Not for long, she thought.

PAUL BLACK

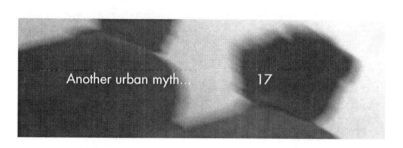

Another urban myth...   17

GEORGIA stirred. She wrapped her arm around Jonathan's chest and ran her fingers through his chest hair. The room was quiet, and the light from the neighbor's porch came through a sliver of space between the old shutters that covered the windows in Jonathan's bedroom. She scooted tighter against him, and her eyes moved into the path of light that cut through the dark room. She twitched.

"What is it?" Jonathan whispered.

"Nothing. Just that light again."

"I'm tired of that light." He focused and created a narrow grav corridor that traced the light beam back to its source. He didn't need to phase for something like that. In his first year at the Agency, his training and development had refined his ability to the point that a small exercise like breaking glass four houses away was no more difficult than blinking.

It shattered, and a dog began to bark.

"You want me to shut the dog up, too?"

"No, please don't," Georgia whispered. She squeezed him tighter and kissed the back of his neck.

Jonathan could feel her breath against his skin. He pulled his knees in, tightening his fetal position. He shuddered and coughed lightly.

"Are you all right?" Georgia asked.

"Yeah, I'm fine."

"You've been quiet all night, and you hardly touched your dinner."

"I'm okay, really."

"How was your ride today with...what's her name? Your new driver?"

"Sasha?"

"Yeah, her. How was it? Did you win?"

Jonathan hesitated and coughed again. "No...no I didn't."

A few moments passed, and all Jonathan could hear was his own breathing. Georgia sat up on her elbow and leaned into his ear. "What are you thinking?" she asked with a slight huskiness that Jonathan found sexy. Very sexy.

"You really want to know?"

"Yesss," she said in a way that sounded special, like it belonged only to him.

"I was thinking about Zvara...his life. About how I have so much in common with him–"

"I was thinking of getting more of his file," Georgia said, stepping on his thought. "There was another section I couldn't retrieve. It had a ton of security around it, but I think with a little effort I could break through. I'm curious about what's inside it."

Jonathan rolled over. "Please don't. You've already risked way too much exposure. I can't let you risk yourself any further."

"Shhh," she whispered, silencing him with her finger. "I know the risks, and I'm willing to take them. If Zvara's message is true, then the more we find out about him, the more you'll understand about what the Agency might have planned for you." She kissed him. "Besides, I'm not in this just for you. I'm in this for *us*."

Jonathan searched her face. "Is there an...*us*?"

She leaned in close and licked the tip of his upper lip. "I'd like to think so."

Jonathan gently crawled on top of her. She spread her legs to let him nestle against her hips. Her skin was warm, and she smelled of sex and sweat and need. "I can't promise you anything," he tenderly whispered.

Georgia put her arms around his neck and smiled that smile. "I know. But tonight, just love me...even if it's for a few hours." She wrapped her legs tightly around his waist.

• • •

Jonathan sat at the kitchen counter and watched the

national netnews. The talking heads were deep into an entertainment segment about the new fashions from Milan. The supermodels stood like perfect statues as their individual platforms hovered about the exhibition hall. Holographic projections of the clothes quick-cut between detail vids of the various collections, all choreographed to the biting fused rhythms of Middle East core and New American electronica. Jonathan tentatively sipped coffee and paid scant attention to the segment. Georgia was devouring a bowl of fruit and yogurt.

"Max," she said, "what is the life date for these strawberries?"

"Approximately 3.8 days for optimum flavor, with a 1.3 day window of spoilage on either side. The current strawberries are at 2.4 days for optimum flavor."

She questioningly glanced at Jonathan.

"Welcome to the big city, New Mexico girl." He began to cough.

"Are you sure you're all right?"

"Yeah, I just pushed it too hard yesterday with Sasha."

"If you haven't been training for that kind of thing, you can't just go into one of those booths and expect to win. She's a ripped little lady..."

"You've met?"

"I met her at the training center. She's pretty cute," Georgia said. She waited to see if he'd rise to the bait.

"I guess," Jonathan said, borrowing his disinterest from the news segment. "She's too ethnic for me."

Georgia pinched his side. "I'm not *too ethnic*, am I?"

"No." Jonathan batted her hand away and hopped off the stool. He slid behind her, wrapped his arms around her waist and kissed her neck. "You're just right."

Georgia reached up with one hand and stroked him behind his head while she took another spoonful. "What are you going to do today?" she asked through a mouthful of breakfast.

"I'm now officially on vacation, winging my way to sunny Tortola," Jonathan said sarcastically. "At least that's what I've told James."

"What about Sasha?"

"I think she's cool. She's too concerned with her classes to care if I'm on vacation or not."

"She's a little old for a driver, isn't she?"

"A little. She told me that they discovered her later than most."

Georgia nodded and glanced at her watch. "I've got to go. James wants my opinion on the new Potential files by noon."

"Oooh, so he's asking for your opinion now, eh?"

She winked. "Yes, he is. I'm advancing quite fast in the Unit."

"Very impressive, young lady."

"Why, thank you, Mr. Kortel." She bounded toward the garage.

"Hey," Jonathan yelled after her. "Meet you at the Nougat tonight?"

"Yeah...call me," Georgia called from the hallway and slammed the door to the garage.

Jonathan turned back to the TVid to find the netnews

had moved on to a science segment. A field reporter was doing a remote from the deck of a ship somewhere in the middle of an ocean. The wind kicked at his coat and blew his hair to one side, which exposed an odd, pre-Biolution era comb-over. The color of the sky was a deep, almost artificial blue. Probably done in post. He pointed to the horizon. "There, 60 miles away, is the start of the Hazard Zone, and beyond that, the former Hawaiian Islands—"

"Shall I turn the TVid off, sir?" Max inquired.

"No, let's see what this is about." Jonathan propped himself back on the stool. "Louder, please."

"Scientists now believe that the biodegeneration of matter that has been taking place since that fateful day 16 years ago has stopped. A research team from the French Oceanic Institute believes that the rate of decay has slowed to an almost imperceptible pace. It appears that, for all intents and purposes, the Hawaiian Islands have stopped merging their matter. This means that scientists may soon physically enter the Hazard Zone for the first time since the event. Who knows what they'll find? With a target date for entry just a few weeks away, the whole world waits in anticipation for the first look at ground zero. For this reporter, it won't be soon enough. I, like thousands of others, lost relatives in the event, and we hope finally to have closure on a terrible chapter for humanity. This is Reynard Moskowitz reporting from the Safe Zone in the Pacific Ocean."

"Off, Max." Jonathan sat and stared at the now blank TVid. Moments passed. He didn't move.

"Are you all right, sir?" Max questioned.

He didn't answer.

"Sir?–"

"Yeah, Max...I'm okay. Don't worry."

"I am not programmed to worry, sir. Just observe changes in body temperature, eye capillary dilation, motor movement–"

"Thank you, Max...for your observation."

"Certainly, sir. Are you leaving this morning?"

"Yes, I'm going out."

"Shall I call the car service?"

"No, I'm going to work out, then walk over to Arturo's and have some lunch."

"Yes, sir."

Jonathan's mind was back in Hawaii.

"Are you worried, sir?"

"Hmm? What, Max?"

"Are you worried, sir, at what will be found at ground zero?"

He smiled at the AI's intuitive question. "No, Max. Not really. I imagine there won't be much to find."

"What if they do?"

"Do what?"

"Find something, sir."

"Well then," he said, rising from the counter, "we'll have to deal with it as it comes, won't we?"

"Actually, sir," Max continued, "only you will."

• • •

Arturo's was slow, and Jonathan found himself enjoying the

outdoor cafe almost alone. A young couple laughed and kissed at a small table near the back of the patio. He relaxed against his chair and let the warm midday sun pour over his face. He could feel it heating his skin, and he removed his sunglasses to enjoy its full effect. The shadows along the street were black, as if light itself couldn't escape from them. By contrast, the areas lit by the sun glowed with the intensity of a billion-K spot. A "Santa Fe sun," as Tarris used to call it. He had just finished his sandwich and was gulping down the last of his tea when he saw Jimbo step from a shop across the street. He was in dark shadow, but Jonathan could spot that red hair a mile away. He began to wave, but a small, pretty woman also stepped from the shop and joined him on the sidewalk. Her hair was pulled back with dark, oversized sunglasses balanced delicately on top.

"Well, well," Jonathan said, "ol' James finally has himself a girlfriend." He watched the woman take Jimbo's arm, and as she shifted a large shopping bag to her other hand, her face entered a shaft of sunlight that cut a path between two buildings. Jonathan slowly lowered his hand as the shock of whom he saw began to wrap itself around his soul. There, in the edge of the midday light like a detached fragment from a nightmare, was Anari – Tamara's best friend.

For a second, Jonathan truly thought he was hallucinating, or that the combination of sun and shadow was only making the woman with Jimbo look like Anari. But as she came fully into the light, the cold truth that Anari was truly standing across the street hit him like a discharge from a Light-Force. He fell back against the chair, his breath caught in his throat. He quickly shoved on his sunglasses and rushed into the restaurant, where he stood at the window, frozen – seized by the cruelty that was unfolding before him. He watched them walk, arm-in-arm, down the sidewalk – Anari laughing, Jimbo bending down every step or two to say something in her ear. They stopped, and Jimbo passionately kissed her before entering another shop.

Jonathan's heart collapsed. His mind struggled to process what he had witnessed. He had always thought that Anari, along with Hector, his former staff at the restaurant, Tamara and her child had been purged of any memory of him. He had allowed the Agency to wipe away part of his past, only to discover that the man he called "friend" had lied to him for his own gain. While the brutal realization that he had been a pawn sunk in, he thought of the warning in the mysterious net message. He had given up so much for the Agency: his life, his past, his love. And when he watched Jimbo tenderly kiss Anari, his pain and hurt began to transform into a new emotion.

A case of 10-year-old Barossa Shiraz exploded behind him.

. . .

Georgia took a deep breath and warily eyed her netport. The last time she had invaded the Agency's system, it had taken all of her skill just to retrieve the basic file on Zvara. Now she was contemplating a hacking that really required someone who did it for a living. She hesitated ...

... and snapped her optic visor into place to enter the Terra-Cray landscape. Stealthily retracing her steps back to Zvara's file, she found everything as it had been. The system's protocols had not been altered, and travel through the domain went smoothly. Too smoothly, she felt. The security codes encapsulating the second file on Zvara proved complex, and after 20 minutes of hacking, she grew nervous. All good hackers knew that the longer the stay, the more likely you pay, and Georgia felt she had spent 15 minutes more than she should have. Just a few bits of data from breaking through, Georgia struggled with the last string of code that would unravel the security subroutine that guarded Zvara's file. Again, she crawled within a megabyte of success, but the code resequenced itself like a drug-resistant, recombinant biological virus. Frustrated and defeated, Georgia noticed a subtle shift in the system to the left of her virtual field of vision. Someone else was hacking the same area — and closing fast on her. Georgia panicked. She wouldn't have time to back out and encrypt her exit path. The hacker's data stream flooded the area, and Georgia could only watch as it entwined itself around the last data sequence she had been hacking.

Astonished, she noticed that the intruder was not preventing her from entering Zvara's file. It was helping her.

She watched, awestruck, as the hacker's data stream resequenced the last bit of code and released the file. Immediately, the hacker's data began to dissipate until only a few bits of data were left from the original stream. They reformed into the words: YOU ONLY HAVE 10 MINUTES.

Georgia instantly dove into the file and began rifling through the volumes of data. Frantically, she caught only glimpses of Zvara's life. An email from one doctor to another expressing concern over inordinate cranial pressure. A memo to Trumble about cost overruns. Grav tests with field ranges 10 times that of a "normal" Level 8. Then a file, which appeared to have had extra security, caught her attention. Its content proved rich, and as she scanned from netmails to meeting summaries to confidential memos, a pattern began to form. Neural tests just before Zvara had assumed leadership of the Agency revealed a tremendous surge in his neurological activity. Surgical notes from a doctor's personal log detailed a series of cranial explorations: its three-dimensional holorecord indicated an experimental implant of bionanoware technology directly into Zvara's cerebral cortex. A handwritten note next flashed by; its rudimentary characteristics stood out like a wrongly struck note amid the symphony of statistical data. It was addressed to Jeffrey Trumble:

Jeffrey,

You are the only one I have left who will listen without malice. I wish to meet with you and the board to discuss my future. I know I am in no position to dictate terms, but my dedication to our culture and way of life should outweigh any protests that you may have to field. I leave my fate in your hands.

Your friend always,
Armando

Georgia continued to scan. If she understood everything correctly, the procedures on Zvara only confirmed her suspicions about the Agency. They also imparted an ominous feeling that Jonathan might soon (if not already) be subject to the same desires that drove the Agency to conduct its first experiments a decade earlier. Engrossed in the data, Georgia suddenly noticed that the 10-minute deadline was rapidly approaching.

Along with the system's security constructs. *00:03:16...*

The virtual domain was easy enough to navigate, but its security measures were some of the best ever designed. Georgia didn't see them coming: she felt them. Any good hacker could sense their presence a nodal point away. Like disfigured ripples in the sea of information, the security sentries could be sensed by the subtle shift of data flow left in the wake of their movement. Agency sentries roamed the vast Terra-Cray network, digital white blood cells that sought and attacked any intruders in the bloodstream of information.

00:02:32...

Georgia sensed their imminence and immediately executed her exit strategy. She quickly downloaded as much of Zvara's file as she could, then bounded from level to level, all the while encrypting her path to confuse the constructs.

00:01:46...

She entered the exit path to the outer layer, but found it blocked by a sentry application. Instantly, she veered off, hitching onto a stream of transfer data. It dragged her to a flow she recognized as a path to the entry hub. She surfed it wildly, executing sharp cutbacks and shifts to keep herself in the swiftest current.

00:00:46...

Passing through the final layer, she emerged at the base level of the system and exited through her inception point. She ripped off her netgear and threw it on the desk. Her hair was saturated. She shook her head in a futile attempt to shake away her nerves with the sweat.

00:00:08.

Georgia leaned back and reviewed her path on the vidscreen. As far as she could tell, the system's sentries never drew close enough to sample her data. She was free and clear. Breathing a sigh of relief, she began to shut down her portal when suddenly her vidscreen shifted color. Her path architecture was replaced with a black screen and a simple two-word message that, in an odd way, gave her a feeling of accomplishment. "GOOD LUCK" glowed for a second in a bright green sans serif, then slowly faded into the inky blackness.

. . .

Jonathan tracked Georgia as she made her way through the current of people around the bar. Her gait was fast, and she didn't display her usual posture of confidence. Even after she had caught her first glimpse of him, she didn't smile. Instead, she only made eye contact, then nervously looked away. Something, he sensed, was seriously wrong.

Georgia slid into the booth, wadded her raincoat and

slammed it against the wall. She ran her fingers through her wet hair, put her elbows on the table and folded her hands. She looked out over the crowd. Then finally to him.

Jonathan swirled the ice in his drink and studied the emotion in her eyes. She averted his stare.

"Well?" he questioned, his voice cool and void of its usual soft timbre. "What is it? What's the matter?"

"Oh, Jonathan. I...I–"

"You went back in, didn't you?"

She hesitated, then nodded.

"I asked you not to! It's too damn dangerous. You're taking way too big a risk. It's not worth it."

"It was," Georgia said firmly.

"What? What did you find?"

She hesitated again, then reached across the table and took his hands.

Jonathan could feel her fear. "What did you learn?" he asked gravely.

"I was able to hack into the other file, but I didn't do it alone."

He winced questioningly.

"I got within a few strings of data, but I couldn't untie the last security sequence, until this other hacker charged in and finished it for me." She pulled away and folded her arms tightly across her chest. "It was Zvara, I know it!" Her leg began nervously jittering.

"And?..." Jonathan pressed. His voice had an edge that

pushed Georgia against the vinyl booth.

"And I discovered something." She couldn't face his glare.

Jonathan mentally pulled her face around. Her eyes widened with shock at his abrupt display. "What did you learn?" he asked sternly.

Georgia, experiencing for the first time the rawness of Jonathan's telekinetic power, sunk back against the booth. "This other file," she nervously continued, "was full of data that detailed experiments they had performed on Zvara."

"Go on!"

"You know when Zvara began his rise within the Agency, just before they made him director?"

"And?!"

"The reason he surpassed Whitehorse was that the Agency had conducted some experiments..." She looked away. Both legs jittered in sync.

"What *kind*?!" Jonathan demanded. His impatience boiled over in a primal display of rage that spun Georgia's head so forcefully she yelped. Unaware that his thoughts had become manifest, he dragged her over the table.

"They implanted some kind of bionanoware!" she exclaimed, her eyes flush with fear. "Jonathan! My neck...my God, you're hurting me!"

Suddenly realizing, he recoiled at his own actions. Georgia fell back, her knees slamming against the bottom of the table. Her face went blank as she vigorously rubbed at her neck.

Jonathan was stunned. He began to apologize but saw in

her eyes that the damage had been done. "Goddamnit!" he raged. He jumped from the booth.

"No, Jonathan! Wait!"

Too late. He already had charged into the crowd, telekinetically shoving people aside, their drinks ripped from their hands by the field disruption. Georgia leaped from the booth like her legs were hydraulic and pushed through the dense mass, trying to keep within his wake; but the crowd, collectively connected to the Net and seemingly oblivious to Jonathan's telekinetics, closed in as soon as he passed and continued dancing like one thick, undulating being. Frustrated, Georgia focused and created a grav field corridor that not only slammed through the dancers, but caught Jonathan off guard. She spun him around and yanked him back so fast his feet dragged on the tips of his toes. She caught him by his lapels. He was shocked at her aggression.

"Don't you ever do that to me again!" she growled, pulling him tight to her face.

"Georgia, look...I'm—"

"Shut up and listen. I went back in because I care for you, Jonathan Kortel. You might think of me as just some fuck buddy, but to me..." He felt her grav field relax, and his feet slowly lowered to the floor. "...it's more than that. Lord knows why – after tonight." She released her grip from his lapels and began to straighten the wrinkles she had caused. "I must be the craziest girl on the—"

"No," Jonathan said, grabbing her hands, "no, you're not. Quite the opposite. You're the best thing that's happened to me since..." He looked down, caught in his own analogy.

"Since...*Tamara?*" Georgia tersely finished.

Embarrassed, Jonathan nodded. "I'm sorry. That didn't come out the way I wanted it to."

"You're damn right it didn't! You know what your problem is, Kortel?" She leaned in close. "You need to just fucking let go!" And she shoved him away.

"Georgia, come on! Wait!" Jonathan pleaded, but she was already halfway to the door. "Damn it!" he said, and chased after her. He caught up and grabbed her arm. "What about these people? They saw us phase!"

Georgia glared back into the bar. "Screw them. These people are so jacked, they don't know what reality they're in." She pushed her way past Jonathan and stormed toward the parking lot.

They tensely walked in silence through the cool night air, Georgia a few steps ahead of Jonathan. She marched up to the car; its doors slowly opened. She stopped and waited for him to reach the passenger's side. Shooting him a deadly look over the top of the car, she said, "Those people back there? They could use a new urban myth!" She climbed into the pilot's seat. Her hands flew over the instruments. The door slammed behind her.

PAUL BLACK

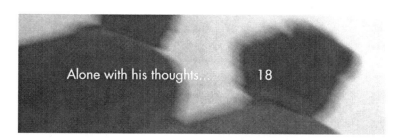

Alone with his thoughts...   18

THE room was draped with a thick blackness, the kind of blackness that masked depth and scale. Jonathan sat on his bed, solemn. He thought about what Georgia had told him, about Zvara and the experiments. He looked at the empty side of the bed, sheets still tucked crisply into the frame.

He would sleep alone, his thoughts his only companion.

The ride to his home from Bar of Chocolate had been quiet. Jonathan hadn't said a word, partly from embarrassment, but mostly from the anger that was building again inside him. Just before they had turned down his street, Georgia broke the silence to tell him that if he wanted to know more about Zvara, the data had been transferred to Max. She didn't know exactly what she had retrieved, just that she had grabbed as much as she could. Jonathan had appeared calm, but a maelstrom raged inside, fueled by the revelations about experiments upon Zvara. Georgia's anger seemed absolute, and she hadn't even asked about what he had discovered. She had just pulled the car up to his house and quietly let his door open onto the sidewalk.

He stared into the blackness, her words replaying in his head. The Agency had conducted bioimplant experiments on Zvara. Had they done so on him? The pieces all fell into place: the cool reactions he had been receiving from key people on the staff, the crippling headaches that struck out of nowhere, and now, the discovery that his friend had been deceiving him. Like a tattoo on his soul, the words from the message kept running through his mind.

Trust no one.

"Max, run the file you received today on Zvara."

A holojection materialized at the foot of his bed. He scanned its volumes of fragmented telekinetic data, beginning with the childhood grav tests and field exercises. The file bore out the rumors that Zvara had been extremely powerful early on, and it appeared the Agency had pushed the young Tel to his limits. Jonathan read through the teen years, with Zvara's prodigal angst in full documentation. Then he entered a period labeled only as the "project" years – Zvara's early 30s – when the Agency tested its theories on level acceleration. The concept was to enhance Zvara's power a hundredfold by interfacing fledgling bionanoware technology into the part of the brain from which it was believed the Tels derived their telekinetic ability. Twenty surgical procedures were performed on him, three of which almost resulted in his death, and for a short time, the bioenhancements showed promise. Zvara started to display an immense power range, able to move massive objects on an obscene scale. But not without a price. His brain started to show signs of swelling, and the telekinetic stress began to devastate his neural system. Thereafter, the Agency's scientific elite abandoned the project. They tried to remove the technology, but the implants had integrated so completely into his brain tissue that removal would have left him a vegetable.

Having ridden a power curve that thrust him to the top of the Agency, Zvara had been the youngest leader the Tel world had ever known. But with the failure of the experiments and the crippling effects of the bioenhancements, Armando Zvara had been left a broken man. Now the poster child for the Agency's failure in producing the Infinite Tel, Zvara's pride drove him to a final conclusion. He approached the governing board and requested that his death be faked, his appearance altered and his identity changed, for he wished to live his life free of the stigma that would have followed him the rest of his days.

"Off!"

The room slipped again into blackness.

The flat bedsheets greeted him with all the comfort of a plague. He moved through the path of light from the neighbor's porch. Its 100 watts of irritation burned itself onto the backs of his retinas. He quickly shot a grav wave up the beam to shatter the light, which sent Toto into a fit that seemed to loop after every fifth howl. His anger grew like a fever, and in a paroxysm of rage, he trained his imaging in the direction of the barking.

A silence settled egregiously over the neighborhood. Jonathan was returned to staring into blackness.

They know everything... 19

HE cautiously approached the lab. At this hour the hallway was at 20 percent illumination, where it would remain for another three hours until 5:30 a.m. Ashton Franks usually arrived at his lab around 6:30, giving Jonathan a decent window to find some answers. Wearing the illegal signature displacer was uncomfortable enough, but telling the cab driver to let him off two miles away infused the whole act with a sense of melodrama that felt like he was in one of those spy arcade virt booths he and Tarris used to play in when they were kids. Jonathan felt a twinge of pain begin to attack the base of his skull. He reflexively pulled the infuser from his pocket, placed it to his neck, and pulled the trigger.

Franks's door appeared no different than the others on this

floor, with its unassuming, brushed-metal surface and industrially designed handle – the kind that revealed no locking mechanism yet probably contained more security technology than most vaults. It did, though, have one glaring contrast: the light suffusing its small frosted-glass window. Jonathan tried the handle. It unlatched with a high-pitched click. The room was dark, except for a lone antique table lamp that spotlighted a netport station on the main counter. Finding the door unlocked, his senses were on point. He scanned the room with his netpad. Nothing.

Relaxing, Jonathan entered the code to lock the door, walked to the counter and spun the netport around. On the screen was a series of field tests, and as Jonathan scanned them, he saw ranges like nothing he could have imagined. He read the name on the tests. His name.

A cold chill spiked through his nervous system. The room grew oddly still.

"Impressive stats," said a disembodied voice.

"Thanks...Sasha?"

Sasha stepped to the counter, grazing the edge of the lamplight. The fluorescent glow cast a sallow hue across her chest and set her stomach in dark shadow. Her low-cut pants exposed an antique navel ring, and Jonathan could barely see the tip of what appeared to be a dragon's tail biotattoo escaping over the top of her belt. The rest of the dragon couldn't be far below. She had stopped short of the circle of light, which kissed her lower lip as she talked.

"Really," she continued, her voice barely above a whisper, "these are scary. The APT's, the Grav Dis...they're all off the charts."

Sasha flexed her stomach. The dragon's tail flicked and disappeared.

"I hadn't seen these," Jonathan said, casually gesturing to the screen. "Now I know why."

Sasha, still partially in shadow, reached to spin the netport around. Jonathan grabbed her arm, clamped down with the force of an eagle's talon and pinned her wrist to the countertop. He leaned into the light to reveal the breadth of his anger. "What the hell are you doing here?"

"The same as you, I suppose," Sasha said without a hint of recognition to his action.

Jonathan tightened his grip. The dragon's tail flicked into view. "Don't bullshi–"

"I'm not," Sasha said, cutting him off with an air of confidence. "If I'm going to work for you, I want to know all I can..." she leaned into the light "...about the Infinite Tel."

"That's not for public knowledge."

"Now who's bullshitting?"

Jonathan felt a razor's edge slice across his knuckles. He looked down, but there was nothing there. Suddenly, a thin line of blood appeared. He released Sasha's arm and examined his hand. His blood looked almost black in the anemic harshness of the light. The dragon's head appeared over the top of Sasha's belt. It smiled and spit a flame of fire arcing across her stomach. She flexed her stomach and the dragon disappeared into the front of her pants, just above her left pocket.

"Neat trick," Jonathan said. He examined his hand. "Where'd you learn this one?"

"I've been around," Sasha coolly replied. She rounded the counter and took his hand. "Now, that didn't hurt...did it?" She tenderly rubbed the blood away with her thumb. Her eyes were fully dilated, and Jonathan sensed something more than desire behind them. She guided his hand to her hip, tucking his fingers into the top of her pants. "Shut up, Mr. Kortel..." she whispered. She grabbed the back of his neck and pulled his ear to her mouth. "...You wanna find my dragon?" Her breath was warm against his ear, and he could smell a faint tinge of honey emanating from her skin. She was riding.

Jonathan dug his hand deep down the side of her hip and slid it to the front of her pants. He gently kissed the side of her neck. Sasha let out a soft gasp as his fingers explored the dragon's lair.

"Oh, God," she moaned and turned her back to him. Her top's design was slit up the back, exposing much of her muscular body. Three small tattoos – Rembrandt self-portraits, each from a different period of his life and perfect in every detail – appeared just above the top of her low-cut pants. Jonathan stopped.

"Whoa," he said, pulling back to admire the workmanship.

"What's the matter," Sasha purred, "not into the classics?"

Jonathan slowly smiled and met her salacious look. "Not really. I'm more of a...*modernist*."

Sasha spread her legs comfortably and leaned onto the counter with her elbows. "Don't worry," she said into the expanse of the lab, "just give them a second....I think you'll like the next showing."

Jonathan watched in amazement as the three masterpieces

transformed into a triptych by the late-20th century artist Roy Lichtenstein. Again, the biotattoos had captured every brush stroke of the pop icon's famous masterwork depicting a stylized paper-era comic, its World War II hero exclaiming his hatred for the Nazis.

Sasha lowered her head to spill her hair across the countertop. "More *your* taste?" She arched her hips slightly.

Jonathan grabbed her hips and pulled her against him. He leaned down to kiss her neck, but jerked away, startled, as the dragon leaped across her back. It slowed just enough to turn its head and wink at him before it danced back to its den.

"If I didn't know any better," he said, "I'd say you're trying to seduce me."

Her eyes almost slits, Sasha turned and smiled sex at him.

Jonathan bent down to her ear and whispered, "There was a time when I would have been very tempted by this, not to mention we're taking quite a risk–" Suddenly, Jonathan felt the heat of her telekinetic presence at the gates of his mind. She had scaled his ego and was descending into his id. A burning sensation nestled at the base of his neocortex. He became aroused faster and harder than he had ever experienced before. He was pressing like steel against the warmth of her inner thighs. Jonathan moaned as the sensation intensified and hovered deliciously between pain and pleasure. He collapsed onto her back, letting his forehead rest between her shoulder blades.

"Who ever said we needed to get physical? *Besides*," Sasha sarcastically whispered, "it's time you started taking some risks–" She froze in midsentence and gasped.

Jonathan raised his head off her back. "Tag," he whispered, "you're it."

Sasha opened her mouth to speak, but Jonathan silenced her with the palm of his hand. He gestured for her to be quiet. A tiny drop of sweat fell from his forehead and landed on the countertop. She licked it off.

The door handle to the lab clicked.

Jonathan quickly motioned for them to hide in one of the huge service lockers. They slipped into the nearest one, cramming between three rollaway carts piled high with diagnostic scanners and grav flux readers. Sasha yipped as her back pressed against a cold metal cart handle. Jonathan quietly closed the locker's door. The latch echoed around the lab.

Ashton Franks was whistling loudly as he pushed a lengthy equipment cart into the lab. The lights came up when the system read his grav sig.

"Oh, shit!" Sasha whispered. "Our sig displacers, they're on the counter!"

"Shh," Jonathan said.

Through the locker's mesh, they anxiously watched while Franks wheeled the cart to the lab's center counter and began to unload small brown boxes. Abruptly, the whistling stopped. He stared at the displacers for a second, then the netport caught his attention. He slowly stepped to it and read what was on the screen. Momentarily his eyes darted between both. He twisted around, his steely eyes keenly searching until they landed on a locker at the opposite side of the lab. He began to approach it cautiously.

"Looking for something?" Jonathan asked. He walked up to the counter.

Franks jerked around, stumbling into the cart he had wheeled in. There was fear in his eyes. "Oh, Jonathan!" he said, putting his hand to his chest, "you gave me quite a start."

Sasha scrunched down, watching.

"Getting in a little early this morning, aren't we?" Jonathan said. His hand glided over the top of the netport.

Franks's eyes shifted to it. "Just getting, ah...head start. You know, end of the quarter and all."

Jonathan coldly studied the Aussie. He spun the netport around and glanced at the screen.

"So...ah...Jonathan, what brings you to my lab so early? Wanting to get a jum—"

"When were you going to share your data with me, Ashton?" Jonathan coolly asked, his attention still focused on the netport screen.

"My boy, I'm not sure what the devil you're ta—"

"Don't fuck with me, Franks." He snapped the netport shut.

"Look...Jonathan...let me expl—"

"Three percent increase in APT Waves? A thousand times the field size of a Level 8?" Jonathan slowly began to step toward the Aussie. "Over a million CTU movements in a second?!" He pinned the Aussie against the cart, his face only inches away.

"Jonathan, please...I can—"

"My God, Ashton. What else do you know? How strong am I?"

"Listen to me," Franks began, his demeanor suddenly shifting from his usual outback hickness to a cold, deadly seriousness. "You don't know what you're dealing with here."

"I don't think *you* know what you're dealing with." And Jonathan telekinetically grabbed Franks's throat and began lifting him off his heels. He field fluxed his arms tight to his body.

The Level 8 Tel balanced helplessly on the edge of his toes, gasping for air. "Jonathan," he groaned, "all I know is...AUGH!"

Jonathan folded his arms and lifted Franks a foot off the floor, hanging him like a freshly hooked salmon. "What else do you know, Ashton!"

"Jonathan!" Sasha yelled, "please don't!" She ran to his side and grabbed his arm.

Franks fell to the floor and desperately struggled for air. "Jonathan!" he said, coughing and spitting. "Just hear me out, for Godsakes!"

Jonathan shook off Sasha's grip and stepped over the Aussie. "To think," he said angrily, "I actually thought of you like a father."

"Please, listen to me," Franks pleaded in an attempt to cut through Jonathan's loathing. He rubbed at his throat. "I only do APT and field testing." He looked up in awe. "But there is someone who might help you."

"Who?"

"Shoalburg." He coughed violently. "He invented the nanogenetic implant."

Jonathan calmed and knelt down. "What the hell is going on? Why am I being kept in the dark?" Sasha stepped up and placed her hand on his shoulder.

"I don't know, son," Franks answered. "There are rumors, but they're only rumors."

"What, what are they?!" Jonathan asked. He seized Franks's wrist. Sasha squeezed his shoulder, and he relaxed his grip.

"I wish I could tell you more," Franks confessed, "but they're holding everyone to a limited knowledge parameter."

"Am I being made into some kind of a weapon?"

"That is the general theory floating around."

With Sasha's help, Jonathan lifted Franks to his feet. The senior Tel straightened his shirt and brushed back his white hair. "You haven't introduced me," Franks said, his eyes on Sasha as she nervously adjusted her top.

"Ashton Franks, Sasha Kuntar. Sasha is a Greener and assigned as my driver."

Franks stuck out his hand, and she tentatively shook it. "Don't be too embarrassed, young lady," he assured. "I have two grown daughters. It's nothing I haven't seen before, you know."

Sasha sheepishly smiled.

"Ah, Ashton...I'm sorry for—" Jonathan began.

Franks raised his hand to cut him off. Like a father consoling a son, he took Jonathan by the shoulders. "I understand." He looked him over. "I wish I could help you more, but there's really nothing this ol' dingo can do. I'm afraid you're on your own." He smiled, stepped back and folded his arms. "Now, you two," he said, pointing at the counter, "get those displacer units on before you forget and walk out of their field range."

Franks stood by as they put on their units. Jonathan turned and faced the Aussie. They warily eyed each other.

"Remember to tighten your focus, my boy, *before* you enter the shift threshold," Franks said. He winked at Sasha. "Less pain, you know."

Jonathan knowingly nodded.

Franks closed his eyes.

"Jonathan," Sasha said. "Do you have to?"

"He most certainly does, young lady," Franks answered, opening one eye. "Get on with it, my boy."

Jonathan began to focus, but hesitated.

"Damn it, son," Franks exclaimed, "just be done with it!"

Jonathan phased.

Franks flinched, gasped and collapsed. Jonathan tried to grab him, but his head bounced like it had landed on an invisible pillow.

"Nice trick...a grav bubble," Jonathan said. He turned to Sasha, who grinned slightly.

"Is he in pain?" she asked.

Jonathan looked at him, his head now nestled in the comfort of field displacement. "No," he said with a hint of disgust.

Franks' heavy breathing began to fill the room.

Goodbye, Jonathan... 20

"SIR, you have a netcall."

Jonathan stopped drying his hair. "Yeah, Max. Who is it?" He threw the towel onto a chair.

"Georgia, sir."

"Put it through." Georgia's holoimage appeared at the foot of the bed. "Morning," Jonathan said somberly.

"Good morning," Georgia said. There was an uneasy pause. "Jonathan...I'm sorry about what happened in the bar."

"No," he said. He tightened the towel around his waist and stepped to the edge of the bed. Her holoimage quivered as the steam from the shower wafted through it. "Don't apologize. It's me who should. I know what I did was unforgivable. It's...it's just...look, I'm in a real weird place right now. I...I just overreacted, and I'm sorry. I hope I didn't hurt you."

Georgia shook her head slightly. Her eyes locked on his as she stared out from the holojection. "I've been assigned."

"Oh?" he said, surprised. "Where?"

"A small town in Wisconsin...it's called DePerre. There's a little 8-year-old boy who's shown some Level 4 tendencies."

"That's pretty young for a Level 4."

"Yeah," Georgia said, sighing. She nervously shifted her weight. "It should be very interesting. There hasn't been this strong a Potential, at this age, in about 10 years. I'm kind of flattered that he wants me to take it on. It'll be my first assignment."

"Who's going with you?"

"James gave me Rolo."

"He's good. You can learn a lot from a guy like that." He eyed the door to the bathroom. "I guess congratulations are in order."

Georgia bit her lower lip. "Thanks," she replied with no emotion. "Jonathan, about last night..." She cut herself off and pulled some hair from her face, tucking it behind an ear. "It's probably a good thing that I go out on assignment right now...you know?"

Jonathan hesitated for a second, then nodded.

She smiled weakly, and the holoimage dissolved.

"Who was that?" Sasha asked, emerging from the bathroom wrapped in one of Jonathan's towels.

"Just catching up on some messages from my property in Chicago."

though the occasional nurse would run from the OR sobbing as a result of one of his tantrums, no one would dispute that tolerance and patience were the only ways to deal with the Agency's resident genius, because Carter Shoalburg was handicapped. He had been born deaf, dumb and blind.

"Good night, doctor."

Shoalburg looked up, which itself was a miracle considering his mind could only "see" what was being fed to his brain from the ocular implants that occupied his once-empty sockets.

"Good night," he said in the even timbre imparted by the nanotechnology that ringed his underdeveloped vocal cords. "I'll see you in the morning, then?"

The nurse looked into Shoalburg's eyes. Even though she had worked with him for more than a decade, she was still unnerved by his eyes. At first glance they appeared real enough, but with time one noticed their androidian quality. Their movement was slightly off, as if with every glance they were processing billions and billions of photons to create his field of vision. She constantly had to remind herself – they were.

"Yes, Carter," she answered affectionately. Carter Shoalburg was 43, yet his insecurity was like that of a 12-year-old. He knew she'd be back, yet he still had to ask. "I'll see you in the morning," she said on her way out.

As soon as the door clicked shut, Shoalburg reached for the direct netlink connectors that had been retrofitted for him. He deftly plucked out his ocular implants and laid them in their special case, its living foam swallowing them like gray quicksand.

"You okay?" She walked to the edge of the bed and ran her fingers through his wet hair.

"Yeah, I'm all right."

"Good," she whispered, and licked his ear. She walked toward the bathroom, but as she neared the door, she let the towel fall to the floor. The dragon on her back acted startled, like a naked cartoon character that had suddenly been exposed. He looked at Jonathan, quickly crossed his legs and covered his body with his arms, then pranced around her side to the comfort of his cave.

"You know," she said, half turning, "I think we need to finish what we started last night in the lab." A flame of bright yellow tattoo fire shot around her waist.

"There's nothing to finish," he said. He coolly looked at her like boring sculpture. The towel floated up to her hand. "Get dressed…" he said flatly.

She awkwardly gathered the towel around her with a look that sheepishly questioned his request.

"You're taking me to the airport."

I got your back...   21

CARTER Shoalburg was considered the best biosurgeon in the Agency's network – some felt in the Tel world. He had conducted experiments that, fully practiced in the "outer world," would have probably won him the Gates Prize. His microsurgical techniques had revolutionized biosurgery, but many of his true achievements could never be fully unveiled to humanity without risking the exposure of the Tel culture. His heritage both empowered and frustrated him, such that if it had been up to him, he would have unmasked their world years ago. His drive was legendary, bordering on manic. And those who worked with him could attest that without his immense capacity for discipline, he might easily have been committed. Outbursts and rants were routine. And even

The ocular implants were more for other people's convenience than his. They worked well enough, processing the same trillions of details as organic human eyes, but compared to the neural connectors that fed his brain the vastness of the world's information net, they might as well have been porcelain.

Having a brilliant mind trapped in a useless body propelled Shoalburg to achievement. In his early 20s, he invented the first genetic nanoimplants. The Biolution had fostered the technology, but his handicap inspired its development, and the secretive Tel culture allowed the experiments that the legal and moral agendas of the outer world never would have sanctioned.

By his early 30s, he had refined the technology and had persuaded the Tel elite to allow for a "leakage" (the calculated release of technology) into the outer world. Soon, his technology revolutionized how medicine dealt with the severely handicapped and rocketed to fame the operatives who had introduced it. It also filled the Agency's coffers with profits from the various publicly traded front companies that had launched the technology. By the time most medical students were just beginning to pay off their loans, Carter Shoalburg had changed the face of medicine. He had risked his own life by experimenting on the only subject he knew he could trust. He was the prime example of his own achievements – seeing, hearing and speaking, all with the aid of a technology that some had scoffed at as flotsam from science fiction. At his age, he should have been at the top of his career, but the Tel culture held him in frustrated obscurity. With the profiteering from his genius fueling the fires of his bitterness,

Carter Shoalburg was not the model company man.

He gently slipped the net connectors into place.

Integration into the world's information net would have jolted other nervous systems into epileptic seizure, but for Shoalburg and the miles of nanoneural connections that threaded throughout his body, it was like tuning in to the evening news. In the virtually limitless dimension of cyberspace, Shoalburg was truly himself. His lack of organic senses meant nothing here. A physical presence was useless; what mattered was the organ that had always served him well – his brain. The Biolution and its swell of technology meant there wasn't anything in the real world that couldn't be done faster and safer in the virtual. For Shoalburg, it was the perfect laboratory. He raised his head in the direction of the door, connector cables dangling from the modified headgear like techno dreadlocks.

The handle clicked.

"Pretty late for a visit, isn't it...Mr. Kortel?"

"How'd you know it was me?"

Shoalburg tapped at his ear and smiled.

"Oh, yeah" Jonathan said. "Better hearing than a dog."

"A bat...actually. And when you spent that month in our lab, I learned your walk. So," he nonchalantly added, "were you going to tell me why you're wearing a sig displacer?"

"How did you?..."

Shoalburg tapped under one of the chrome net connectors in his eye socket.

"Right...the system."

"*The* system," Shoalburg affirmed. He leaned back and tracked Jonathan around the lab.

Jonathan pulled out his netpad and punched in a sequence of numbers. "Can you see me now, Carter?"

"Yes, yes. There you are. Smile..." Shoalburg pointed to the upper corner of the lab.

Jonathan turned and searched for the camera. A fly landed on a light sconce. "Where is it?"

Shoalburg pointed to the sconce. The fly buzzed off and landed on a cabinet.

"The sconce? That's pretty obvious."

Shoalburg laughed a little, then pointed to the cabinet.

"The fly?" Jonathan questioned, slowly stepping toward it.

"Kind of gives a new meaning to the old phrase, doesn't it?"

Jonathan reached for it, but it flew off into a dark part of the lab. "So," he said, turning back to Shoalburg, "how do I look?"

"Like you could use a haircut."

Jonathan smiled. "Hey, check into the main system. Am I showing up there?"

Shoalburg paused as he moved through the Net. "Nope. You're invisible to the main system. I can see you here in the lab, but they can't."

Jonathan intently studied the chrome connectors where Shoalburg's eyes should have been. "Say, Carter," he asked, "can you ever see...like us?"

"You mean in dimension and color? Sure," Shoalburg said. He pointed to the ocular implant's case. "These implants give me an almost perfect representation of the world – maybe a little richer in color, that's all. And, I'll never have to regen when I get old. Now, what's on your mind, Jonathan? You didn't come all the way to California to play spy and talk about my handicaps."

"That's true," Jonathan said, nodding. He pulled a chair beside Shoalburg. "Tell me, Carter, what do know about bionano implants?"

"I'm the father of it. You know that."

"What about for the brain?"

Shoalburg shrugged. "Depends. Neural sensory augmentation, no problem. Making someone a genius," he smiled, "that's got to be mother nature all the way."

"Okay, not a genius. But how about stronger..." Jonathan leaned closer, "...in *level?*"

Shoalburg shrugged again. "That's touchy territory, Jonny. They experimented with it before my work came onto the scene–" He stopped himself.

"I know about Zvara," Jonathan said softly.

Shoalburg nodded. "Well, who do you think tried to extract that technology out of Zvara's head? God, what a butcher job that was." He laughed. "No, if you're thinking about asking me to–"

"No, Carter. I'm not." Jonathan tensely rubbed his hands together. An uneasy quiet filled the lab.

"Jonny. What's wrong? You in some kind of trouble?"

"No. Nothing like that, at least...not yet."

Shoalburg frowned. He quickly turned to Jonathan, the connector cables whipping around and slapping into the counter's edge. "Awww, man...they didn't try nanogenetics on you, did they?"

"I don't know," Jonathan said coolly. "Did they?"

"Only one way to find out." Shoalburg rose from his chair. "Lets hook you up." He began to walk away, but was yanked back by the tether of cables. His rotund little frame bounced to the counter. "Damn! Excuse me, Jonny. You may not want to watch this."

"I've seen worse." Jonathan watched in fascination as Shoalburg carefully removed the net connectors from his eye sockets. "Doesn't that hurt?" he asked.

"What, these?" Shoalburg questioned. He rolled the two units around lazily in his hand and they clanked together. He clumsily set them on the counter. "I've done this so many times, it's as painless as removing a hat."

Shoalburg gingerly searched for the box that contained his ocular implants, and Jonathan saw for the first time the great scientist as he truly was. He reached over and guided Shoalburg's pudgy hands to the case.

"Thank you," Shoalbug said. He slipped the units in and faced Jonathan. "You *do* need a haircut."

Shoalburg walked to an area of the lab that looked more like an operating room than a science station. He patted the platform. "Hop up here and let's have a look at you."

Jonathan climbed up and began to lean back. Shoalburg swung a large, articulated armature into position over him. "Don't worry, this is totally painless," he said with a sly grin. The armature came to rest just above Jonathan's chest. Its sinuous tip whined as it sequenced though a set of three ominous heads.

Jonathan shot up.

"Easy there, I'm just kidding," Shoalburg said, pushing him back down. "Just be still for a second while I scan you." He shoved aside some carts that cluttered the lab and stepped behind a small console. "Now, don't move."

The 12 seconds it took for the scan seemed like 12 years to Jonathan. Shoalburg emerged from behind the console and stepped to the platform, his eyes glued to the screen that hung behind Jonathan's head. He intently watched the data cascade down the screen.

"Well, I'll be damned..." Shoalburg said softly.

"What?!" Jonathan shot up again.

Shoalburg's ocular implants shifted alienly in his direction. Jonathan could have sworn he heard them click into place. He swung his legs over the edge of the platform and sat there staring. "Well?" he finally asked.

"Hold on, I'm checking this out," Shoalburg said, his attention glued to the screen at the scan station. He leaned on his elbows and diligently studied the images. He whistled to himself. "Damn, this is some good work."

Stunned, Jonathan didn't answer. He hopped off the platform and paced the floor. Finally, he asked, "How bad is it?"

"That all depends on your point of view," Shoalburg said, still studying the data. "If you don't mind not being completely organic anymore, it's no big deal. But if you do..." he slowly trained his implants on him, "then you have a ton of bionanoware growing in your head that's been genetically coded especially for Mr. Jonathan

Kortel." He leaned toward Jonathan. "And you may not want to yank it out of there." Shoalburg blinked in a mechanical sort of way, like the act was more for show than reflex, and began walking over to another console. "It's not that bad, really."

"What?..." Jonathan asked, still grappling with the reality of his situation.

"Having implants. I've had them most of my adult life. I couldn't function without them. And there are a million people out there with my technology in them, all living happy, normal lives." He tapped in a sequence code at the station. "Roll that net connector cart over, will you?"

Jonathan wheeled the cart to Shoalburg.

"The only problem in your case, Jonny," he said, removing his implants, "is that me, and the other hundred million or so handicapped people who have my nanoware, know *why* we have it." He slipped the connectors into his eye sockets. "You don't."

"There's a rumor going around saying this stuff's supposed to make me into some sort of weapon."

"Possibly. They tried to make Zvara one." Shoalburg paused for effect. "After they'd tried to make him the 'Infinite Tel.'"

"What do you know about this Infinite Tel?"

"That whole business was started by Jacob Whitehorse.... You know about him and Zvara, don't you?"

Jonathan winced. "More than I ever want to."

"Right. So when Whitehorse left and started the Rogues, he was on a quest of sorts – to find the Infinite Tel. A real Don

Quixote thing." Shoalburg suddenly jerked to attention. "Hey, what the...aughhh!"

"What's the matter?" Jonathan asked, stepping to him.

"Nothing. Sometimes you run into data that's real hard to process, even with all my implants." Shoalburg stood quietly motionless as he filtered the stream coming off the Net.

"So, what about the Infinite Tel?" Jonathan pressed.

"Hmm? Oh, yeah...sorry. The Infinite Tel supposedly can not only manipulate gravity, but alter matter as well." He abruptly faced Jonathan, the connector cables wildly following his motion. "I'll believe that when I see it." He smiled again. Suddenly, Shoalburg's teeth clenched and he jerked forward, almost into Jonathan's arms. "Oh, God! That hurt!"

"What happened?"

"I was retrieving some data from the Agency's archives when I got hit with what felt like a predator stream." He rubbed at his head and sat down in the station's chair. "Man, I haven't felt that in years."

Jonathan sat next to him and put his hand on his shoulder. "Carter...tell me the truth. What am I?"

"Whoever did this to you did a hell of a job. This was no amateur procedure like they did on Zvara. Yours was done by a seasoned biosurgeon." He reflected for a moment and said, "I'll bet it was Adrian."

Shoalburg stood and pulled down a screen that was hanging above the console. "Now, let's see if you're a weapon, shall we?" He scrolled through the data faster than Jonathan could manage, pausing every second or two, then plowing ahead. "Aha, see these?" He waited for Jonathan to catch up. "These can control your vision center...and, and those?" he said, enthusiastically pointing. "They can control your motor functions. But I don't understand how they would make you more powerful....Here!" He nudged Jonathan, barely able to contain himself. "These can increase the flow of adrenaline into your system. It's the same thinking they had with Zvara, but that backfired when his brain started to swell." He rubbed at his temple.

"Maybe you should get out of the Net for a while," Jonathan said.

"No! No, that's okay. I can stay in here forever. Listen, if they've found a way to control the swelling and the residual side effects, you might well be on your way to being Mr. I.T. But if they haven't, who knows what this stuff will do." Shoalburg shrugged. "Beats me." He leaned back in the chair and folded his arms. "As a package, this stuff could have been intended for a number of things. Level enhancement. Sensory enhancement. Yeah...they could be prepping you for power. You'd be one helluva weapon. At your advanced level, you could wreak some havoc." He sighed. "In any case, I can't tell with this equipment. I need a nanogenetic reader, and not this one." He slapped at the console. "This is out of date, and what they've put into your head is quite advanced. It's breakthrough stuff, for sure." Shoalburg paused, then asked, "Are you experiencing any light flashes, headaches, that sort of thing?"

Jonathan slowly nodded.

"The technology is growing. They give you anything for the pain?"

Jonathan reached into his coat pocket and showed Shoalburg the pneumatic infuser.

"Typical," Shoalburg said, shaking his head. "That drug's nothing more than a masker. But watch yourself, you can get addicted to that shit. Over time, your body's going to grow tolerant of its masking effects, so get ready for more pain....I'm afraid it's going to get worse before it gets better."

Jonathan sighed. "Carter, is there anyone in the system who could help me find out exactly what I've got?" He tapped the side of his head.

"Except for the people who did it? Nah. I'm your best bet. Besides, you'd be taking a big risk...I assume you're doing this covertly?"

"Yeah. They think I'm on vacation. And those who did know, don't." Jonathan winked at Shoalburg.

"You Level 8's and your erasing....Oh, excuse me, Level 9. Or is it higher?"

"Hell, I don't know. I've been kept in the dark so much, I have no idea anymore." Jonathan leaned forward and put his head in his hands.

"Jonny," Shoalburg said, reaching over and patting his arm, "what do you want...really?"

Jonathan looked up mournfully, then smiled. "You know, you're the first person who's asked me that. Seems like everyone else just wants a piece of me...."

"I remember when the rumors of your discovery came out. Man, it tore through our world like wildfire! You're supposed to be the one, you know."

"One, what?"

"The one to reveal us...you know, to the outer world. Come on, from what I've heard, nobody's going to mess with you. You're way too advanced."

"But they're not teaching me, Carter...I'm mean they are, but they aren't. They take me to a certain level, then slam on the brakes. And if I want to go further, it's virtually impossible. They hold me at arm's length. It's driving me fucking crazy!" Jonathan jumped up and kicked his chair into the lab.

Shoalburg sat quietly facing forward as Jonathan paced about the room. Finally, he started to chuckle.

"What so funny?" Jonathan asked.

"Oh, nothing. It's just that you and I are a lot alike, you know."

"How's that?"

"We're both freaks."

Jonathan stopped.

Shoalburg kept staring into cyberspace. "The Agency doesn't want us, yet at the same time, they need us." He finally turned in Jonathan's direction. "I make them money...*lots* of money. Plus, they know I'd go biothermal if they tried to mess with me." He smiled. "I can do a lot of damage if I want to." He tapped at the connectors. "But you? You're in your own league, Jonny boy. Something's up. They're hiding it from you, and I'm afraid you're going to have to go to the top to get your answers."

"Takeda and Trumble?"

"The dynamic duo themselves. God, what a freak show. How we let them stay in power is beyond me." Shoalburg stretched his arms above his head. "Looks like you got a bit of a road ahead of you."

"What do you mean?"

"Well, you can't just walk up to those guys and ask, 'Excuse me, what the heck are you doing to me?' They'll be prepped, you can bank on that."

"Bank on that...on what?" Jonathan questioned.

"It's an old expression. One my grandfather used to use. When there were banks, they were perceived as secure. It's where you kept your money...when there was paper money. Get it? Banked on?"

Jonathan nodded hesitantly.

"Never mind. Just be smart about Takeda and Trumble. They know their stuff. And don't let that fatherly routine of theirs fool you. They're ruthless bastards."

Jonathan put his hand on Shoalburg's shoulder. "Thanks, Doc. You've always helped me when I needed it."

Shoalburg gingerly reached for Jonathan's hand and patted it. "Us freaks got to stick together."

Jonathan laughed. "Hey, Carter?"

"Yes, sir?"

"If I need you, can I...ah, depend on you?"

Carter looked in Jonathan's direction and smiled. "Of course you can. I got your back."

"My back?"

Shoalburg shook his head.

"Let me guess, another old term...from your grandfather?"

Shoalburg smiled.

"It means...you'll watch out for me?"

"Close," Shoalburg replied. "It's old military speak. More like, I'll protect you...while you walk point."

Jonathan smiled in approval. "I may need it, Carter."

"Don't worry," Shoalburg said, removing the connector units. He closed his eyelids as he fumbled for his ocular implants. He slipped them in, blinked several times, and then faced Jonathan. "I'll be there for you."

"I know, Carter," Jonathan replied. "I know."

PAUL BLACK

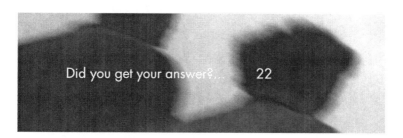

Did you get your answer?... 22

REAGAN International Airport was choked with Beltway insiders, middle-aged Japanese tourists and Hare Krishnas, who had made a recent comeback once they ditched the robes and finger cymbals. The new breed of devotees had donned a more approachable style, which included contemporary clothing and a bit more hair. They had kept the ritual of chanting, though, and their mantra reverberated in Jonathan's head 20 gates after he had passed them.

Jonathan picked his way through the masses like a salmon fighting upstream. He looked at his netwatch for no special reason, a habit brought on by being part of an organization that prided itself on precision.

Fatigued by the flight from California, he slowly shuffled along the conveyor walk, trapped between a young Hispanic family and a few government types. He was preoccupied with the technology that was currently entwining itself around his cortex. Even though he sensed no evidence of its presence, he had an odd, nagging feeling, as if an imperceptible headache had taken permanent residence and was oscillating somewhere near the base of his skull. He felt for the infuser in his coat pocket, but quickly fought off the urge.

The young mother began straightening the sullen posture of her little girl, who fought every attempt at correction. She finally swatted the child on her butt, and the girl gave out a yelp that snapped Jonathan back to reality. The little girl looked up at him as tears ran down her face. Jonathan began to grin, but a bolt of sharp, jagged pain carved a path through the back of his skull. Startled at its severity, he lurched forward and almost dropped his bag. The little girl ducked behind her mother's leg. The pain struck again, this time with twice the intensity. This second invasion dropped Jonathan to his knees, but when he landed, the pain instantly vanished. The government types, still busy on their netphones, never looked over. Relieved, he stood, but the moment his head cleared the edge of the conveyor's handrail wall, the pain struck again. Jonathan landed heavily on the moving floor, and the pain disappeared. Instead of standing again, Jonathan grabbed his bag and started to crawl down the moving sidewalk on his hands and knees. The little Hispanic girl giggled as he passed. People nonchalantly stepped aside, still engrossed in their netphones as if a man crawling along were an everyday occurrence at Reagan.

Jonathan emerged from the conveyor and the pain struck again, though not as crippling. He struggled to his feet and bolted toward one of the exits.

Sasha, you better be on time, he thought.

Running into a crowded area where several large hallways converged, he felt a force upon his body that slowed his momentum as if the ground beneath his feet had suddenly adopted the gravity of Jupiter. At the same time, his back was lacerated with a sensation like a thousand tiny knives, and the pain in his head became almost unbearable. Jonathan lost his grip on his bag as his nervous system began to shut down. He felt himself scream, but heard no sound. He forced his head around and could see through breaks in the forest of people a figure at the end of one of the hallways. The man stood motionless, watching him collapse to the floor.

Jonathan sensed he was about to pass out. Desperate, he resorted to something he rarely did in public; he created a field flux corridor and directed it right at the figure. As the corridor traveled the length of the long hallway, it punched a path through the crowd and sent luggage and people careening to both sides. It struck the mysterious figure and held him like a giant fist. The forces on Jonathan's body vanished. He slowly began to stand, but was hit again with the same savage pain to his head. *Always in twos,* he thought.

A second dark figure stepped into view just at the edge of the flux corridor that held the first. He slowly crossed his arms.

Jonathan sent another flux corridor down the hallway. It seized the new figure like the other, almost knocking him off his feet. Jonathan's pain instantly vanished.

Tired of playing a game that brought him down to the level of an 8, Jonathan prepared to do something he had done only once. Risking major exposure and possible harm to himself, he phased and reversed his own grav field. The time before he had slowly moved himself a distance of about 12 feet. This hallway was more than 100 feet long. He only had a few seconds to execute the move before the two at the end of the hallway recovered. He instantly phased, betting their file on him didn't contain one of his talents.

Launched like an Olympic long jumper, Jonathan sailed down his flux corridor, legs leading and arms trailing. He landed, with a slight step, two feet from his antagonists. He mentally grabbed them and yanked them off their feet. "Bonhiem? Lewis?" he said quizzically, looking them over. "They sent you two?"

Both of the Agency men were in a state of awe. They had never seen a Tel move himself through the air before.

"Not in your files, gentlemen?" Jonathan asked.

"N-no!" Lewis exclaimed. "There's nothing about...what you just did!"

"My God..." Bonhiem said, "...it's *true*."

Jonathan slowly lowered them. Some of the people who had witnessed his feat were approaching them, pointing and talking, while others were on their netphones. And the chaos from Jonathan's flux corridor was beginning to draw attention. Suddenly, security alarms went off.

"Gotta go, boys," Jonathan said. He stepped away from them. "You know I have to do this."

Both men meekly nodded, then crumpled to the floor. Jonathan sprinted for the exit, projecting a field corridor that crashed through the crowd; but just as he was about to plow his field into the exit doors, his back was again riddled with the same sharp, hideous pain. He fell to the floor in convulsion. *Triangulation*, he figured.

With the security alarms blaring, people screaming, and his body slowly going into meltdown, Jonathan breached Tel protocol and cast a broad displacement field. He prayed that he'd hit his mark. The innocent people would just have to become what his grandfather referred to as "collateral damage."

He went into phase. The gravitational disruption flowed like a sound wave in water. It enveloped everything in its path: people, suitcases, trash cans, news kiosks – everything that wasn't welded, bolted or chained down within 100 feet of Jonathan's hypothalamus was displaced by the disruption. He watched, detached, as everything caught in the wave's path lost its gravitational integrity and floated briefly like some kind of gruesome, public water ballet. As the wave passed, anything affected dropped to the floor, which, depending how high it had floated, could be a harsh fall. Jonathan's heart sank as he watched a teenage girl float to the top of a hallway ceiling, only to drop violently like a puppet whose strings had been cut. His pain and convulsions vanished as the wave passed down a wide corridor that led to the Nations Air terminal.

He had only seconds before security would descend upon him. Jonathan sent a powerful grav field toward the exit. The narrowly focused field slammed against the ridged doors, which were now in auto lockdown. They vibrated, shuddered, and exploded, sending plexi shards, metal and glass spraying over the passenger loading area outside. He phased himself through the spray of debris and landed in the middle of the street, crunching and sliding on the remains of the shattered doors. He was searching desperately for Sasha's limo when he felt his head yanked to his right.

"Jonathan! Over here!"

Forced to look in the direction of the yell, Jonathan saw Sasha standing up through the sunroof of the limo. She was in one of the inner lanes, stuck in a sargasso of traffic.

Suddenly, the blare of a horn, followed by the screech of six air brakes locking in sequence, cut the air with a deafening shrill. Jonathan twisted around to find a two-ton *You-Go/We-Park* bus skidding uncontrollably toward him. The huge vehicle began severely listing as its back end jackknifed. To Jonathan, everything instantly slowed: the bus, skidding at him in a cranked-down celebration of the chaos theory, and Sasha, waving creepily at him in a slow-motion, frantic sort of way.

"*Jonathan!*" Her scream had an unnatural, guttural edge.

He phased over the cars to land in a sprawl on the limo's roof.

"Holy shit!" Sasha exclaimed. "How did you do tha—"

"Just drive!" Jonathan yelled.

Sasha shot down into the pilot's seat while Jonathan

crawled through the sunroof and into the back. "GO! GO NOW!" he screamed, landing on the floor of the limo.

Sasha jumped the sidewalk and swerved into the outer lanes.

"Mask us before they read the car's ID!"

"I'm way ahead of that!" Sasha yelled. She gunned the limo into the Interway, weaved through the late-night traffic and barely missed the rear bumper of a recycle hauler.

"So," she asked sternly, her image appearing on the screen in the back, "where am I taking you?"

Jonathan sat pensively as the car glided along.

"Ah...yes? An answer, today—"

"I'm thinking!" Jonathan barked. "We can't go back to my house."

"Can't come to mine," Sasha added sternly. "They'll have it all secured up, too."

Jonathan shrugged. "I...I'm out of ideas here..."

"I know!" Sasha blurted. She jerked the toggle and the car veered sharply over six lanes, barely making the exit ramp. Jonathan was thrown against the door, his legs hitting the roof of the cabin.

"Sorry," she said from the rear screen, "but I just remembered a place that might be safe."

"Might be?!" Jonathan questioned, straightening.

"You got any better ideas?"

"All right, fair enough." He caught her staring. A grin had spread across her face. "What...what the hell's so funny?" he demanded.

"Nothing. It's...just..."

"Just what?" There was a raw seriousness in his voice.

Sasha's grin was replaced with a soft look of concern. "You really are what they say you are."

Jonathan turned away and wiped the blood from his upper lip. "I guess."

"You're meant for great things. You know that, don't you?"

Jonathan didn't answer. He stared out the window while his hand searched his pocket for the infuser.

. . .

They were enveloped in a part of the city where Jonathan had never been, and by the look of it, neither had anyone else for the last 20 years. Old warehouses crowded gutted bodegas; exposed retrofittings undulated in the night wind like mechanical cilia.

Sasha piloted the limo down a narrow alley, swerving around trash and splashing through puddles, which struck Jonathan as odd, since it hadn't rained for a few days. She pulled up to a loading dock that looked like the last thing to have left it probably ran on gasoline. A single mercury lamp surreally flooded the area with the kind of harsh yellow light that could burn through the epidermis and create a sickly pale translucency that revealed every vein in its bluish glory. The whole scene reeked of decay and urine, the kind of stench that was tasted more than smelled.

Sasha got out and smiled over the top of the limo. "Here

we are," she said.

Jonathan stepped into a puddle that didn't respond like water. "Charming," he said as he inspected the underside of his boot.

Sasha hiked herself onto the loading dock and approached a small panel to the left of a giant rusted roll door. The panel had protruding buttons that reminded Jonathan of the old telephone in his grandfather's house. She tapped in a number.

"Yeah?" a scratchy voice asked from the speaker.

"Is Kreet there?" Sasha yelled at the panel.

"Yeah..."

"Can I talk with him?"

"Guess so..."

There was a long pause. Sasha nervously grinned at Jonathan.

"This is Kreet."

"Kreet, hey, it's Sasha."

"Miss Sasha. To what do I owe the honor?"

"Listen Kreet, I need your help. I need a place to crash."

"Well now, Miss Sasha, that's going to cost–"

"Don't fuck with me, Kreet. This is serious....I've got *him* with me."

The speaker went dead for a second. Its paper cone crackled, "Jesus..."

A buzzer echoed from somewhere inside the platform, and the roll door started to rise.

. . .

The elevator jerked to a halt and threw Sasha into Jonathan's side. He grabbed her to steady both of them. She affectionately squeezed his arm. The cage door opened onto a large room that had been segmented into six living areas by crates, prefab packing grids, bubble pack and anything else that could serve as a wall. The room in front of them looked like a kind of kitchen, and there were four people milling about. All heads turned when they emerged from the darkness of the elevator. One guy, startled by Jonathan's presence, dropped his cup of coffee.

"Welcome, Miss Sasha," said a little man, his voice casually Bostonian. He was leaning against a concrete column and wearing a bright red scarf that wrapped his neck twice before it spilled down his side into a small pile on the floor behind him. Its biofabric slithered a vaguely erotic scene of a dancing woman who Jonathan swore winked at him every time he moved.

"Thanks for taking us in, Kreet," Sasha said.

Kreet didn't respond. He studied Jonathan. The others slowly rose to their feet.

"So this is Jonathan Kortel," Kreet said. He began walking toward them; his scarf deftly avoided his feet. "Welcome to the hotel Kreet."

"Thanks," Jonathan said. He reached to shake his hand.

"Nooo, sir," Kreet replied, his hand still buried deep in the large pockets of his canvas jump pants. "No offense, boss (it sounded like *bass* to Jonathan), but I'll bet the electro-jump from a guy like you could light this place up for a week." There were snickers all around. "Here." A can of beer flew into his hand from the counter. He offered it to Jonathan.

"Thanks," Jonathan said. "I think I will." The can floated over to his outstretched hand.

"What kind of hotel is this?" Sasha demanded.

"I know. You only drink white wine," Kreet said evasively.

A paper cup floated to Sasha and hung in front of her. "Thanks," she said, taking it.

"It's not every day that we have such an honored guest," Kreet said. "Let me introduce you to my roommates. Jonathan Kortel, this is Rocket...." He pointed to a gangly boy of about 20 with long, bright red curls that spiraled down the sides of his head. "This is Bixx...." A thin X-ray of a girl – maybe 17 – bowed her head. "And this is Sanjiv." An older Indian man smiled, his white teeth a glaring contrast to his almost black skin.

"Ah...hello everyone," Jonathan said hesitantly.

"Mister Kortel?" It came out more like *Meester Korvel,* and had a Slavic edge to it. The X-ray girl had cautiously raised her hand.

"Not now, Bixx, it's late," Kreet scolded.

"No, it's all right," Jonathan said. "Yeah, Bixx. What's your question?"

She hesitated. "Is it true?...You know..."

Jonathan looked to Sasha for help. She shrugged. "Know what?" he questioned.

Bixx hesitated again. "That you're...faster than light?"

Jonathan smiled, slightly embarrassed. "Yeah, Bixx...it's true."

Rocket whistled. "I told you!" he said to Sanjiv. "You owe me big time!"

Jonathan took a swig from his beer.

The room fell into a silence that seemed impenetrable.

"Daaamn..." Kreet eventually said under his breath. "You're bending time."

"If it's okay with you all," Jonathan said, "I'm pretty tired. I'd really like to get some sleep." He glanced at Sasha and took another swig.

"You can have my room. I'll sleep on the couch," Kreet said. He looked at Sasha. "It's a *big* couch."

"Nice try Kreet, but...ah..." There was a sudden awkwardness in Sasha's voice.

"I'm sure Kreet won't mind us doubling up...would you?" Jonathan interrupted.

"Ah...no, no please," Kreet said, bowing. "My shit-hole, your shit-hole."

· · ·

Jonathan leaned back against a poor excuse for a pillow, but a T-shirt stuffed with underwear would have done, considering that he felt like crap. Anything that was soft and could cradle his aching head was just fine with him. Sasha pulled off her top; the dragon was nowhere to be found.

"Why do they live like this?" Jonathan asked.

"You mean, Kreet?" Sasha replied. She slipped on what a

century earlier would have been called a Guinea-T.

"Yeah. They're all Tels. They can live better than this. I don't get it."

Sasha crawled onto the old futon. "They want to live like this."

Jonathan frowned and downed the dregs of his beer.

"Did it ever occur to you that just because the Agency takes you under its wing doesn't mean that you'll like it?"

"Yes, but—"

"But nothing," Sasha said. "Tels come from all walks of life. The Agency hasn't found a pattern that explains the shift, so...some people just can't adapt to a new way of life." She cuddled up to him and wrapped herself against his side. "Not everyone was successful like you." She nestled her head on his chest.

Clearly uncomfortable with her show of affection, Jonathan started to push her aside, but she rucked her leg over his hips and squeezed even tighter. He watched as she slowly rose and fell with his breathing. "Hey, ah...Sasha. About the night in the lab...look, don't get me wrong, that was...ah, intense, but I need to focus right now. I can't...Oh, how can I put this without digging a hole here?...I'm not sure it would be good if we got, you know...close. I mean, we're already kind of close...I guess what I'm trying to say is, there are some things I've got to take care of....Important things. And I'm not sure how it's all going to turn out. I don't want you to get hurt. Understand? Sasha?..." He felt her gentle snoring through his chest. He chuckled and gently kissed the top of her head.

. . .

In the dark quiet of the kitchen, a low industrial hum emanated from deep within the building and filled the floor with the kind of vibration that, once felt, was hard not to notice. Jonathan had sensed it through the futon, and it had kept him in a state of quasi-sleep for the better part of the night. Having opened every cabinet in search of a clean glass, he wiped out a bowl, leaned against the counter and waited for the gray liquid coming from the faucet to begin resembling something close to water. The pain at the base of his neck turned cold as he felt, more than heard, what sounded like the loading sequence of a Light-Force weapon. The water became clear.

"That's an older model, isn't it?" Jonathan asked into the darkness behind his back.

There was no answer.

"I'll bet it's a Hitachi 2300 – the old ones with that field imager that takes forever to recycle."

Quiet blackness.

"You know, if I wasn't such a nice guy, I'd explode your heart right now...*Kreet*."

"How'd you know it was me?"

Jonathan slowly turned around. "Just a little Tel intuition." He folded his arms and relaxed against the counter. He could barely make out Kreet's figure in the dim light of the kitchen. Kreet had an old-style Light-Force leveled directly at him. "Kreet," he said, "what do you hope to accomplish with this stunt?"

"Just a little test for Mr. Big Time," Kreet said mockingly.

"I told you earlier that I'm FTL. You're going to gain noth–"

"Shut up...just shut up!" Kreet exclaimed. "How do we know you're not just bullshitting us? Hmm? We've seen guys like you before – waltzing in all full of yourselves and boasting about your high levels of power." His voice jumped an octave. "People like Rocket and Bixx and me – we don't come from any fancy backgrounds. We come from the streets. We work our asses off just to get noticed for a level jump. But you, you just appear out of nowhere and land right at the top."

Jonathan shifted his weight and put his hands in his pockets. "I don't get this, Kreet. What do you have against me? I haven't done anything to affect whether you jump or not....Hell, I don't even interface with your area of the Agency."

Kreet laughed. "The Agency's like any other corporation. It's designed to keep people like us – the ones who really get things done – in their place. It's guys like you who make it impossible for us to get anywhere in our world. You should know better," Kreet's voice was filling with anger. "You just go with the flow, as long as it fits your needs. You never came up through the ranks. Ever drive a car, Kortel? Or put in a year straight in the Pit?"

Jonathan didn't answer.

"Thought so. You get all the breaks. You get the best assignments, the best instruction....You even get the best women...."

"Ohhh," Jonathan said softly, "so that's what this is really about." He peered into the darkness at Kreet's silhouetted figure. "This is about Sasha....You've got a bone for Sasha, don't you." He started to laugh under his breath.

"Shut the fuck up, Kortel."

"Easy, tough guy. You ever discharged one of those? It's not a toy, you know."

"I've discharged more of these than you ever will."

"Well then," Jonathan said, stepping away from the counter and folding his arms across his chest, "what's stopping you?"

Kreet didn't answer.

"Come on, Kreet. If I'm not as fast as the rumors say, then there'll be one less fancy Tel for you to deal with." He took a step toward him. "Then again, if I am FTL..." He took another step. "...you'll just have to find out what happens...won't you?"

Kreet still didn't answer.

"What's the matter? You said yourself you've shot more Light-Forces than I ever will. Go for it!"

The low hum from the building suddenly shut off. The room fell into a thick, tense silence.

"Hey, Kreet, some of us are trying to get some sleep..." Yawning, Sanjiv suddenly appeared in the room. He hit the lights.

The flash from the weapon split the air like a silent lightning bolt had erupted in the loft. Sanjiv jumped back so hard he slammed into a concrete pillar. Sasha, in her bare feet, ran from the bedroom and skidded to a halt beside Jonathan. Bixx sheepishly peered around the wall of the kitchen, and gasped as she gazed at the bizarre scene captured like a photograph.

"Oh...my...God," Sanjiv uttered.

In the center of the kitchen was Kreet, suspended four

feet in the air. His long scarf cascaded to the floor and looked oddly like a tether that kept him from floating away. Hovering just out of his hand was the old Light-Force gun, its white needle of laser light extruding from its silver barrel. His legs were caught in sort of a half scissor kick, the look on his face sheer terror. The whole scene reminded Jonathan of a trick from the old kids' magic show he used to watch on the Retro Channel. He took a long, slow sip from the bowl.

"What the hell is going on here?" Sasha demanded. She began to approach Kreet, who looked like a sculpture in the full light of the kitchen.

"I wouldn't get too close there," Jonathan warned. He took another drink.

"Oh, my God," Sanjiv repeated. "This is unbelievable!"

Sasha walked back to Jonathan and patted him gently on the chest. "Let him go," she said.

"Better move first," Jonathan warned. "That's an old gun, and there's no telling what its discharge will do."

Everyone shuffled behind one of the freestanding walls that divided the kitchen from Sanjiv's area.

"Will it be loud?" Bixx asked shyly.

Jonathan just smiled.

With a flash, Kreet dropped to the floor while his weapon completed its discharge. The beam went directly into one of the cabinets, debiolizing it into a liquid state that resembled melting plastic. It dripped and oozed over the dishes piled in the sink.

Kreet struggled to his feet, entangled in his scarf, as

Jonathan stepped from behind the wall. He mentally seized Kreet, raised him off the floor and held him tight, though he allowed his head to be free. Jonathan circled Kreet, eyeing him with contempt. The others cautiously stepped into the kitchen. Unconsciously, they stopped at the edge of the light that illuminated Kreet like a theater spot.

"So," Jonathan said as he came around to face him, "did you get your answer?"

A large dark spot appeared at Kreet's crotch. "Jonathan...sir, please...I...I never meant for it to go off. I-I was just fooling around—"

Jonathan motioned for the young Tel to stop. "Don't say any more, just listen. If you weren't Sasha's friend and helping us right now..." Kreet began to choke. Sasha started to protest, but Jonathan shot her a look. Bixx gasped slightly. "...you would have been facing God before you knew what hit you." Kreet choked for air when Jonathan released his throat. "Let this be a lesson to you. Don't fuck around with things you're not ready for." He stepped up and glared into Kreet's face. "Make myself clear?"

Kreet nodded. Sweat dripped off his forehead.

Jonathan walked over to the counter and picked up his bowl. "I'm tired," he said with his back to the room. "I'm going to bed." He swirled what little water was left and downed it in one gulp. He quietly placed the bowl on the counter and stepped through the makeshift curtain into the bedroom.

Kreet fell to the floor gagging and coughing.

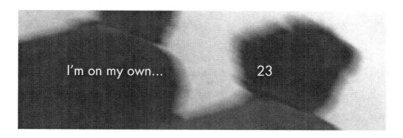

I'm on my own...   23

BIXX was seated at the kitchen table quietly eating while Sanjiv scrambled eggs in a small metal bowl. Rocket was in the shower enthusiastically singing to himself, oblivious to whatever key the song might have been before he wrapped his lips around it. Kreet, his back to the curtain of his bedroom, reverently sipped his coffee and stared blankly across the table. His scarf hung neatly on the back of his chair, the dancing woman replaced with a serene pastoral image of the Swiss Alps, clouds cycling lazily through its peaks. The air was filled with the kind of tension that revealed itself in stilted conversations or awkward pauses. It hovered over them like a living thing.

Jonathan pulled the curtain aside and emerged from the

bedroom. All movement instantly stopped, and the room fell into an even deeper quiet. He surveyed the kitchen and felt the tension like a sunburn on his soul. Rocket's voice sliced the air in a futile attempt at a high note, then cracked a bit as he struggled with the range. Kreet winced and spilled coffee over the tops of his knuckles. Bixx began to giggle.

"Does he always do that?" Jonathan asked to no one in particular.

"What, sing in the shower?" Sanjiv questioned. His attention was clearly focused on pouring the precise amount of milk into the bowl.

"If that's what you call it," Jonathan answered. He stepped over to the pot of coffee, poured a cup and listened to Rocket's rendition of *Crying Train*, the last major hit from Nympho Scooter Pie. He hadn't heard the song in years. It had been one of Tarris's favorites – one they used to listen to when they took Tarris's dad's car out on midnight joy rides. With Tarris high on Jack and Nympho blaring from the car's Muzak system, they would tear across the back roads of the Midwest Interway with all the car's protocols disengaged. To Jonathan, it seemed a lifetime ago.

"He does that every time," Sanjiv said. "Drives us crazy." He poured the raw eggs and milk into an old-fashioned skillet, which hovered above an antique open-flame burner. The eggs crackled when they hit the pan.

"Could be worse," Kreet said. "At least he sings good songs." Bixx giggled into her bowl of cereal.

The shower shut off and sent a low rumble through the

floor's exposed piping. Rocket rounded the partition wrapped in a large green towel. He was drying his hair with a microdryer, its high-pitched whine barely audible.

"What?" he asked as all eyes landed on him. Bixx giggled again. His eyes met Jonathan's, and he clicked the dryer off.

"You like Nympho?" Jonathan asked.

"Ah, sure...I guess." Rocket averted Jonathan's gaze and took a seat at the kitchen table. He grabbed a banana, peeled it back and took a bite that practically vanquished the whole fruit. Everyone kept staring.

"What?" Rocket asked, barely managing the word with his mouth so full of banana. Bixx began to laugh, and everyone broke out.

"Aw, fuck you all," Rocket exclaimed. He stormed out of the kitchen and headed to the sanctuary of his cubicle.

"Oh, Rocket, come on..." Bixx called and bounded after him.

The chorus of *Crying Train* kept looping in Jonathan's mind, and he began to think about Tarris. He missed his friend. To Jonathan, he was the only one he could trust – really trust. But now he was strung out, forced back into addiction by the same people Jonathan was growing to loathe. He kept thinking of Jimbo's words to him on his flight back from France, "We found Tarris."

"Hey...Sanjiv," Jonathan said pensively, "you're a techno-guy, right?"

"Systems specialist, to be exact," Sanjiv replied, vigilantly watching his eggs. "Why do you ask?" The skillet left its position above the flame and floated to the table. It tilted to slide the eggs onto a plate, then moved to the sink, where it settled into a large bowl of dirty water that hissed violently and sent steam and the smell of burnt eggs and curry into the room.

"I need to retrofit something. It's kind of...well..."

"Off the netdar?" Kreet offered, finally giving Jonathan his attention.

"Yeah..." Jonathan replied, looking down at him, "...*off* the netdar."

"What do you need?" Sanjiv asked.

"I need a sig displacer that can mask for any platform or system."

Sanjiv and Kreet exchanged glances, and looked in the direction of Rocket's area.

"What?" Jonathan asked. "Rocket knows this kind of stuff?"

"No," Sanjiv replied. He smiled at Kreet. "Bixx does."

. . .

Jonathan watched Bixx diligently pore over the sig displacer. She hummed as she worked, testing and retesting – calibrating the sensitive device to mask Jonathan in any platform's environment.

Sanjiv leaned in to Jonathan's ear. "Don't let that innocent act fool you," he whispered. "She can do things I still can't figure out."

Bixx giggled in her little-girl voice, her hands not skipping a beat as they danced over the displacer.

"How's she doing?" Sasha asked, coming to Jonathan's side.

"Hell if I know," he replied. "I got lost after she tore down the drive board."

Bixx giggled again. She scanned the displacer for a tenth time and flipped up her headgear. "There!" she declared. The connections hissed from uncoupling. "You should be able to walk into a session of the Joint Chiefs and not be detected." She proudly handed Jonathan the displacer.

He held the unit up and inspected it like he knew what he was doing.

"Let's test it," Bixx said with a girlishly sly grin. She snatched the displacer from him. "Rocket!" she declared, suddenly taking charge. "Let's jack this in and see what we see."

"Let's hope we *don't* see," Rocket said. He pulled his headgear over his face, and his hair protruded through the straps in a patchwork of clownish red clumps.

Bixx clipped the sig displacer to her belt and stepped into the middle of the room. "Rocket, are you online?"

"Yeah, baby."

"Well? What *don't* you see?"

"I don't see you!"

"Good. Now scan through the different platforms and tell me what the ranges are...if there are any."

Rocket dutifully scanned through the various platforms that were used by the Agency and most any other network.

"Well?..." she demanded impatiently.

"Hold on! I'm not a genius like you."

Bixx shied. "Sorry," she said.

"Not a damn thing," Rocket announced. "Baby, you're a genius!"

Bixx clapped with glee and looked to Jonathan for approval. She slipped off the displacer and mentally passed it to him.

"Thank you, Bixx. This is extraordinary work." Jonathan collected the device as it floated into his hands.

"I'm glad she's on our side," Sanjiv said, chuckling.

Bixx just grinned.

"Why does a Tel at your level need a sig displacer?" Kreet asked. His voice carried an edge of accusation.

A silence descended on the group like a thick blanket of seriousness. Jonathan leveled his gaze at Kreet. "I have some...*unfinished* business to take care of. Why?"

Kreet stepped back reflexively. "I...I didn't mean anything. We won't tell anyone, honestly!"

Jonathan slowly eyed the whole group.

"Please don't!" Bixx blurted, and she covered her face. Rocket slowly lifted the eye trodes of his virt headgear. Sanjiv folded his arms tightly across his body and stared at the ground.

Sasha stepped over to Jonathan. "You don't need to," she whispered. "They're not going to say anything."

"All right then," Jonathan said to the group. "Let's just keep this between us...shall we?" He pulled the blanket aside and stepped into the bedroom.

The tension lifted as a collective sigh went through the group. "Excuse me," Sanjiv said, "I need to use the bathroom." He hurried out.

Bixx began whimpering into her hands, and Rocket came to her side. "Don't worry, baby," he said in an attempt to comfort her. He shot a sad look at Sasha.

Sasha stormed toward the bedroom. She mentally whipped the blanket aside, almost tearing it from its hooks, and found Jonathan packing his gear bag with relaxed precision.

"You were really going to do it, weren't you?" she questioned sternly.

Jonathan straightened but kept his back to her. He stood for a moment, then sighed. "I'm not in a position to trust anyone."

"These people just gave you a place to hide."

"*These people* have no interest in my well-being—"

"They're the backbone of the Tel world," she said, angrily biting off his words. "Think, Jonathan! They just altered a sig displacer, possibly jeopardizing their futures! They're not doing it out of some sense of duty. These are smart, ambitious people. They've been given a gift that's alienated them from the rest of the world, and they just want the same thing we all do. And guess who they think might lead them out of this absurd secrecy all of us exist in?!"

Jonathan turned and severely regarded her. "You done?" he asked.

"I don't know why I'm—" Sasha cut herself off and scoffed.

"You know," Jonathan said, his voice turgid with

aggression, "it would be nice if just *once*, someone would think of my situation." He stepped closer. "I'm the one who has all the mystery technology growing in his head! I'm the one who's lost practically everyone who was ever important to me!" He was almost touching her face. *"I'm* the one who has everything to *lose* here."

Sasha could feel his rage. It was like heat against her skin.

"I should go back out there and erase all of them!" he declared, pointing to the curtain. "It would be for their own good." He turned and resumed packing his gear bag.

Sasha folded her arms and trained her attention at his back.

Jonathan flinched in midfold and angrily spun around, but his arms slapped to his sides and his body went rigid.

Sasha walked up and stopped inches from his face. "Those people are *my* friends," she growled.

Jonathan's look of surprise dissolved into a steely mask of anger. Sasha felt her windpipe begin to constrict, as if invisible hands had wrapped around her neck. She gagged and slowly dropped to her knees. "I know, Sasha," Jonathan said quietly. He knelt and took her face in his hands. "That's why I didn't erase them." His face softened, and he gently released her throat. She let out a small gasp. "Please don't ever test me again. I don't like being forced to demonstrate my level...especially with someone I like." He softly kissed her forehead, stood and walked to the curtain.

"Jonathan," she said hoarsely.

He stopped, but didn't respond.

"Let me go with you. I can help you...."

Sasha suddenly felt herself being lifted to her feet.

"From now on, I'm on my own," Jonathan said. He stared at the floor, and his shoulders slumped. "Hell," he lamented, "I'm not sure if what I'm going to do will even work..."

He turned to look at her, and for the first time Sasha saw in his face something she had never seen before.

Fear.

She began to speak, but Jonathan motioned for her to stop. His demeanor hardened, and, without looking, he reached back, and the gear bag flew into his outstretched hand. The curtain flew open.

"Sasha, please remember..." Jonathan hesitated, then shook the thought away. He hiked the gear bag onto his shoulder. "Goodbye," he said coldly, and quickly stepped from the room.

PAUL BLACK

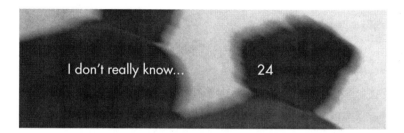

I don't really know...   24

JIMBO pensively studied the data stream.

His netphone hummed, and he glanced at the ID. "Hi, baby," he answered. "Why are you calling so late?"

"Oh, I don't know," Anari replied. "I was getting off from the club early, and I'd thought I'd call and leave you a good-night message. But you picked up."

"I can cut off and let you call back."

"No, I'm glad you answered. Although, I wish I could see you when I call. So why are you working late?"

"Just reviewing some field results from one of our latest assignments. Nothing special. A lady in New York had shown some ability, but she turned out to be nothing much at all...just a

Displacer. And you know I don't want you visually calling 'in system.' It's just safer that way."

"I know, I know. Too bad about the woman. A trip to New York would've been fun."

"Don't get your hopes up on this one. This lady's more talk than anything else." He shifted to a new file and a new data stream.

"Say, Jimmy..." Anari's voice was tentative. "Have you heard from Jonathan?"

"Hmm?" he questioned, his mind lost in the flux parameters of a new Potential in Idaho. "What'd you say?"

"Have you heard anything from Jonathan?"

"No. He's on vacation. He went to that island where you and I went last year. Why?"

"No reason..."

Jimbo looked up from the netport. "Bull. I can hear it in your voice."

There was a pause. "I had lunch today...with Tamara–"

"Anari, I've warned you about that! You're only going to frustrate yourself and possibly hurt Tamara in the process. Is she still having those dreams?"

A longer pause followed. "No," she said. "I don't think so."

"You don't think so, or you don't *know* so?"

"We didn't really talk about it. She hasn't mentioned them for a long time."

"Good, because if they start up again, I'm going to have to send out a Level 8–"

"Jimmy, please don't. You people have put her through enough all ready. Just let her have her life–"

"Anari!"

"Okay! Okay!"

"Look, baby, this is my job. Hell, it's my life. We have to protect ourselves. I took a huge risk with you. My God, if the Agency found out I let you go – free and unerased – I'd...I'd..."

"You'd *what*?"

"I'd be screwed for sure," Jimbo said, his voice rising. "It would be erase city. Nothing left. A clean, goddamn slate for ol' Jimbo."

No response.

"You don't want that, now...do you?"

More silence.

"*Anari*?"

"No! Of course I don't. It's just that...well, it's so hard to see Tamara sometimes, you know, knowing what she was...what she and Jonathan had together."

"What they had was never going to work out."

"You don't know that!"

"Oh, sure. A hooker into 'riding' with a guy like Jonathan Kortel?"

"She doesn't trick anymore, and she hasn't ridden in years. That was a cheap shot!"

"Okay, I'll give her that," he said, backing off a bit. "But you've got to admit, it would have never worked out...*never*."

"I've seen it happen."

"Where, in a romance vid?"

"No. Katrina married that doctor–"

"Yeah, after he promised to augment her."

There was a long pause, and Jimbo resumed his study.

"It was different between them," Anari said quietly. "You know that."

Resolved, Jimbo slowly shut his netport. "I know," he said, rubbing at his temples. "They did have something special."

"And you people took it away!"

"*Us* people had to take it away! Jonathan is special, Anari. I've told you a million damn times. We did what we had to do. End of story!"

Anari began to cry silently.

"Oh, baby...please don't..."

"You never saw them...how they looked at each other. We all saw it. They really...were..."

"Were what?"

"In love...true love." A sob escaped, and she gave in to it. "A love where their backgrounds didn't matter to them."

"That doesn't exist, Anari. It's only in the vids."

"They had it, Jimmy. You should have seen it....It was...beautiful."

"Look, Jonathan Kortel thinks too much with his other head. Maybe Tamara isn't your typical dirty girl, but believe me, they would have never lasted. He would have dumped her as soon as he got bored with her. Come on, think about it, what could a girl like Tamara Connor offer a guy like Kortel? They come from two totally different worlds. I know you've said she's been working on her degree, but even after she gets it, she'll still be an ex-prostitute – smarter maybe, but still a prostitute. We probably did him a favor by erasing her. Breaking up is such a pain in the ass anyway."

Solemnity fell over their conversation.

"I gotta get back to work," Jimbo finally said. "Are you going to be all right?"

"Yes..." Anari said coolly.

"Okay, then. Good night, baby."

"Yeah, sure..."

The netline abruptly severed.

"Jesus, what a bitch," he said into the empty room. He clicked to the next file.

Jimbo's screen filled with the image of Shirley Valentine, a Northern California medium who had claimed on a local TVid talk show that she was telekinetic and telepathic. A month earlier, Jimbo had dispatched two Recruiters to investigate her claims and discovered that she was as telekinetic as the average Shih Tzu. Shirley was mostly a media hype, and strictly out for the money. People like her were often left to continue with their sideshows. The Tel world had learned that allowing charlatans to amuse the masses only reinforced the notion that telekinetics was the stuff of tabloid journalism. It provided a simple and effective deflection to a relentless issue, as well as a great source of amusement to many in the Tel world. And when someone did come around who was a true Potential, he or she never lasted long enough in the public spotlight to do any damage.

Scrolling further only revealed more boring documentation. Jimbo leaned back and stretched. Glancing at his watch, he pulled the netport closer and dove into the last file. Lost in concentration, he never heard the latch move on the outer office door.

The hum of the netport drive filled the void as the HVAC system reached the optimal temperature and shut off. The drive whined and whirred, processing teraquads of data for Jimbo to study. The desk lamp buzzed just under an audible range.

"Working late tonight?"

Jimbo almost jumped out of his chair. "Shit, motherfucker! Jonathan, you scared the crap out of me!" He snapped the netport shut. "What the hell are you doing here? You're supposed to be in Tortola!"

"Yeah, I know. But a funny thing happened to me on the way to the islands." Jonathan slowly paced the office and glared at Jimbo with gelid disdain.

"Oh yeah...what happened?" Jimbo's senses were sharply alert due to the system's failure to announce Jonathan's approach.

"I was having lunch the other day, and I saw the weirdest thing." Jonathan stopped and leaned against a cabinet. "There I was, sitting outside, taking in the afternoon...actually thinking about Tortola..."

Jimbo apprehensively shifted in his chair.

"...when I looked across the street, and guess what I saw?"

Jimbo shifted again. "I don't know...what did you see? Where were you?"

Jonathan stepped to Jimbo's desk and leaned on it with

all the burden of his anger on display. "I was at *Arturo's*...James."

Confused, Jimbo didn't respond. He carefully studied Jonathan's emotional state and nervously smiled. "Yeah...so?"

"Oh, come on, *Jimbo*..."

Jimbo's nerves shot to attention. Jonathan never called him that. Ever.

"Man, what's up?" Jimbo asked, testing.

"You don't know what I'm talking about?" Jonathan asked mockingly.

"No...I don't."

Jonathan shook his head. He began to laugh a little under his breath. "Goddamn you," he said more to himself than to Jimbo.

"Jonathan...hey, what's the matter? Oh *shit*–" Suddenly, Jimbo's tongue was yanked from his mouth almost to the point of tearing. His body rose over his desk, and his arms slapped tightly to his sides. His legs flailed madly, sending his chair slamming against the windowsill behind him. As his tongue led his body's slow forward movement, blood began to drip from the sides of his mouth. Jonathan was still staring at the desk, his arms tightly folded as if this action was causing him pain, too. He finally looked up and regarded Jimbo with callous hatred. "You goddamn, motherfucking son of a bitch," he said.

Jimbo came to a halt, his eyes on level with Jonathan's. His tongue was stretched to its anatomical limit, and blood poured from his mouth. Tears streamed down his cheeks, and his eyes were filled with terror.

Jonathan didn't say a word. He just stared into his former

friend's eyes and searched for a reason. "What's the matter," he asked, "Tel got your tongue?"

Jimbo tried desperately to speak.

"Let me answer that for you with another rhetorical question." Jonathan leaned forward till he almost touched Jimbo's tongue. "How's *Anari?*"

Jimbo frantically began to groan.

"Yeah, thought that might shake you up a little." Jonathan leaned back against the cabinet to watch Jimbo squirm in his telekinetic grip. "How long did you really think you'd get away with that one?"

Suddenly, the window behind Jimbo's desk exploded into a spray of fragments. The bits of glass stopped in midair, then slowly collected together into a shape that to Jonathan resembled one of those old disco balls he had once seen in a New York dance club. It glittered in the night air reflecting the lights from the campus's buildings. Jimbo tried to look back at it. Jonathan released his tongue.

"Fuck!" was all Jimbo could manage at first. He coughed and spit blood, speckling the top of his desk and netport. "Jonathan," he eventually gasped, his tongue swollen, "let me explain!"

"Explain what?" Jonathan asked. "That you're a selfish, manipulative bastard?"

Jimbo began to slowly back toward the open windows. "Jonathan," he yelled, "what the hell are you doing?!"

Jonathan didn't answer and followed Jimbo to the window.

Jimbo continued floating out of the office until he stopped

eight feet outside the window. He futilely wriggled within Jonathan's hold as he hung 20 stories above the campus. One of his feet kicked the ball of glass fragments, but it didn't move.

Jonathan stepped to the window and folded his arms. He eyed the Southerner whom he dangled in the night breeze. The hatred had left, replaced with a deeper emotion, one that took him by surprise. Tears welled at the corners of his eyes.

"Why?!" Jonathan demanded. "Why did you do it?!"

"We had to!" Jimbo pleaded. "There was no other choice!" He coughed and watched his blood fall 200 feet to the pavement.

"But there was a choice when it came to Anari!" Jonathan exclaimed. "Sure, you can screw me over, but yourself – that's different!"

"Jonathan, it wasn't like that! You've got to believe me!"

"I really want to, James, really. From the bottom of my heart, I want to believe that your reasoning has some...some viable purpose – something I'm not seeing." He looked at him wildly. "Well?!" he screamed. "Does it?!"

Jimbo, knowing he was caught, couldn't respond. Resolved to his fate, he stopped fighting and relaxed.

"That's what I thought," Jonathan said in disgust. He slammed his fist on the sill.

"Jonathan!" Jimbo cried from his purgatory. "Let me explain."

"Yeah, I'm listening."

"Man," Jimbo started, "when you came on the scene, it rocked our world..."

Jonathan rolled his eyes.

"...no, really! Listen to me. Jonathan, you gotta understand...." His voice dropped to a serious register. "...You're like nothing we've ever seen. You're off the charts."

"How far off?"

Jimbo hesitated. "That's classified, man. Really, I have no idea." He fell about three feet, and jerked to a halt. "NO! Shit...goddamn it, Jonathan, listen to me! I'm not bullshitting you! Only Takeda and Trumble know. Everyone else is too fragmented. We only gather parts of the puzzle, but they have the big picture!"

"Tell me, James, what else is going on?! What other things are being conveniently kept from me?"

Jimbo shrugged. "What do you mean?"

"Was that KFBC sign an accident?"

Jimbo reluctantly nodded. "All right, Jonathan. Look...do you really think all your training takes place in a classroom? Don't be so naive! How else are we going to test you?"

"God, James, people could have died!"

"No! No, not with you there! Besides, it's a calculated risk—"

"And the bus in San Francisco?"

Jimbo looked away. "I..I don't know about that one. But..." he looked back to Jonathan "... the French guard was."

Jonathan fell back. "James," he said, aghast, "I killed him."

"Like I said, man...a *calculated* risk."

Jonathan fell into despair with the realization that he couldn't be sure of anything. What had been a test, and what had been real? He stepped to the window and deathly eyed the Southerner. His despair morphed into something more deadly.

"What about Anari, James?"

"Yeah," he acknowledged, "I fucked that up big time. But you gotta understand, I was fucking lonely...SHIT!" Jimbo had fallen another four feet. "OHHH! Man! Don't do that!"

Jonathan raised him slowly to his eye level. "Just tell me *why*."

"Buddy, pal, friend...you've been there! Haven't you?"

Jonathan didn't grace him with an answer.

"All right," Jimbo said, coughing. Blood dripped from his mouth. "What can I say? When I first saw her...I...I just wanted her, all right! Can't a guy just want a girl that bad?!"

Jonathan dropped his glare. "Yeah, James..." he said, reflecting on what he had with Tamara, "...a guy can."

"Then you understand!" Jimbo said, desperately reaching for rapport.

"You know what I *understand*, James?" Jonathan leveled a savage glare at Jimbo. "That it's about damn time I started living my life."

Jimbo's heart palpitated. The wind punched his face. "Look, Jonathan, I'll do whatever you want!" he exclaimed in panic. "I'll even erase Anari!" Jonathan's eyes narrowed, and Jimbo knew he had only minutes, maybe seconds, left. "Jesus, Jonathan, please, you're on the system right now! They're recording this....They'll hunt you down!"

"We are?" Jonathan asked mockingly. He pulled his netpad

from his pocket and opened his coat to reveal the grav sig displacer strapped on his belt. He smiled. "To the system, I'm not here." He glanced at his netpad. "And according to this, your section of this building is experiencing some..." he looked back at Jimbo with a hint of pleasure "...technical difficulties."

Reverting to his Southern Baptist roots, Jimbo closed his eyes and began to recite the 23rd Psalm.

Jonathan leaned out of the window. "Don't worry," he said, not hiding his disdain, "I'm not going to kill you..."

Jimbo pitifully stopped in midverse.

"...I'm going to do something *a lot worse.*"

Jimbo gasped. "How far back?!"

Jonathan's eyes narrowed more. "I don't really know..."

The life drained from Jimbo's face. "No, *please!*—"

Instantly, Jimbo's body stiffened, as if it were in some kind of cataleptic lockdown. Jonathan phased and focused his rage, wiping the Southerner's memory from his being. He gave no thought to precision or accuracy; he was out to get even.

In the brisk night wind, Jonathan stood at the window with detached numbness and observed Jimbo convulse. Like a marionette in the hands of a child, his body shook spasmodically. Spittle built at the corners of his mouth and his eyes rolled back in their sockets. Jonathan had cast an unusually broad erase field, which might wipe away 30 or more years of life. He didn't know. He didn't care. The man in front of him had taken away all that had been dear to him, and as Jonathan figured it, the law of karma had caught up to James McCarris.

SOULWARE

Jimbo's body gave one final, violent jerk, then caved. His head fell forward, and a mixture of vomit and blood gushed from his mouth. The wind whipped his red hair about.

Jonathan stepped back as he brought Jimbo's limp bulk through the window and into the office. He slowly lowered him to the floor, almost reverently settling him onto the tile. He looked down at the man he had once called friend and reflected on the night they first met.

"What happened to you?" he asked.

Jonathan knelt and checked Jimbo's breathing. It was labored, but steady. And as he studied the inert body, he was overcome with an odd mixture of emotions. Jonathan actually still cared for James McCarris – even pitied him. He couldn't really fault him for thinking with his dick rather than his heart; he had done it himself more than he cared to admit. But to Jonathan, Jimbo had come to represent his whole Agency experience and, unfortunately, had also become the recipient of his wrath. He thought of Tamara and began to break down, but rapidly quelled the emotion. Jimbo wasn't the only metaphor for his pain, and there was still more karmic justice to dispense.

Jonathan slowly rose and reviewed his netpad. The office remained off-line to the system, but not for much longer. He shot a glance at the shattered window frame, and the ball of glass fragments glided into the room. They settled onto the floor in a small pile by Jimbo's feet. Edges of the shards caught the light from the desk lamp and reflected hot shapes of light about the room. Jonathan began to leave, but he glanced back at Jimbo quietly sleeping off his telekinetic judgment. He had no idea what would be left of Jimbo's memory. Nor did he care.

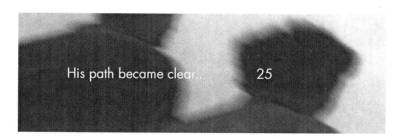

His path became clear...   25

THE limo splashed through fresh puddles left behind by a
front that had passed through the D.C. Zone, and the sky was
littered with broken clouds that marked the approach of another
line of storms. A deep rumble of thunder echoed like a backdrop
on the stage of the dark East Coast night. Jonathan piloted through
the streets, his mind, his soul, his whole being consumed by a
deep, almost instinctual rage. With his motivation fluxing between
need and revenge, the Jonathan Kortel who had entered the Agency
full of hope and trust had now descended to a primal state of
mind. All that was dear to him had been ripped from his life. He
had nothing to lose, because in his mind, there was nothing left to
lose. His thoughts were a spastic collage, hyper-jumping between

the images that represented the life he had loved and the life he now had. Living in a cold reality of bitterness was not what he had expected from his life, but if this was the hand he was dealt, so be it. He had crossed this threshold of anguish before, but this time he had a strange sense of renewal, of cleansing. This fresh bitterness slipped on his soul like a finely tailored suit, and for the first time in his life, Jonathan Kortel felt justified in wearing it.

He punched in an ID sequence on the limo's netport, and Carter Shoalburg's image appeared. He was crowded into a small council station; his chrome net connectors reflected the light from a small lamp.

"Carter, are you picking up my sig?" Jonathan asked.

"Negative, Jonny. I'm deep in, and you're nowhere to be found."

"Good. When I get closer, I may need your help....Are you still up for this?"

"Hell, yeah!" Shoalburg said. "Don't worry about me. You just watch yourself, you hear me?"

"Thanks, Carter, I'll owe you one."

"You'll owe me nothing, Jonny," Shoalburg said sincerely. "I just hope you get your answers." He paused, his image frozen on the screen like a mutated humanoid bug. Shoalburg's blank expression gave nothing away, but Jonathan could sense that the famous Tel had something on his mind.

"What are you thinking?"

Shoalburg hesitated. "Be careful. These two are ruthless sons of bitches. Believe me, I know."

"I appreciate that, but I'm not worried. I know you've got my back."

Shoalburg smiled and tapped the side of his headgear. His image cut out.

. . .

Jonathan parked the limo a few blocks from the downtown *Citenikelet* building. It was one of the few street spaces left in D.C. A light rain began to fall as he walked down the sidewalk that led to the loading dock area. Stopping just short of the entrance, he checked his netpad for the vid readouts from the building's security grid. Shoalburg had effectively masked him from the security cameras, and the modified sig displacer was working perfectly. "Thanks, Bixx," he said quietly, and pocketed the netpad. The collar of his coat sensed the rain and tightened slightly around his neck.

It was 2:00 in the morning, and there wasn't a soul around. The wind from the storm had kicked up, swirling dust and trash into little tornadoes that Jonathan disrupted. The rain intensified. Water began rolling down the ramp of the loading dock in waves, and droplets pelted the back of his coat with a relentlessly manic syncopation. He ducked under the platform's overhang, and his coat's biofabric mesh expanded and shifted to its "dry out" setting. He approached the set of doors that led to the lobby level.

"Carter," he asked into his netpad, "can you unlock these doors?"

The center door clicked twice.

"Like that?" Carter said with a cocky smile from the pad's tiny screen.

The hallways were dim from the repressed lighting, and Jonathan's boots squished unforgivingly against the freshly polished travertine. He approached the main elevator banks and stopped. He cautiously peered around a corner. The lobby of *Citenikelet Investments* presented itself in a vaguely Greek motif. The main foyer was ringed by ten massive Corinthian columns that rose five stories from the lobby floor, and with its severe lighting reflecting harshly off of every surface, it seemed to have been designed to give visitors the impression that they had just entered the gates of heaven. Two stories above the lobby floor, the firm's holovid promo was still projecting its 30-foot-tall corporate hype. A guard would have been dwarfed in the cavernous expanse, but suspiciously, the security station was deserted.

That's weird, Jonathan thought. He clicked his netpad to life and whispered, "Where's the lobby guard?"

No response.

"Carter?" he asked, looking down at the pad.

The screen's pixelated static greeted him with the coldness of a New England winter.

"Carter?" There was a trace of panic in his voice. "I need the elevator!" His nerves jumped on edge with the realization that he was utterly and completely solo. He glanced at his watch: 2:21:06 a.m. With only about an hour left of masking time and Shoalburg out of the equation, what little safety net he thought he had was gone. The loss might mean his presence had been detected, but it also could be just a signal disruption caused by the building's complex web of interlink hubs. His heart began to race. He glanced back down the hallway to the loading dock, to the false comfort of a life to which he knew he could never return. He shifted his attention back to the remarkably simple oak doors that distinguished the private elevator car to the penthouse. His heart pounded erratically against his chest. His breathing was shallow and rapid. It was now or never. All that Jonathan was – all that he would be – had come down to this moment.

A memory came into his mind and tugged at his heart like an insistent child on the pant leg of a parent. He thought of the last time he had seen his mother and father alive. And his path became clear.

PAUL BLACK

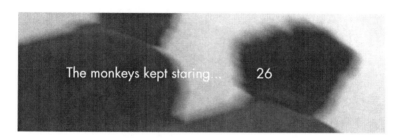

The monkeys kept staring ... 26

JONATHAN'S access to the private elevator's security codes had vanished with Shoalburg's signal, and with his limited masking time, he couldn't even consider the 70 flights of stairs. He keenly trained his telekinetic force at the beautifully hand-carved elevator doors and began to pry them apart.

Takeda and Trumble weren't casual with security. They knew their positions within the Tel world were fragile at best, so Jonathan figured the entrance to their private car would be heavily reinforced. He phased and focused a tight field against the doors. The thick oak veneer began to splinter, which revealed a honeycombed titanium skeleton. He focused more tightly, and the doors started to give. Blood began to run from his nose.

The titanium doors buckled and compressed like sponges to expose an opulence reserved for the privileged few. Jonathan sprinted into the cab's burled wood luxury, slamming into one of its fabric walls. Polynesian hand-carved monkeys glared at him from perches above the cab's leather floor. He frantically searched for the elevator's emergency door, running his fingers along the ceiling trim until he found the release catch. It was cleverly disguised in the rope molding. He clicked it and jettisoned the door onto the elevator's roof. Peering up through the escape hatch, he could see the elevator shaft rising the height of the building. At every floor were emergency lights, demarcating the perfect path to the penthouse.

Jonathan stepped directly under the opening, pressed his arms to his sides, looked up and quickly slipped into phase.

The monkeys kept staring.

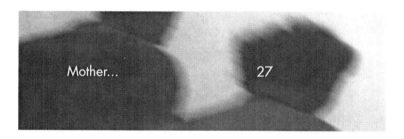

Mother...   27

CYRIL Takeda poured himself another sherry. The squeak of the cork being replaced severed the living room's calm just as the concerto started. Jeffrey Trumble looked over his reading glasses and frowned.

The Burton of Kendal chimed once. 2:30 a.m.

As the second movement ended, the solo of German violinist Mansford Drural began. His artistry was legendary, and this particular movement always left Takeda melancholy. He threw back his sherry and slammed the glass onto the bar. Trumble looked over again, glanced at his watch and sighed. They never heard the initial cracking of the stress on the striations in the wood.

Mansford Drural reached the apex of his tenuto.

The two wooden doors of the penthouse elevator blew so completely free of their frames that they flew into the room like cardboard. One slammed into the Burton of Kendal and obliterated its 18th-century mahogany body. Its master painted arch dial went sailing across the room and shattered against a Queen Anne desk. The other door carved a deep rut to the subfloor of the living room and skidded to rest at the foot of Trumble's ottoman. It bunched his grandmother's Victorian rug into an accordioned mass of ornate cadmium flower patterns.

Jonathan slowly floated up from the dark shaft and through the shattered door frame.

"Good evening, Jonathan," Trumble said, casually considering him through the distortion of his lenses. He delicately removed the glasses and folded them away into the breast pocket of his robe. "We've been expecting you."

"It's morning, actually, Jeffrey," Takeda corrected. He generously poured himself another drink.

Trumble waived him off.

"You know, Jonathan," Takeda said; "you could have just asked for the access codes. There was no need for theatrics."

"Grandmum would be heartbroken to see her rug this way," Trumble said.

Jonathan glided into the center of the living room and landed gently in the middle of the gouge left by the elevator door. His knees bent slightly as he settled down. He viciously eyed the two Tels.

"So, my boy. What can we do for...augghh!" Trumble

desperately reached for his throat.

"Jonnnathaaan..." Takeda sang, wagging his finger.

Seething, Jonathan focused on Takeda.

"Manners, Jonathan," Takeda said disappointedly. "Haven't we taught you anything?"

Jonathan released Trumble, who gasped for air.

"You *know* why I'm here," Jonathan said in a low, measured voice.

"My God," Trumble said. He rubbed his throat. "Is that any way to treat your elders?–"

Jonathan's glare cut him off. "What's in my head?...*Fucker.*"

Trumble cautiously shot Takeda a questioning look, then turned back to Jonathan. "Well, my boy," he began, "that's not really for you to, hughhh–" Trumble let out a gasp as his body seized. His back arched and his hands shot straight to his sides. Motionless in the large chair, he sat like an old-style mannequin in a bathware display. He started to vibrate, slowly at first, but picking up speed until he was violently shaking. His eyes rolled back into his head: first his right, then his left. Foam curdled at the edges of his mouth and began splattering about.

"*Release* him!" Takeda screamed.

"I asked a question," Jonathan demanded.

Cyril Takeda took a step forward. "You," he said coldly, "are in no goddamn position to bargain."

Trumble's body was now a blur.

Suddenly, Jonathan's vision shifted and the room's darkness became blacker, as if he had just donned a pair of solar goggles.

The darkness shifted again, and what little edges of blurred light his eyes previously picked out of the black vanished. Jonathan was instantly gripped with shock as the realization hit: He was completely blind.

Trumble stopped shaking, but the residual force threw him out of the chair like a rag doll. He landed in an unconscious heap on his grandmother's rug. His arms flapped limply to his sides, coming to rest in contorted positions.

Panicked, Jonathan stumbled back. He caught his foot on the edge of the gouge left by the door and fell to the floor.

"I think *you're* the one who's *fucked*," Takeda commented.

Jonathan's hearing quickly faded. All he could sense was the soft, rhythmic swoosh of his own blood as it pulsed through his now-useless ear canals. He felt his throat go numb. He tried to speak, but he couldn't form a sound. He was cripplingly void of all his senses.

Takeda trained his attention on Trumble's body. It slowly rose off the rug, floated to the couch and gently settled onto the soft cushions of the heirloom. Trumble's arms folded themselves across his chest.

Radically disoriented, Jonathan groped across the floor on his hands and knees. His fingers caught in the gouge, and he fell to his face. His chin struck the polished hardwood with a crack.

Takeda sighed loudly.

At that moment, Jonathan's senses mysteriously returned. Startled, he squinted at the sudden reintroduction of light to his brain.

Takeda came and stood over him. "How does it feel," he asked, "to be defenseless?"

Jonathan crawled to face him. His chin swollen and bleeding, he tried, still squinting, to look up at the Agency leader.

"If you think I'm bluffing..." Takeda said just above a whisper. A sharp, deep pain instantly gripped Jonathan's chest, and a throbbing shot down his arm. He frantically clawed at his shirt, gasping for air. "...here's a little glimpse of *eternity*."

As if a switch had been thrown, Jonathan's heart abruptly stopped. He collapsed backwards, landing with his legs bent underneath him and his arms out to his sides. He felt his organs begin to relax inside his body, and his eyes focused on the ornate vine pattern carved into the woodwork of the living room's ceiling. He gasped and took his last breath.

"Mother..." he softly exhaled.

His vision faded to white.

PAUL BLACK

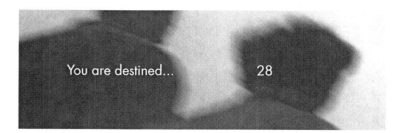

You are destined... 28

CRASHING.

Hard.

Like a thousand body bags slamming to the ground.

A screech...no, a squawk.

Wind. A sound like chimes.

Heat. Burning, but not.

Light. Intense brightness.

Trying the eyes.

"Shit..."

Standing. Vibration in the feet.

Feet. Sunk into...wet.

Jonathan cautiously opened his eyes. There was a rushing sound, as if the air itself were being drained away. Then everything repeated itself, but not as before: He now had a sense of where he was.

A beach.

The waves crashed, and Jonathan's vision returned, but the color seemed muted, like a faded photo from the past. The ocean's green, the sky's blue, the sand's silver – all *distended* somehow. The beach stretched to the horizon on either side. He looked down at feet buried in the sand, warm between his toes. He turned, but the physical sense of turning was missing. A forest of palm trees rose behind him and ran the length of the beach as far as he could see.

He had an urge to walk down the beach, but something inside him prodded him to head toward the palms. As the ground rose, his legs responded, but with a leaden detachment. He entered the forest and pushed his way through the undergrowth. It was slow going at first, but as he made his way, the trees began to thin. Looking up, he saw the sunlight cutting through the canopy of fronds, and he began feeling shafts of warmth with each step. Time had seemed to pass. A minute? An hour? A lifetime? He didn't know. And strangely, he didn't care.

He emerged onto a large grassy area where beds of flowers, infant palms and a bench – sitting in the center of a concrete circle – all greeted him with a vague sense of purpose. He stepped forward. His foot struck an object. Startled, he looked down. It was a child's toy. He picked up the little red truck and spun its front wheels. It made a familiar sound. A sweet sound. A haunting sound.

His bottom lip began to quiver. The warmth he had enjoyed surrendered to a cold that seemed for him and him alone. He knew where he was.

Hawaii.

His heart pounded while he desperately searched the yard. It continued to rise, past beds of roses and heather, to a house. Jonathan realized it was his parents' house. Then he saw the pale green door that led to the kitchen, to milk and cookies, to the waist of his mother, where he had buried his face when he wanted the world to vanish. Jonathan ran as fast as he could, occasionally stumbling, but feeling no pain of his toe being stubbed or his ankle rolling over. He stopped short of the threshold and paused to take in the home. His fingers ran over flaking paint and loose-fitting hardware, and he stepped into the kitchen and found everything in its place. A search of the house unearthed tangible memories of a life he had experienced too briefly, but had longed for his entire life. The only thing missing was his parents.

If I'm dead, he thought, *then surely this is hell.*

Suddenly, Jonathan's mind began to fill with a strange sense of doubt, as if his lucid self were rising to the conscious surface – a hint of reality that beckoned for his attention. He ran back down the hill and plunged into the forest. He fought through the palms, the sounds of the beach growing more intense until he glimpsed it through the maze of trunks. He stopped, barely at the edge of the beach, hidden (he hoped) at the lip of its density.

A figure was on the beach. It was a woman.

She faced the horizon, her feet at the perfect point where a wave lost its momentum and fell back to rejoin the sea. She turned. Jonathan recognized her. He fell to his knees and started to weep. "Mother..." he said, again the child he had been. He started to wail, letting go of all that had held him for so many years.

His mother spread her arms. Jonathan burst from the palms. He didn't care if he was dead. He didn't care if this was hell. He just wanted to hold her.

As he got closer, he could see that she was dressed as he had last seen her, more than 20 years ago at the Honolulu airport. She wore her crisp, white lab coat and khaki short pants. She even wore her favorite belt with its silver buckle of the stylized naked woman, the one that had adorned the mudflaps of old trucks. She had loved that belt.

Painfully prudent thoughts gripped his rational self, and he stopped just out of arm's length. He fought the emotional urge to hug her, to kiss her, to simply nuzzle her face, and smell her lab coat and soak in all the comfort her arms could bring. One more time.

"Mother...what's happening?" His mouth formed the words, but he hadn't heard a sound. Was it in his mind? He didn't really know.

"Don't be afraid, darling," his mother assured. Even though she had moved, he didn't have the sense that she had. She was now barely a foot from him.

"Am I...dead?" he asked. He searched her face, which he noticed had no visible signs of age – the soft crow's feet that he remembered from their final embrace were gone. Her brow was void of the concentration lines that her profession had etched over the years. Her face, in fact, was smooth, almost like a Kabuki dancer – ageless as well as genderless.

She smiled, and Jonathan's heart filled with an awing sense of love that seemed to radiate throughout his body.

"Mother," he softly asked, "what should I do?"

"You are destined for a different passage, son."

Behind her, Jonathan could see dark, featureless figures moving in and out of the surf's mist. They were beckoning to him. He shifted his attention back to her. "I've missed you so much..."

She brought her hand to his face, touching it tenderly with the tips of her fingers. "It's not your time," she whispered, and knowingly smiled.

Jonathan looked into her eyes and suddenly felt his whole being – the sum of all that he was – rush through them and into her soul.

His vision dissolved to black.

PAUL BLACK

You might know him...   29

"**HAVE** a nice trip?" Takeda asked.

Jonathan, his clothes drenched with sweat, gasped for air while his heart came back on line. Takeda was glowering over him.

"You've been gone for five seconds," he mused. He straightened and walked back to the bar to pour another sherry. "I believe your original question was 'What's in my head, fucker?'" He raised his glass in mock toast, "Only the best," and threw back his drink.

"Why?" Jonathan said roughly. He rubbed at his chest and started to cough violently.

"Why?" Takeda retorted. He wiped his mouth with the sleeve of his robe. "Because you're very, very special, Jonathan. In fact, you're one of a kind. Oh, we've had powerful Tels before," he placed his gloved right hand into the pocket of his robe, "but never anything like you."

Jonathan began to rise, and was instantly jerked into a standing position. His arms were held tight against his body by a force that felt eerily like it was coming from inside him.

Takeda chuckled.

"What will this technology do to me?" Jonathan asked. "Am I...a weapon?"

Takeda hesitated and smiled. "Let's start with the first question, shall we?" He calmly walked over to him. "The genetically tailored bionanoware that we implanted is currently integrating with your cerebral cortex, brain stem, cerebellum...basically, everything from your neck up. In time, the nanoware will spread and fully merge with your central nervous system. It's intelligent nanoware, Jonathan. Or as the lab boys affectionately call it, *soul*ware."

Jonathan flinched.

"Oh, it won't be painful..."

"Tell that to Zvara."

"Zvara," Takeda said, "was an experiment, nothing more." He resumed pacing. "Currently, the nanoware can control most of your base functions...sight, hearing, speech. Or motor control, such as you're experiencing right now. But soon it will be able to augment your higher functions, as well. Thought, reason...the like."

"And my gift?" Jonathan questioned.

Takeda stopped and eyed him. "Especially your gift."

"Now the second question," Jonathan said. "Why?"

Takeda slowly smiled. "Lights!" The living room lights dimmed to 10 percent of their illumination. "Jonathan," Takeda said out of the darkness, "do you know how powerful you are?"

"No...not really."

"You are, without a doubt, the most powerful Tel ever to exist."

"How powerful?" Jonathan thought he sensed Takeda smiling through the darkness.

"I thought you'd ask. Stream file Kortel 0005!"

A 10-foot by 10-foot holojection instantly appeared in front of Jonathan. Its lucent glow highlighted every exposed edge and gave the room a dated look, like a celluloid silent he had seen in history vids. The feed began to stream. Test after test, case study after case study, the file was an endless torrent of telekinetic data. The grav results, APT waves, field flux levels – all beyond normal parameters. For several minutes, Jonathan scanned the massive holochive. It became almost overwhelming. Takeda stood motionless, warily studying his reactions.

Halfway through, Jonathan began to formulate the complete picture. His level strength was immense, and if he read correctly, his ability bordered on evolutional. He was, he concluded, more than just a Tel.

He was something new altogether.

"God..." he said under his breath.

"Not quite yet, Jonathan, but who knows?" Takeda said flippantly. "Keep reading. I think you'll find the last part *very* interesting."

The streaming came to a file marked "SECURED" and stopped.

"Release!" Takeda ordered. "Voice authorization: Takeda alpha."

The file launched, and Jonathan began scanning through its abstruse gravity charts and quantum mechanics computations. After a minute, he looked at Takeda who had been intently watching him. "I...I don't get it. This stuff is way over my head."

Takeda grinned and motioned excitedly for him to keep reading. He was almost gleeful with the anticipation of what Jonathan would find.

Jonathan continued to read the rest of the file. Just before the last page streamed, he gasped. "Stop!" he ordered. The file froze. "Prior page!" It sequenced back.

Takeda started to chuckle.

"Holy ssshit!" Jonathan exclaimed just above a whisper.

"Holy shit is right," Takeda said smugly.

"This can't be. This is impossible!"

"Oh, it's not only possible," Takeda came closer, "it's *quantifiable*!" He stepped between the holojection and Jonathan, his silhouette rimmed with a glow that gave him a transcendental presence. "Before you came to us, you brought down a 500-ton airliner that had been partially torn apart by a Tactical Short Range Bioweapon. The warhead of that missile contained a biogenetic agent. When you field fluxed, you altered the molecular properties of that agent."

"But James told me that his equipment hadn't recorded

anything," Jonathan argued.

"James lied," Takeda said. "And by the way, you were a bit excessive, don't you think?"

"How bad is he?"

Takeda shrugged nonchalantly. "He's eating intravenously right now. We might recover some of his memories....It's hard to say."

Jonathan looked away.

"These results are unassailable," Takeda continued. "You have altered matter at the molecular level!"

"You haven't answered my second question," Jonathan said.

Takeda paused. "Control," he said with such casualness that what he had said barely registered with Jonathan.

"Excuse me?"

"You're not a weapon, Jonathan. Our world has no need for anything like that. Our arsenal is built on influence – financial, political, it doesn't matter, as long as it serves our needs. Do you really think we would let someone like you do anything to disrupt the order that we've been building for the last hundred years? We could have revealed ourselves years ago, but what would that have accomplished?" Takeda paused as if inviting Jonathan to answer. "Probably the destruction of our kind. If we reveal, our human cousins will fear us and eventually hunt us down like animals. Jonathan, who do you think has been saving man from himself? If it hadn't been for our influence, this world would have been a charred, dead planet 50 years ago. We've been controlling the dynamics of mankind ever since we went under. Who do you think influenced the decision for Khrushchev to turn those warships around in 1962? Who stopped the freighter in New York harbor 12 years ago? Who prevented the space stations from colliding last year?" He was now inches from Jonathan's face. "The Tels."

"What about Hawaii?" Jonathan asked gravely.

Takeda's demeanor suddenly shifted, and Jonathan could tell he had struck some kind of Machiavellian nerve in the Agency leader. "Jonathan, Hawaii was...a *calculated* action."

Jonathan thought he felt his heart stop again.

Takeda cautiously stepped back, his hands still in the pockets of his robe. "You must try and understand," he said with all the solemnity of a father consoling a child, "with Hawaii, we...oh, how can I put this?...*let* it happen, more than made it happen."

Stunned, Jonathan glared at Takeda. It was almost too much to comprehend.

"Now, Jonathan," Takeda said, "before you make any rash moves..." He took his right hand from his pocket and showed off a small device. It caught the light from the holojection and glowed a steely blue against Takeda's black glove. "I still control you." His fingers closed around it. "I know you don't understand it now, but, someday, perhaps you will. Hawaii, Jonathan, *has* changed the world. It has put into motion more security measures than a thousand interventions."

"You murdered a million people!" Jonathan said, hardly restraining his rage.

"And by doing so," Takeda said, "there are finally in place safeguards to prevent atrocities of unimaginable scale! No war could have accomplished this!" He was pacing again. "Such a war would have cost more lives and caused more sorrow, not to mention risking the complete annihilation of this planet! We live here, too, Jonathan, and we certainly can't trust *them* to take care of it." Takeda faced the holojection and spread his arms wide. "Look at you, Jonathan! You're the next step!" He spun on his heels to face him. "With your power, there's no limit to what we could do! New technology! New advances!" He stepped closer. "My God, you might even take us to the stars!"

"Cyril," Jonathan said with loathing, "I would rather die than help you."

Takeda slowly folded his arms and tapped the controller on his lower lip. "Don't be so melodramatic," he said with all the weight of his power. "You need to start thinking about the big picture – and *your* place in it."

Jonathan began to sense an extreme heat building inside his body. It started spreading into every cell, radiating from the center of his chest to his extremities. He felt like he was being cooked alive. He tried to phase, but the ability, which had become second instinct to him, had vanished.

Takeda looked down his nose. "Come on, Jonathan. Don't waste your life. We don't know when another one like you will come around again."

Sweat came from Jonathan's every pore; his body desperately tried to extinguish the heat that was consuming him. He was shaking, even in Takeda's telekinetic grip.

"Go...to...hell...Takeda," he barely managed.

Takeda sadly shook his head, and with a sigh that summed

his frustration, he pressed a small green button on the controller.

The heat instantly intensified, surging toward Jonathan's head. His lungs felt filled with a fire that was licking at the back of his throat. "Oh my God!" he screamed. Takeda, his finger poised on the green button, gave him a "had enough?" look.

Suddenly, the room exploded with a vision-crushing flash. Takeda was thrown off his feet like he had been slammed by an invisible truck. The controller flipped end-over-end out of Jonathan's field of vision. The heat, and Takeda's telekinetic grip, abated, and Jonathan collapsed to the floor. The flash, he realized, had been a Light-Force.

Takeda was visibly shaken. He began to stand, but was struck again with another blast. At each discharge, the beams deflected off the field wall he had induced and struck the ceiling in bright explosions. Its wood and fabric turned into gooey upside-down puddles that dripped and hissed as they struck the floor.

A numinous figure slowly approached with each successive cratering of the ceiling. Jonathan's eyes were partially blinded by the Light-Force's discharges, which rendered it impossible for him to distinguish the attacker in the dark room. Then the silhouetted form walked into the glow of the holojection, and his nerves spiked.

"Jesus, Takeda!" Georgia exclaimed. She fired off another round into his field. "Won't you just die!" She glanced at Jonathan. "You look like shit."

"Nice to see you, too," Jonathan said, coughing and wiping the sweat from his face.

Takeda was pressed flat against the floor as Georgia let off one more round. This discharge slammed his head violently against the wood, creating a horrific gash that ran the length of his face. Suddenly, her handheld Beretta began to whine down, and in a manner that resembled a ballet move, she flung it over the bar while pulling from behind her back a weapon Jonathan had never seen before. Its matte black surface was featureless and seemed to absorb the holojection light. To Jonathan, it appeared she was holding a shadow.

Seeing his opening, Takeda grav'd and caught Georgia before she had time to fire the weapon. He lifted her off the floor and spread her arms and legs out in his own version of a telekinetic crucifixion. Jonathan tried to phase, but was slammed to the floor by Takeda's unyielding wrath. Something in his arm snapped.

"You're not the only one with nanoware!" Takeda raged. Blood poured down his face. He glared at Georgia, and her limbs began to stretch to the boundary of their structural integrity. Jonathan watched in disbelief as Georgia's left arm acquiesced to Takeda's will and slowly started to separate from her body. Blood spurted from her shoulder joint as the skin and muscle began to shred. She screamed an inhuman sound, like some wild animal being torn apart.

In the horror of the moment, Jonathan felt a strange sense of clarity press upon the edge of his mind. The bionanoware gestating deep in his neural system had reached its first stage of development. Reflexively, the telekinetic ability that had so long dominated his thoughts slipped away to join the rest of his body's autonomic functions. In its place came a new, more powerful ability: one that fed off his heritage and expanded his Tel perception. It was like a cataract being removed from his mind's eye.

Jonathan simply thought about being free of Takeda's grip, and the field wall that had kept him pressed to the floor vanished. He looked at Georgia, just milliseconds from tearing apart, and his mind almost occluded from the torrent of memories that jammed his consciousness. His heart went out to her. Instantly, the telekinetic force lacerating Georgia disappeared. Takeda fell onto his back, while Georgia crumpled to the floor.

A new pain moved through Jonathan's body. Its recondite wake trailed a neural sensation that seemed strangely inorganic – more technical in nature. Like an electronic digital signature, it pulsed with an androidlike rhythm. Jonathan desperately tried to grasp what was happening to him. It seemed that phasing was not part of the equation anymore, and thought – or even emotion – could become manifest. He looked at his hands. They were shaking in sync with this new pain. Suddenly, there was a deep, almost subsonic rumble behind him, but the sound seemed compressed, like a miniature clap of thunder. Then Jonathan felt a thin edge of biting cold air whoosh past his head.

Takeda groaned.

Jonathan torqued in his direction and recoiled in awe. In the dim light of the holojection, Takeda was wearing a look of complete surprise. He was on his knees and appeared to be in a queer state of being, like his body was out of focus. Jonathan rubbed his eyes, thinking them affected by the extreme heat. But when he looked again, the Agency leader seemed to be morphing, becoming...transparent.

Takeda was beginning to look like a medical hologram. He sorrowfully examined himself, and gingerly stuck his fingers *into* his chest. He grinned at Jonathan with a childish look that asked, "Isn't this amazing?" But his expression changed as he registered the horror of his imminent death. His form quivered for a second, and in the time it takes for a heart to beat, his matter delicately dispersed into a fine vapor that glittered blue and pink in the glow of the holojection. His black gloves dropped silently to the floor.

Jonathan heard behind him a small click. It cut through the numbness of his shock and filled the room with a soft, audible hum that barely registered at the threshold of his hearing. A leather sole scuffed into position, accepting a shift in weight. He turned to find Georgia, her left arm barely hanging at her side, in the quiet glow of the holojection. She was holding the shadow weapon.

"Georgia!" Jonathan exclaimed. Every muscle in his telekinetically exhausted body collectively relaxed as she stepped fully into the light. "Oh, God, am I glad you're–"

"I've always hated that name," Georgia said with a strange monotone to her voice. She slowly stepped toward him. The weapon remained raised.

"Georgia?..."

Georgia kneeled down and cringed when the fingers of her shattered arm met the floor. The tip of the weapon's barrel came to rest inches from Jonathan's nose. She studied him with a detached severity. "You're not the only one who's lost someone they loved," she said finally. "I, too, lost someone dear to me." She stood and leveled the weapon directly at his face. The edges of its black housing were devoid of any reflections. "You might know him," she said, grimacing from the movement. "His name was Jacob Whitehorse."

A harsh sensation tore through Jonathan's nerves like shards of jagged glass. He peered into Georgia's eyes, but found they held no memory of him, and as he searched her face, he suddenly realized these eyes were identical to some he had looked into once before — on a balcony in Chicago, a long time ago. They had the same pupilless feature. The same intense black. The same intense hate.

"Georgia, please..."

"*My* name," she said, with a surge of power and pride, "is Kaya Whitehorse!"

The humming stopped...   30

CAREFUL to keep the shadow weapon trained at Jonathan's head, Kaya Whitehorse took a few steps back. She clicked a button at the tip of the trigger. The humming rose an octave.

"Georgia...I...I mean Kaya. Please!" Jonathan pleaded. "It was self-defense! Your father forced me—"

"Forced you? What a joke!" she exclaimed. "My father offered you your future. Your *true* future! But no, you had to choose the Agency. And look what that got you." She smiled smugly. "What's it like being a puppet?"

"You should know," Jonathan said coolly.

Kaya Whitehorse's eyes narrowed. "For the record, I *loved* Tarris." She relaxed and let out a snicker that seemed to define her disgust at a bad memory she had kept locked away. "You know, my father really believed that you were the one to lead us out of this absurd existence, and he was willing to do anything for your—"

"Like kill anyone who got in his way?"

She hesitated. "If needed."

"What about us?" Jonathan asked, trying to connect with the woman he had known.

Kaya Whitehorse's eyes softened as she regarded him with what seemed to Jonathan a glint of compassion, but they quickly narrowed with resolve again. "Oh, don't worry, baby," she mused, "you were a damn good fuck. But like most male Tels, you're easy to lead around." She began to laugh.

"You know I'm faster than light."

Her laugh dissolved. She stood like a warrior at the end of a long and arduous hunt. "This is a Matter-Force weapon, Jonathan, and unless you're the Infinite Tel, this ought to do to you what it did to ol' Cyril there." She flicked the barrel toward the gloves. "You know," she said with a sigh, "I am sorry you miss your parents so much." She leveled the Matter-Force rifle at his chest. "Maybe there's something I can do about that."

The humming stopped.

Kaya Whitehorse discharged the shadow weapon: its spatial-altering wave radiated directly into Jonathan's chest. The ebony wake consumed any light, and the recoil knocked her to the floor, screaming, her left arm spinning to rest somewhere in the middle of the room.

Jonathan instinctually phased, and his vision detonated

into a bright field of white. His mind, his soul, his whole being flooded with beautiful, brilliant music of ten thousand upon ten thousand angels in full chorus. Still on his knees, Jonathan spread his arms to receive the Matter-Force wave like a miscreant accepting God's love. The wave slammed into his sternum and began to curl and spread in two equal directions along an invisible path that arched back upon itself directed by the curves of his outstretched arms. Within a nanosecond, it appeared he was hugging a giant oil-filled bubble, which continued to grow until it enveloped Kaya Whitehorse. Her figure wriggled and deformed as the bubble washed over her. Then the Matter-Force wave collapsed upon itself and crushed Kaya, along with all matter within, into subatomic oblivion.

Her death scream echoed in Jonathan's mind.

Jonathan collapsed to his hands and knees. A sharp tingling ricocheted throughout his body, and his head throbbed from the spatial-altering trauma. His vision slowly clarified. Disoriented and shaking from paroxysm, he surveyed the room. The holojection seemed to be the only thing moving. Jeffrey Trumble lay motionless on the couch, and both Takeda and Kaya Whitehorse were gone. He collapsed onto his side and threw up. His netpad spilled from his pocket. He clicked it on, and Carter Shoalburg's face pixeled up on the tiny vidscreen.

"Carter," he said weakly, "I think I need a little help here..." He felt himself starting to go under.

"Hold on, man," Shoalburg said. "Some friends of yours are heading your way."

Jonathan tried to focus on Shoalburg's tiny image, but his vision was too blurred. "Thanks, Carter," he said.

Shoalburg smiled. "I told you I'd have your back."

The netpad slipped from his fingers. *It's done,* he thought. But even as he wavered on the edge of consciousness, Jonathan Kortel felt a foreboding sense of doubt crawl into bed with his soul. With one last glance around the room, his attention came to rest on the holochive, its brutal data still quivering in the center of the room.

He smiled, then carefully wiped the vomit from his mouth. "Off program," he uttered, and quietly passed out.

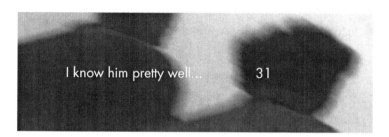

I know him pretty well... 31

JONATHAN awoke to a blurry, whitish-green light that was obliterating his field of vision. A black silhouette of a head eclipsed the light and appeared to grow as Jonathan's eyes began to focus.

"Kreet?..." he asked, his voice cracking a bit.

"Who'd you think you'd see?" Kreet replied. "God?"

"The thought had occurred to me," Jonathan quipped. He tried to sit up, reached to rub his eyes and noticed the biomed regeneration unit that cradled his arm.

"Easy there, killer. Just lay back down," Kreet said. "You're in no shape to be getting up."

"What...what happened?" Jonathan asked hoarsely.

"Your forearm took the brunt of the fall, fracturing your

ulna in two places," a familiar voice replied. Kreet stepped aside
to reveal Sasha, who was sitting on the edge of the table next to him.
She was wearing a black sleeveless T-shirt, military rip pants and
dull gray work boots. Rocket and Bixx stood behind her. She smiled
affectionately. "How are you feeling?"

"Okay, all things considered," Jonathan said. "Hey, who
did my arm? This looks like a pretty high-end unit."

Sasha motioned behind him, and Sanjiv stepped to the table.

"I thought you were a systems specialist," Jonathan said.

"You never asked what kind!" Sanjiv replied with
a laugh.

"Hey...ah...can I have a moment with Jonathan?" Sasha
asked the group.

They nodded knowingly and shuffled out of the makeshift
medical area. Sasha hopped off the table and came up to Jonathan's
side. She took his hand. Jonathan began to speak, but stopped
himself. She smiled and pulled his hand to her face, holding it
tight against her cheek. "I'm glad you're all right," she said. She
kissed the back of it, and her expression changed. She placed his
hand at his side. "I have something for you." She hesitantly removed
an old PDA from her pocket. "I'm supposed to give this to you now."

Sasha helped Jonathan sit up. He took the small pad, and
she stepped back in a gesture that gave the perception of privacy.
He clicked it on. The bearded face of Armando Zvara appeared on
the tiny LCD screen. Jonathan had never seen him smile.

"Hello, Jonathan," Zvara's image said. "If you are seeing
me, then more than likely, Trumble or Takeda, possibly both, are

dead. And, I would venture to say...you know what you are now."
He paused and pulled at his beard. "This will be a difficult time
for you. You are now a fugitive in the Tel world, and you will not
be able to stay in New America. Time is critical, so you must act
fast." He cleared his throat. "I sent Sasha to assist with your crossing
in any way that she could."

Jonathan glanced at Sasha, who nervously pulled stray
hair from her face.

"Now, I know you are probably thinking that you had
already crossed when you killed Jacob Whitehorse on that balcony
in Chicago. That is what the Agency wanted you to think. Your real
crossing, Jonathan, could only come when you fully knew what
you were. And now that you do, it is time for you to develop into
what you are destined to be. But not yet. First, you will have
to...disappear for a while. There are Tels in Russia who will help you
with this – you will have to trust them. Sasha has all the file work
and identity protocols that you will need. When the time is right,
we will contact you." Zvara pondered his next thought. "Jonathan,
let me be frank here....I do not know if you will ever be able to
come back to New America again. It is hard to say at this time
what the fallout from this situation will be. We will monitor it
and try to keep you informed. And, Jonathan..." Zvara's voice
became grave, "...I do not need to remind you that you are still
human and quite killable. So watch your back, keep your field up,
and good luck." The image cut out.

Jonathan sat quietly staring at the blank screen.

"Are you all right?" Sasha asked.

Jonathan shifted uneasily on the table. "Yeah," he said softly, "I'm all right."

Sasha handed him a small envelope. "Here's your new ID card, itinerary and travel passcard. And also a chip with software to teach you to speak Russian....We think it will be able to dialog with your nanoware. There's a series of words that will automatically create the interface. If not, there's a vid for backup, along with all your contacts." She gingerly removed a tiny device from her pants pocket. "This is for you. Hang onto it. You never know when you might need it."

It was the controller.

Jonathan cautiously took it and the envelope. "I want to go through San Francisco," he said solemnly.

Sasha smiled tenderly. "I knew you would. It's already been arranged."

"Hey," Jonathan said, grabbing her hand and gently pulling her close, "how well do you know Zvara?"

"Oh...I know him pretty well." She kissed him softly on the cheek.

"Really?" he questioned, pulling away. "How?"

Sasha hesitated slightly. "Because," she said with an intuitive grin, "he's my father."

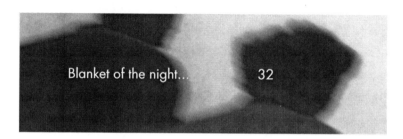

Blanket of the night...   32

A lone seagull rode a current of air as the Pacific Ocean released its might against the jagged rocks of Point Reyes. The wind blew hard against Jonathan's face, and he could taste the salt on his lips after each relentless gust. He looked to the edge of the world at the sun starting to slip beneath the horizon, its dying rays of gold and yellow extending between the breaks of a storm building a hundred miles out to sea. Lost in his thoughts, he watched the sun disappear completely, never noticing the blanket of night being pulled over the earth.

He turned and slowly walked to the memorial. The small acreage in the Point Reyes National Park seemed a fitting place, since it was one of the nation's westernmost points. It, along with three other locations, had been put to a national netvote, and five years after the event, the International Memorial for the Victims of Hawaii opened its doors to anyone who wanted to pray or reflect or say goodbye.

Jonathan, as he had done once before with thousands of other relatives of survivors, entered the Great Hall and approached the small kiosk. Its simple design had a quiet dignity that was apropos to its patient wait for the next visitors to use its gigantic database to help their healing. He entered his parents' IDs, then looked around the hall at the 360-degree holojection that had been taken by the Freedom 10 Space Station only days before the event.

The kiosk chimed. "As a courtesy to the survivors," a pleasant, yet authoritative female systems voice announced, "will anyone who is not a family member please leave the Great Hall at this time. The doors will automatically close in three minutes. Thank you for your cooperation." An elderly Japanese couple sadly glanced at Jonathan, bowed, and quietly left the hall.

Jonathan sat on the large wooden bench in the middle of the expanse. The kiosk chimed again, signaling the closing of the hall's doors. The lights dimmed. The Freedom 10 holojection disappeared, and Jonathan found himself alone in the memorial whose curved walls camouflaged any concept of depth or space in cavernous darkness.

A moment of silence for the dead.

His parents appeared in a huge holojection that floated 20 feet in front of him. Jonathan had opted for the simpler

SOULWARE

memorial, though he could have had their images morphed into an introduction where they said "hello" and "we love you" or some other absurd beginning. He always felt that his parents talking back to him from the grave was horrific, at best. He just wanted to remember them as they were: Jonathan Sr. and Sarah Kortel, career scientists, father and mother of Jonathan Jr. He quietly watched their lives played out through family pictures, home vids and any public records that might have captured them. Having been a fairly high-profile scientific couple, their careers came to public attention every now and then, and the memorial tribute producers had spared no expense in their research. He had to admit they had done a pretty good job of capturing, as far as he could remember, the essence of his parents. The music and the editing had all been designed to pluck the heartstrings without being too morose, or too over the top. The producers also had strategically placed another moment of reflection at the end of the program. After his parents' memorial finished, Jonathan quietly wept in the darkness.

The lights came up and the doors slowly opened, and the Freedom 10 image went back to reminding the generations how the Hawaiian Islands once looked.

. . .

Jonathan slowly returned to the spot at the cliff. He looked to the southwest, where the islands used to be. He picked up a small clump of dirt. The wind was now gusting, whipping his hair and forcing the seagulls to tack erratically in the air.

"Goodbye, Mom...goodbye, Dad," he said into the wind.

He recited the Lord's Prayer and stood quietly with his thoughts while the dirt filtered through his fingers. The seagulls squawked, and the ocean continued its relentless bombardment while the world was tucked in for the night.

FEBRUARY ~ 2 YEARS LATER

PAUL BLACK

Do the right thing...   33

ANARI sat at the VIP bar and rested her chin in her hand. It was a Thursday night, and Liquid Courage was suspiciously vacant of the automotive conventioneers who wore their paunches like badges of honor. They had descended upon Chicago for two weeks of dealing, drinking and any other kind of devilment overweight, fortyish salesmen could get themselves into. A lone dancer slithered apathetically across the stage; the sequins at her crotch refracted little rainbows about the dark room.

"Who in the hell did her tits?!" Anari asked.

"Karmenowski," the bar back said with a knowing grin.

"I should have guessed," she declared. "He should be shot for that aug job. Those things look absurd."

"You can take the girl out of the country..." the bar back started.

"That's so sad," Anari said. "She's going to regret those in about 10 years."

"Maybe she'll be screwing another doctor by then," the bar back offered and laughed.

The door to VIP slowly opened, which wasn't an odd occurrence in itself, but Anari knew that the doorman was on break, and nobody got into VIP without being checked by him first. It didn't matter how important you were...nobody just *walked* in.

The man wore a high-end biocoat still wet from the evening's light snowfall. She contemplated calling security, but figured what the hell: the night was a bust, and she needed to pay the rent. She followed him at a distance, watching the living coat reform into its dry-out setting. *Money,* she thought. He slipped it off and chose a dark booth against the back wall. He kept his face out of the narrow spotlight that judiciously illuminated the top of the table.

"Neat trick," Anari said as she slid beside the booth.

"Pardon?" the man asked.

"Opening the doors to VIP...neat trick, because they're voiceprint controlled, you know. Was there a doorman out front?"

"No."

"Then how'd you open them?"

The man hesitated. "I have my ways," he said dryly.

"Well, usually I'd have to ask you to go see the doorman, but since we're dead and all..." she leaned on the table, trying to get a better look at him. He retreated into the darkness of the booth.

"...I guess we'll make this our little secret, okay?"

"Thank you," he replied.

"So," she asked softly, "what are we drinking tonight?"

"Oban, with ice, no water, please."

She paused for a second before punching in the order.

"Something wrong?" the man inquired.

"No, no..." Anari said, and she quickly headed for the bar.

. . .

"Anything the matter?" the bartender questioned.

"Hmm?" Anari asked, staring into space.

"Anything the *matter*?" He handed her the drink.

"No, nothing. I was just remembering something..."

Anari walked back to the booth. The man hadn't moved. "One Oban, with ice, no water," she said, presenting the drink. "Do you live here, or are you in town with the convention?"

"I used to live here, but I'm in for...business."

"Cool. Are you going to stay with us long?" she asked in an effort to make conversation to relieve the boredom.

The man hesitated again. "I don't know..."

Anari thought she detected a touch of sadness in his voice. There was an awkward pause, the kind two strangers share when they realize that their conversation is really nothing more than forced small talk.

"Well then, I'll come back and check on you in a little bit." She began to leave the table.

"Anari..." the stranger beckoned.

She stopped in midstep. "How do you know my real name?" she asked, charging back to the booth.

"It's me, Anari," the man said tenderly. "Jonathan." He leaned forward, and the spotlight flooded his face in harsh contrasts. He had aged a bit, but the sharp angles of his jawline still announced his boyish charm.

Anari almost dropped her tray. Her legs started to buckle. "J-Jonathan...I...I–"

"It's okay, Anari. I know you haven't been erased. James told me everything...before the–" He stopped and smiled. "Please...sit with me?"

Anari composed herself. "Sure," she said. She cautiously settled into the booth, careful to keep a fair distance between them. She studied him for a moment. "Oh, Jonathan," she finally said, "it's so good to see you again." Tears welled in her eyes.

"Anari, please don't cry..."

"I'm not even sure why I am," she said.

"Mia?" her voice pin interrupted, "are you going to be there a while?"

"Give me a fucking minute, will you Trev?!"

"I'm cool to that, baby. I'll send Tissy. She needs the scratch."

"Sorry," Anari said, focusing on Jonathan.

"Hey, if you gotta go..."

Anari scooted over and hugged him. "No," she said into his chest, "I can hang for as long as you want."

SOULWARE

Jonathan returned her hug, but it was restrained, and Anari could sense it.

"How've you been?" he questioned. He took a sip from his drink.

"I'm all right. Just working and living...you know the drill." Anari pulled back and folded her arms tightly across her chest.

"Anari," Jonathan said, "when was the last time you heard from James?"

"Oh, God, I don't know...at least two years ago. Since I was a secret, I never knew what to expect. Our relationship was pretty strange, you know, with your culture such a secret and all. Then one day, Jimmy just quit calling. I kind of figured he got tired of all the sneaking around. For a long time I was always looking over my shoulder...thinking he'd send someone to erase me. But after a couple of months I quit worrying. I guess he just got busy and forgot about me." She noticed Jonathan seemed to react to this comment, but she couldn't figure why. She looked painfully at him. "Did he ever say anything to you...about me?"

Jonathan struggled for an answer. "There was an accident," he replied flatly. "His memory was...ah...damaged."

"Oh no," Anari said softly. Tears came into her eyes again.

"In a sense he did forget you, along with about 27 years of memories. They say with time he may recover close to 60 percent of them, but they never really know what a Tel will remember until the recovery process is over."

"When will that be?" Anari asked between sniffles.

"It's hard to say..."

Anari forced a smile. "Well, it's been a long time now....Maybe someday he'll remember me."

"Maybe he will."

Anari wiped her nose with a cocktail napkin. "Jonathan, why are you here?" She already suspected the answer.

Jonathan's demeanor changed, and he leaned back against the booth. "I think you already know the answer to that question, don't you?"

"Oh, Jonathan, don't do this...don't try. She's moved on. She's got a new life and a new job. She's not the same Tamara you knew." A seriousness came over Anari. "Especially after what the Agency did to her."

"I'm not with the Agency anymore. I haven't been for some time now."

"What happened?" Anari said with surprise. "Where have you been?"

"It's a long story..."

"Are you in some kind of trouble?"

Jonathan sighed. "Yeah, you could say that."

"Jonathan, what happened? What did you do?"

"Let's just say that I'm not the golden boy in the Tel world any more, and keep it at that."

"Okay," Anari said, nodding, "but you're all right, aren't you?"

"For the moment," he said gravely.

They both became silent. Anari's thoughts drifted to Tamara. "She's done well for herself," she finally said.

"I'm so glad to hear that," Jonathan replied. He smiled. "Tell me about her....What's she doing, and how's Nicki?"

"Oh, Jonathan, Nicki's so big now. She's got her mother's body for sure, with those long legs and all. You should see her..." Anari caught herself and quickly turned away.

"That's why I'm here, Anari...to see Tamara."

She hesitated, then looked back.

"Anari, what? What is it?"

"It's...it's just that you two had such a love for each other. Everyone saw it. It was different....It was...true."

Jonathan concentrated on his drink and took a big gulp. He leaned against the booth and watched a lone dancer shuffle about the stage to a retro tune that sounded like Desperate Sense. "If you really believe that, Anari, then let me just try. If we had it once, we might be able to have it again."

"It doesn't work that way, Jonathan, you know that—"

"It might."

Anari looked at him, confused. "What are you saying?"

Jonathan pensively swirled his ice. "There's something you need to know. I'm not going to get into the technical details, but basically, when a Level 8 erases a person, most of the time it takes. There's full erasure and that's that. But once in a while, an erasure doesn't take fully. Now, this varies from person to person, but there can be 'leftover' memories still present in the person's mind. Depending how much is left over, a Level 8 may have to go back and finish the job. But that gets tricky. Erasing a person who has already had the procedure can be dangerous, even fatal."

"So that's why Jimmy never wanted to do it on Tamara!"

"What?!" Jonathan exclaimed. He grabbed her shoulder.

"Ever since the procedure, she's not been the same girl. I mean, she is...it's just that..."

"What, Anari? Just what?"

"She's...sadder, that's all. Nothing manic, just sadder. Like she's in a state of being perpetually bummed, which is weird, because the way I understood the procedure, it shouldn't change her personality....Should it?"

"No, no it shouldn't. It only destroys memory, nothing else." Jonathan leaned back, thinking. "Anari, is there anything about her that seems odd, like headaches or sleeplessness?"

"Well, there's the dreams—"

"Dreams....What kind of dreams?"

"Strange ones, real disjointed. She says they've really affected her...and I think her love life, too."

"Why's she say that?"

"I'm not sure. She closes up when I try to help. It's like she's embarrassed or something." Anari processed her last statement. "Oh my God, Jonathan!" She put her hands over her mouth. "They're about you! Her dreams!"

Jonathan didn't respond. He sat against the booth with his eyes shut.

"One way leftover memories come forward is through dreams," he said, his eyes still closed. "They're sometimes called repressed dreams." He leaned forward and looked at Anari. "In this case, though, it's not the mind suppressing a trauma or something.

It's more of a leakage, due to the procedure not taking fully."

Anari sat quietly contemplating. "What do you think?"

"I think that if there's a chance in hell of getting back some of my life, I'm going to take it. I haven't come this far, and risked this much, not to at least see if there's anything left between us." He leveled his gaze at her. "And if you have any compassion for us, you'll tell me where she is."

"Do you think that's fair?—"

"Fair?!" he blurted. His drink shattered and sprayed Scotch and glass across the table.

Anari jumped back against the booth. "Easy, Jonathan. I'm just saying, would it be right?"

"I'm sorry," Jonathan said. He wiped away the ice and glass with his napkin.

Anari noticed that some of the ice appeared to shift – the melted water separating from the Scotch and reforming into tiny cubes.

Can't be, she thought. *Must be the light.*

"I...I just have to see if there's any possibility," Jonathan continued. "I don't think I could live with myself if I didn't at least try."

Anari could see the intense pain and torment in Jonathan's eyes. She also knew that her friend had never been the same since the procedure, and every time she saw Tamara, it cut into her heart a little bit more. Anari reached over and stopped Jonathan from wiping off the table. She took his hands in hers.

"Hey..." she tenderly began. Jonathan stoically looked at her, trying not to display what his eyes already revealed. "Give me your netpad." Anari entered Tamara's work address and handed it back, but as Jonathan took it, she held on and shot him a firm look.

"Don't worry," he said. "I'm not going to force it if it's not right. I would never do anything to hurt her."

Anari smiled. "I know you'll do the right thing, Jonathan." She leaned over and kissed him on the cheek.

I don't really know...   34

A cold winter wind blew up Michigan Avenue and slammed hard against the broad shoulders of the city by the lake. Its citizens, as they had for hundreds of years, braced themselves for the onslaught of frozen nose hair, sordid gray snow, and relentless overcast from what meteorologists affectionately called "the lake effect."

Jonathan watched this world go by from the cozy warmth of the coffee shop booth he had occupied for the better part of the afternoon.

"Need a refill, hon?" the waitress asked. She stood expressionless with her right hand on her hip, her left hand dangling an antique coffeepot like she had a million of them to spare. Her makeup appeared to have been applied with an acetylene torch, and probably not since her last raving. The topiary that was her hair had assumed a shape that could only be grown on a steady diet of biogel and electric shock.

"Hmm?" Jonathan asked, prying himself away from the scene outside.

"Coffee?" Her eyebrow slowly raised.

"No thanks," he replied.

"Suit yourself." She sauntered back behind the counter; her hair bounced in sync with her steps.

Jonathan glanced at his watch. 4:45:34 p.m. He gathered his coat and walked to the counter.

"What, you're leaving us so soon?" the waitress asked sarcastically. "And just when we were getting to know each other." She handed Jonathan her netpad. He punched in his tip and handed it back. She raised her eyebrow again, and her mouth stopped chewing on what was left of a straw. "Mister," she exclaimed, "you only had a couple cups of coffee!"

"For taking up your booth for so long."

"Honey, come back and stay as long as you want!"

He smiled and pulled on his coat. It cycled through the presets for the harsh environment it was about to encounter.

"Damn, that's a fancy coat! Say, what are you, government or sumthin'?" She gave him the once-over.

"Something..." he said bluntly, and the collar of his coat tightened slightly around his neck.

. . .

Jonathan quickly crossed the street, bracing himself against the hard, driving wind. He slipped between the CitiCabs and CitiCars and tentatively approached the gallery. When he reached for the door handle, he noticed his hand shake a little. He couldn't tell if it was nerves or the bionanoware, though he wasn't sure if there was a difference anymore.

The gallery was quiet, only two other people looking at the art. A young girl, who was wrapped so tightly in winter clothes that it was impossible to tell where her neck ended and her head began, studied a giant holographic tampon. It dripped blood that splattered into a puddle on the floor, then went in reverse so that the blood flew back onto the tampon.

Jonathan drew beside her. "Interesting," he commented.

"It's called 'Life's a Bitch,' by the artist Koe-9," the girl said without taking her eyes from it.

"Hmm," he mused, pretending to care. He walked from piece to piece, diligently studying the assortment of paintings, holojections and three-dimensional sculptures as if he might truly buy one. He rounded the corner of a wall that displayed the torn remnants of a hundred T-shirts like the one Sasha had worn in their virt-booth bike ride, and stopped when he saw the back of Tamara. She was discussing the works with an elderly man who had an air about him like he could buy out the whole place. Jonathan quickly averted his face and started reading the vidbrief on the T-shirt piece.

Who Cares, by Albert Foster Milton Glaser.

"Do you like it?"

A wave of metallic cold swelled through Jonathan as his heart processed the sound of Tamara's voice. "Yes," he said. He turned face to face with the woman he loved and was struck at how little she had changed. Slightly older, a bit more weight, and definitely dressed more conservatively. What hadn't changed, though, were her eyes. Their crystalline blueness cut to his heart, just as they had when he had first met her.

"We'll be closing soon," Tamara said in a crisp, professional manner, "but I still have a lot of research to do. Please feel free to browse the work." She started to walk away. "Oh, I'm sorry. I'm Nicole, and you are?..." She extended her hand.

"Jonathan." He reached for her hand, and an arc of static jumped between them.

"Oh," she exclaimed, "I'm so sorry! We keep it so dry in here – for the protection of the work, you know." They held for a second, and she contemplated him like a piece in a portfolio.

"Is there something wrong?" Jonathan asked.

"No, not at all. It's just that you look...familiar, that's all. Do you live in the city?"

He smiled again. "No, I'm just visiting."

"Well, I'll be over here if you have any questions." She gestured to a small desk at the back of the gallery.

Jonathan noticed her diploma on the wall. "You have a master's," he said.

"Why yes," Tamara said, slightly put off. "At The Pudder Gallery, all associates are required to have at least an MFA."

"I'm sorry," Jonathan said, clearly embarrassed. "I didn't

mean to sound so surprised."

"It's all right. I've worked hard for it, and I'm probably a little touchy about it." She curtly smiled and left for her desk.

. . .

While the elderly man closed the door behind him, Jonathan stepped away from the tampon holosculpture and slowly approached Tamara's desk.

"You sure like our little sculpture," she said, keeping her attention firmly on her netport. She tried to restrain her amusement.

Jonathan watched as she assiduously went about her research. *She did it,* he thought. Pulled herself out of a life that would have dragged most others down a path of addiction or tragedy – and usually both. He affectionately studied her, and his heart filled with a strange mix of pride and relief. Although he would never have admitted it, he was always fearful that her life might turn for the worse. But here she was, accomplished, independent, and more beautiful than he had ever remembered.

Tamara sensed his stare. "I can make a great deal on it for you," she said half laughing. She glanced up and read his look, as she had a hundred times before, and did that thing with her head where she tilted it to one side and gave a tender, questioning expression.

"It's interesting, but I'm not sure where I'd put it. I am, though, curious about these...in here." Jonathan motioned to a small room off the main gallery.

Tamara smiled in response. She rose and walked briskly toward the room. As he followed, Jonathan watched her stride and remembered.

Tamara and Jonathan entered the tiny gallery, and the spotlights brightened to highlight three paintings that hung conspicuously alone on the wall. The halogens bathed the paintings' surfaces in a cool light and created dark tapestries of highlight and shadow in the texture of the oils. Tamara and Jonathan stood for a moment and studied the lone figure that dominated each canvas.

"What do you think?" Tamara asked, considering the middle one.

Jonathan didn't answer. It felt so good to be close to her and hear her voice and smell her presence once again. He closed his eyes and took her in.

"Well?..." she pressed.

"They're..." Jonathan hesitated "...sad."

Tamara scrutinized Jonathan from the corner of her eye as he leaned in to read the artist bio. He got as far as the name – and stopped.

"These are yours," he said, unable to conceal his surprise.

"Yes," Tamara said, giving him her full attention, "they are."

Jonathan pulled back and settled on the third painting. A dark, faceless man looked mournfully through layers of vermillion and indigo and coal.

He gasped under his breath.

"These," Tamara continued, shifting into professional

mode and gesturing casually to the middle painting, "are actually from some—"

"Dreams," Jonathan blurted.

Tamara's arm hung in midgesture as if held by a puppeteer's string. "Why, yes!" she said, her eyes wide with astonishment. "I painted these from my dreams. How did you know that?" Her arm slowly lowered.

"Just a lucky guess," Jonathan said. He tore his attention from the paintings to find her intently staring at him. Her eyes searched his face as if it held the antitoxin to her pain. Their intensity startled him, and he reflexively stepped back. Tamara cocked her head again and gave him that look. It cut through to his soul.

"Tam..." he started, but her netphone hummed, and she pulled it from her pocket.

"Excuse me...will you?" She stepped away, still staring at him in puzzlement.

Jonathan intently studied the figure in the paintings. There, in violent strokes, was Tamara's anguish. While his eyes passed over the complex interplay of color and form, he listened—

"...I'll be right home, honey, I'm just finishing up with a customer....No, no, remember, Michael is taking us to dinner tonight....No, he's the one you said you liked....Yes, dear, Mommy likes him, too....Now wash up and be ready when I get home....I love you, too. I'll see you in a few minutes. Bye-bye." She snapped her netphone shut and returned to Jonathan. "I'm sorry. Now, what were you about to say?"

Jonathan glanced back at her eyes, which had lost their curiosity and returned to a cool professionalism. A simple sense of peace washed over him.

"Nothing," he answered softly.

"Well, you certainly have an eye for art," Tamara said. She headed back to her desk. Jonathan slowly followed. "You're the first person to have picked up on the fact that I painted those from my dreams." She pulled a small card from her drawer and handed it to him. The heat from his fingers triggered the gallery's holopromotional. Tamara's image appeared in the center of the card. She was standing in the middle of the gallery in a crisp suit, then walking through the art, all the while explaining the virtues of investing with the Pudder Gallery.

He watched for a moment, then quietly pocketed her.

"They're a bit silly, but they do the job quite effectively, don't you think?" she said. She folded her hands in a businesslike manner.

Jonathan barely smiled.

"Now, if you make up your mind on my paintings or anything else you've seen," she turned and coyly smiled to the tampon holosculpture and back, "just ask for me."

Jonathan thought for a second. "I will, Miss?..."

"Connor," she said, extending her hand. "Nicole Connor."

He took her hand with both of his, and for the second they held, he desperately fought for balance between what his heart said was true and what his soul knew was right. He turned to leave, but as he approached the door, she called to him. "Are you staying long in Chicago?"

The simple question stopped Jonathan and held him like the Ice Age had returned and spread across his heart. He hadn't really thought past coming to the gallery. "I...I don't really know," he managed. He couldn't face her. He smiled to himself, opened the door and joined the rest of Chicago in battling a typical Midwestern storm on a typical Midwestern night.

ACKNOWLEDGEMENTS –

I would like to thank the following for their assistance, inspiration and patience: Bryan Pudder, Tim Evans, Patrick Florer, Chris Molina, Doreen McGookey, Shanon Pinkston, Bruce Warner, Max Wright and of course, all the great folks in my writers group.

For the Russian transcriptions: Edward Topal and his book *Dermo*, and *www.insultmonger.com* (for expert translations of Russian cursing and its many levels). For the hunting references: The International Hunter Education Association for its invaluable website and the New Mexico Department of Game and Fish. For future trends in technology: *www.socialtechnologies.com* and its wealth of future forecasts and models of global trends. And to NASA News and the Langley Research Center website for its white papers on the future of commercial aviation.

Thanks, too, to the following, all of whom got me through when I needed the right element at the right time: William Gibson, Rudy Rucker, Alexander Besher, the sound track from *Run Lola Run*, Stephen Hawkings and his book *The Universe in a Nutshell*, *Wired Magazine* (pick an issue) and (thank God for) Merriam-Webster.com and the Merriam-Webster Unabridged Dictionary.com.

To my publicist Kelly Kitchens for all her time and hard work. Special thanks to my editor, Jay Johnson, for his faith in the *Tels* series.

And to Trish, with love, whose patience and support kept me together when it seemed everything was going to shit.

Dallas, 2004

ABOUT THE AUTHOR

Born and raised outside of Chicago, Illinois, this was Mr. Black's second work of science fiction, published in 2005. Today, he lives and works in Dallas, Texas, where he manages his own graphic design firm and feeds his passion for tennis. He is currently working on a new book of near-future fiction. Please visit his author website at www.paulblackbooks.com.

PAUL BLACK

THE TELS

BOOK ONE IN THE TELS TRILOGY

THE YEAR IS 2101 A new revolution has spread across the human landscape. The
Biolution and its flood of technology has changed almost every aspect of life. Also changed
is the face of terrorism.

Throughout his life, Jonathan Kortel always sensed he was different, but never imagined
how different, until two rival factions of a secret group called the Tels approach him out
of the shadows of government. He has a gift that could change his life, and possibly the
world, forever.

This is his story. A battle for the loyalty of a man who could change the course of human
evolution. And the struggle inside this man as he comes to terms with his destiny. Deeply
intriguing and powerfully suspenseful, Paul Black has created a future described as "one
of the best science fiction novels" by Marilyn Meredith of Writer's Digest. Part X-Files,
part cyber-thriller, Paul Black unveils a dark and compelling view of a world.

NOVEL INSTINCTS
w w w . p a u l b l a c k b o o k s . c o m

Available at all online retailers including **Amazon.com** and **BN.com**.

PAUL BLACK
NEXUS POINT

BOOK THREE IN THE TELS TRILOGY

DESTINY AWAITS. Jonathan Kortel is the most powerful telekinetic ever. There are others like him, and they're called the Tels. Able to manipulate gravity, they exist out at the edge of the next century, where the Biolution and its wave of new technology have changed life forever.

Blamed for the deaths of the Tel leadership, Jonathan escapes to a life of anonymity. But there's something strange happening in space that threatens all life on earth, and only Jonathan Kortel has the ability to stop it.

Here ends *The Tels* saga, author Paul Black's fascinating near-future series, introduced in his award-winning 2003 novel *The Tels*. *Nexus Point* continues where *The Tels* and *Soulware* left off, following Jonathan Kortel as he fulfills his prophetic destiny.

NOVEL INSTINCTS
www.paulblackbooks.com

Available at all online retailers including **Amazon.com** and **BN.com**.

LaVergne, TN USA
07 September 2010
196161LV00009B/1/P